A CYCLE

OF

FALLS

by

FRANCIS VOIGNIER

Cover design by Francis Voignier
Cover art: iStock

This book is a work of fiction. Any relation to living individuals, at the exception of public figures whose names are respectfully used in the context of their professions, businesses, and/or social influence, is purely coincidental.

Library of Congress Cataloging-in-Publication Data
Voignier, Francis 1954 – United States
A Cycle of Falls/Francis Voignier
ISBN-13: 978-1-952858-03-1
ISBN-10: 1-952858-03-8

Fiction – Mystery – Metaphysics – Philosophy

francisvoignier.com
Dolosse & Writs, Eureka CA, USA

CHAPTERS

My deepest appreciation
goes to the mind that knows itself

NOTE FROM THE AUTHOR

In my usual style, I once more find myself stepping into the metaphorical unknown with a story set in a place as far removed from my native France as it can possibly get, but which, for some unexplained reason, feels very familiar and dear to me.

It is fitting that Tasmania should be chosen for this book as the last hallowed grounds standing before the madness of a corrupt humanity; *she* is beautiful and wounded, qualities that betray her unique strength in highlighting the balance that must be maintained for world sustainability.

This work belongs to the realm of the imagined, and thus mustn't be confused with reality as seen from the eyes of the inhabitants of this wonderful island and state.

That being said, imagination rarely strays from the real when it comes to tackling environmental issues and the mechanics of global, financial powers. And so, who, may I ask, is better equipped in dealing with restoring the balance than a group of international lawyers adept at straddling a multiplicity of outcomes? An odd choice, I admit, but such is the nature of paradox. I forever remain the messenger. Enjoy!

~Francis Voignier~ May 5, 2022

1 – VERTEX

All stood up as one—the meeting had adjourned, cut short by a subtle, common acquiescence to some silent and deep order. As everybody prepared to return whence they came, to name but one, Henri Desgardes Esq. nobly lifted his intercom, tapping out the numbers for his Executive Assistant commanding a car promptly to take him to the airport. The wheels of his progress—such as they may have been—were now in motion.

As for me, well... I was already in my place, in the now empty room, getting the lowdown on Henri's future. Believe me when I tell you there was nothing in the slightest new about it.

— o —

It was an early spring by Quebec City standards, the streets abuzz with unrestrained exuberance. All knew too well it couldn't possibly last, but for today, they were all too happy pretending winter was finally over.

I looked out my fourth floor office window into the far southerly distance, wondering what the weather was like in Tasmania...

— o —

The meeting was about two things—business as usual and unusual business, one being a front for the other. Of the twelve of us present, Leduc, Marchand, and I—the chief partners—knew of both sides intrinsically, while the rest, referred to as Front Shield, juggled all cases, impervious to the distinction. The unusual part of what we did exhibited all the characteristics of business as usual under the motto: *research and gather information, raising as little dust as possible*. The details were simply lost in the shuffle.

I'm John Lehman—the firm is my brainchild.

— o —

Henri Desgardes had ascended to the top of Front Shield, having been with us for exactly a decade when he informed the team he wanted out. The end of the meeting was reserved to a few kind words in honor of his invaluable services; a small token of appreciation—the norm in the field, as it were—although I must confess that such rituals often concealed their true face when too much confidential information was seen growing legs; hence the saying, *you may leave, but you never do*. It was how Henri found himself on his way to conducting unusual business in Hobart exactly a day after having officially walked out.

In spite of the appearance of trickery, there wasn't a single trick involved. Henri always followed his own vision and we were all the better served by his assurance. Did I not say he was joining an extraordinary woman into connubial heaven, teamed to a prestigious position as partner to one of the city's most successful law firms, Garner, Lewis, and in due time, Desgardes? Well then, let me tell you that his wife-to-be, Elizabeth Garner, a brilliant attorney, was no other than the daughter of founder Abraham Elliot Garner, a dear friend who fell to his death exactly a year to the day Henri set a permanent foot on Tasmanian soil. The events that precipitated the senior partner's demise were precisely what the unusualness of said business was attracted to, and the reason why lovely Ms. Garner contacted me. Behind the scene, Lehman, Leduc & Marchand was known as Vertex, or rather, a branch of it, an entity only reachable via the back corridors of power.

Well, I admit that Jean Leduc, Eric Marchand, and I did our part in helping Henri and Elizabeth break the ice; but isn't that what friends are for!

— o —

As a long time intimate of her parents, I met Elizabeth when she was a newborn; and even though we saw each other only in brief flashes as she grew into a lively teen, and later, a dangerously attractive woman, we managed to stay connected the way families remain tight throughout prolonged absences. Her recent call was hardly a surprise, and of course by then Abe's death had generated much suspicion among those with a finer nose for the intricate scent of suspense. Take it from me, the local media and law enforcement were awfully quick at writing off the whole thing as a mundane accident. A man of Abraham Garner's mettle didn't just fall to his death unless he got help.

— o —

Liz, as she went by to close ones, never assumed Henri Desgardes was instrumental to her father's case anymore than Henri knew the first thing about Vertex. They simply fell in love at a time when the Front Shield attorney became annoyed at his stalemated prospects of joining the partnership, in contrast to his irreplaceable skills and accrued seniority begging for his advancement. There was reason for it, but for timing's sake, let's just say that the job opening in Hobart wasn't totally coincidental. After all, Abe Garner was also Vertex.

— o —

In recap, the first half of the meeting addressed ongoing federal environmental cases, whose research elements stealthily tied into the Tasmanian situation. It was merely child's play to conceal reports within others and unload them at the appropriate place and time. Vertex referred to those as *carrier cases*, for they did just that, haul information in the invisibility of the open. If someone ever asked, not that they would, it was a brief matter of whisking it off as a mix-up.

— o —

So, what is Vertex? In a nutshell, and at the time of these recollections, it was a conglomerate of international teams sharing tools and a strong core philosophy, which saw to the sustainability and management of the planet's resources. Breaking it down, the partners and I were *Vertex Quebec*, while the Garners represented *Vertex Tasmania*. Following that model, Liz could just as easily have called Cape Town, Sidney, or Beijing; although Quebec was the natural choice.

Abe was working on a Vertex case at the time of his death, meaning that his trip into the Tasmanian wilderness wasn't merely for the sake of quenching a thirst for adventure. According to Liz, he was following the proverbial slime trail of malfeasance, one that inconvenienced a formidable client in ways the common mind could hardly fathom. Nothing to do with the predictable evils, I was told, but that surely meant it was a lot worse.

As things stood, only Liz, her team partner Jack Lewis, and I knew of the freshly open case; although, many a Front Shield attorney and their Executive Assistants had been hard at work in both hemispheres.

———— o ————

2 – RANCH ACACIA

Desgardes checked his bags through customs and hurried towards the gate. No direct flights from Quebec City to Hobart meant a series of interminable stopovers in Montreal, Los Angeles, and Sidney.

He and Liz hadn't seen each other in months, relying instead on their cell phones screens for random moments of intimacy. I'm well placed to tell you they missed each other with the kind of joyful apprehension that made them relish as much as loathe the wait.

Fortunately, they would connect in Sidney, where Liz had been conducting business for the firm—a well-deserved redemption on the last leg of a gruesome flight.

— o —

Garner, Lewis, & (soon to be) Desgardes occupied the eighth floor of the Shadforth Building at 111 Macquarie Street, across Franklin Square and Sullivans Cove. It had been the firm's sole address since its erection in 1978, the year of Liz's birth. Henri knew the place well from his many visits; his first, three years prior, on his virgin trip to the city on behalf of a *carrier case,* need I say—specifically tailored for the occasion. As hosting coordinator, Elizabeth Garner introduced the members of her father's firm to the Quebec team, taking charge of addressing everyone's needs with commanding confidence. Technically, Liz, just like Henri, was Front Shield, but there ended the similarities, as she belonged to Vertex first and foremost. As expected, she immediately took to liking Desgardes, who, based on the files in her possession, proved to be the man she had hoped he was. She was partial to a face that didn't lie, especially on an A-report, and to the fact he was, like herself, a recent divorcee. It seemed only natural that she should shortly thereafter request that Henri, Abe, and I join her for dinner at her place.

— o —

I knew Henri had the best chance at charming Ms. Garner—the two were a match—but one could never be too sure when it came to the nature of the heart.

For now, I was pleased with my choice.

— o —

Henri and Liz soon grew into a long-distance relationship; but let's be clear—the business mind rarely wishes to see its affairs hijacked by the heart, unless said heart can sit at a conference table.

When I mentioned that some ice-breaking between them was necessary, I meant that at the time of Abraham Garner's death, someone had to raise the ante on the value of joining the Australian law firm. With Liz in her father's chair and no-one in hers, it became obvious that the relationship had found its raison d'être. Still, some convincing was required for Liz to see Henri as the logical choice to filling the vacancy. As to relocating to Hobart, it was asking much of Desgardes, a dear friend who had pledged to remain with us to the end; but the devil was in the nuance: Jean, Eric, and I couldn't make it obvious we wanted him in Tasmania—it all had to come

7

from Liz—yet, the time wasn't right for her to know their relationship was the pivot on which to solve her father's unfortunate end.

The key moment poked its face when Eric Marchand took a health leave of absence and his post was controversially filled by Front Shield second-in-line, Bryan Sackman. I admit it was a vicious move, and though Henri took it with rare stoicism, I was assured the hit had fully reached his pain department by the cold that blew from his office to mine for months on end. It cost me an irreplaceable friend, but I gathered that though he might never forgive me, he would eventually come to see the larger picture.

— o —

Liz lived in an oversized house on Darling Parade, in Mount Stuart, an area blessed with a spectacular view of the larger Hobart and the ranges across River Derwent. Her ex-husband, Jack Lewis's brother, James, had left it to her as part of the settlement. It was by no means located in the most affluent neighborhood, a distinction belonging to Tolmans Hill and Sandy Bay, but Liz loved the place and the scenery across her living room window.

Henri didn't get at first why she chose to live below her means; surely, a regal residence in a gated community was the appropriate option. But Hobart was no Quebec City, notwithstanding a posh neighborhood had no emotional value to Liz. It all made quick sense to him after learning she grew up on a distant family ranch, home schooled and motherless—Helen Garner passed when Liz was nine—raised by the hand to groom and ride horses, connect with the wild, and rise impervious to status and pretence. She was, as her father often humored, *a chip of the old block but with far better looks.*

— o —

It was at the ranch, in Acacia Hills, south of Devonport, that Liz met the men and women destined to become her larger family, the successful lawyers and doctors with their just as affluent clients and patients that gathered at summer parties, drinking and laughing under the stars. I couldn't help witness how quickly she recognized the larger than life energy that enrobed these meetings, the communal aura that brightened at the peak of midnight to gently linger with the mist of the early hours, and how quickly she focused on her father's infidelity, spying on him as he and an unidentified woman walked under the moon until they disappeared in the shadow of trees and a candlelight flickered in the rear cottage.

Those parties left with her mother.

When they returned years later, gone were the walks and the lights at the cottage. By eventually confronting her father about his regressions, Liz at last understood that Helen, then incapable of love-making, not only encouraged the affair, but empowered herself through it by asking to be told every intimate detail, a request Abraham deemed he was in no right to refuse her.

— o —

I attended many of those gatherings starting with the first one. Abe and I had studied at the Faculty of Law at Oxford, followed by HEAD in Paris. Within weeks, we had become fast and lasting friends. It was also a time at

9

which we were made aware of Vertex's general principles and aims.

The first such congregation of like-minded friends at Ranch Acacia coincided with the establishment of both our law firms and Helen's pregnancy with Liz. I must stress that the fact Abe and I met Helen at *Les Hautes Études Appliquées du Droit* is of great importance—we even flipped a coin as to who would seduce her first. As it was, I never stood a chance, well-knowing a second round wasn't in the stars; but what's not to cherish in the thought!

— o —

Fast forward to when Liz wished to follow in her father's steps and join the firm under Garner, Garner & Lewis, having opted to study at Oxford and HEAD just as we did, and to the time she met Jack Lewis's younger brother, James, the man she, in her words, married too early and divorced too late.

— o —

The ranch was sold and razed to make room for new construction, as the winds that blew from Bass Strait carried with them the promise of big trade with Asia and the U.S. The gatherings continued elsewhere, but the years at the old estate forever remained a window into an extraordinarily vibrant and potent past.

——— o ———

3 – SAVAGE RIVER

As it went, Abraham and Harold Freeman—a seasoned guide and long-time friend from the days of Ranch Acacia—reached the remote community of Corinna by boat via the Pieman River. The old Arcadia II cruise ship had picked them up at the mouth where they had helicoptered from Hobart. All had been arranged stealthily with some of the tools available through the back corridors of power, namely—influence and proven discretion.

The aim of the trip was to reach the mining township of Savage River the back way, with plans to connect incognito with a Vertex agent embedded in the giant iron ore-extracting facility.

Abe was technically on vacation from his job at the firm, and the hike, in spite of its enigmatic purpose, had all the innocent makings of a rainforest packing trip. The trick was to not be seen by any of the six hundred or so employees of the mine when internal documents—as toxic as they could possibly get—changed hands.

— o —

Perhaps, a different plan could have been drawn, other arrangements made, such as meeting outside the facility when the informant was off-duty, but I wouldn't say Abe's logic swayed to the side of bad judgment—he always was a pillar of commonsense and integrity. No, there was soundness to his reasoning; likely, no saner options were available. Undoubtedly, he qualified as the best man for the job; he was extremely fit, perseverant, while owning a rare gift of sentience for his environment—plus he teamed with Freeman, the top wilderness guide on the island, and one of Vertex's most dependable and rugged go-to individuals.

— o —

The hike was an insane sixteen miles along the Savage River, with nothing but treacherous terrain edging white waters. Abe was clear that the only way to make it undetected was to travel upriver under deep canopy, since the Corinna/Norfolk road was heavily used by company personnel, while flying within reasonable distance from the mine was subject to radar scrutiny due to ongoing helicopter traffic in and out of the operation. It was a busy place patronized by heavy Chinese interests, which in part were the reasons why Vertex got involved to begin with.

— o —

In Harold Freeman's own words, after kayaking back down the Pieman from Corinna to the mouth of the Savage and taking off on foot from there, the two progressed steadily, nearly covering half the distance on the first day. It took much longer before the forest opened onto the southernmost part of the open mine, a half-mile wide terraced wound carved by monstrous machines. But it was hardly over, since the equipment repair facility where Yang Wu, the Vertex connection, worked as maintenance engineer, was another half day hike along the cliff edge overlooking pits and tailings dams. The plan was for Abe and Harold to come down a rarely used service road at dusk, right when the man closed his office

12

and walked to his parked car on the shadow side of the building. Wu would leave the documents atop a service panel pending a confirmed visual between parties. It was imperative that no direct contact, exchange, or signals be made, even if another two men walking out of the forest at that exact time was out of the realm of possibilities. Let it be told that Vertex took no unnecessary chances.

— o —

What drew unusual business to *Branched Resources*—the mega company that ran the mine—were the rumors from various ecological groups that the firm was at the negotiation table, hammering out the details of exploiting the entire Salvage River Regional Reserve and National Park, as well as portions of the Tasmanian Wilderness through backroom deals with the state, for the purpose of satisfying China's endless demand for high-purity iron ore, under the promise of a healthy job market and increased tax revenues.

The deal essentially translated into a no-holds-barred industrialization of Tasmania, teamed to an ecological disaster of unprecedented scope. From Vertex's standpoint, the destruction of fern trees and huon pine forests, as perceived through global, environmental sensibilities, was the mortal chill that guaranteed the irreversible compromise of the planet's ecosystem, with greed at the controls of existence's undoing.

Vertex's role in such matters was usually to ward off the established politics of obscene fortunes with a flurry of cases fronted by powerful lawyers, the kind of individuals with the mettle and audacity to successfully back desperate causes; but greed and corruption weren't openly China's angle, which isn't the same as saying that China never exploited the vulnerabilities of sins by means of a mindset even more pernicious. And for the sake of shedding light on the unseen, *Branched Resources*'s Savage River pits, a once Chinese-owned operation turned Australian company, remained under the control of a Chinese operating director. You get the drift; "once owned" didn't necessarily mean lost.

A quick look into the mine's finances revealed that although *Branched Resources* showed a 100% profitability rating, vulnerabilities abounded. Seasonal rainfalls and pit instabilities often halted production, with no stockpiles to buffer the cost. In other words, finances teetered on the capricious edge of demanding the impossible out of management and crews, a detail that fared poorly against a claim of exceptional safety standards—a minor lie, mind you, considering the implications of what a poor financial report could do to prestige and fortunes. Moving forward with the vision of increased production through the acquisition of public land via doctored leasing, was thus seen as the necessary one-way win the company's top executives and main stockholders had been gambling for. Undoubtedly, major lenders, notably top world financial institutions and the Chinese government itself owned one side of the negotiations, while the other was occupied by state political interests.

Abraham Garner as well as the larger Vertex naturally saw the acquisition of any internal documents depicting broadened mining operation into off-limit areas as the must-have tool capable of meshing judicial gears into exposing corruption. It was Vertex's core purpose to move the corrosiveness of backroom deals into the spray of Front Shield's decontaminants, and strip the truth clean for all to see.

It's well known a proper villain is tuned to the key of the dangers summoned by his trade, endowed with natural defenses capable of registering the slightest of tremors. My point is that in spite of the absence of foul play in Abraham Garner plunging to his death off the west wall of the lower tailings dam, the fact remained that the incriminating documents never left Yang Wu's hands. No doubt someone was well aware of Vertex's progress.

Harold Freeman resigned himself to being forced into the role of the confused hiker, while Abe was pronounced dead upon boarding the helicopter that carried his body to North West Regional Hospital in Burnie.

Last we heard, Wu was transferred to the Southdown Prospect operation in southwestern Australia. Vertex, because of identity security concerns, stayed clear of the engineer, opting to locate the files—if they still existed—via other means.

———— o ————

4 – THE CASE

Jack Lewis gave Henri and Liz a week to sort their things and enjoy the town before taking care of business. Not much of a break, I admit, but time was of the essence.

— o —

What did we, in Quebec, expect of Henri Desgardes? Primarily, we wanted to make sure he was made of a strong enough fiber to become one of us. We knew he was highly capable, based on his unique abilities, to follow in Abraham Garner's footsteps and eventually walk in his shoes, but we couldn't be sure until he got there. Only Jack Lewis was made fully aware of our intentions; Liz was kept partially out of it for reasons that should be obvious to most, mainly that she couldn't be tempted by an inopportune moment of misplaced confidence to share too much, too fast—something she would naturally know not to do—but I'm talking about the guilty kinks of intimacy here. Not that we didn't trust Liz, for she was one of us, but as I said, Vertex didn't take any unnecessary chances.

— o —

Officially, Harold Freeman was suing *Branched Resources* for the loss of his friend under the claim that the lack of warning posts and the failure to shore up the dam wall had caused his demise. Another related suit concerning toxic waste being dumped into Bass Strait at

Port Letta, the sludge separation plant and ship-loading dock at the receiving end of the pipeline that connected the excavation site with the main island and Asia, was attached as potential fodder for the main case. We were aware each lacked the traction to make a splash, but together they had enough weight to command the interest of a powerful law firm and, of course, the media.

All knowledgeable parties agreed that the Hobart Firm would keep operating under Garner & Lewis until Henri's immigration papers got sorted out. For now, he would intern under the terms of his business visa, while retaining a token employment with us in Quebec, the relevant details having been fine-tuned ahead of the parting ceremony. As things stood, the suit against *Branched* was used as transitional material legally tied to both firms, meaning Henri was responsible for sharing his findings with Lehman, Leduc & Marchand, which put the cases within the ballpark of international concerns.

The grounds for it rested on ecology now being a global reality, allowing cross-border entities to fly under the stamp of extraordinary status—notwithstanding *Branched Resources* had some explaining to do in regard to its public image as a green-operating model.

— o —

Straight from the tip of his bat, Desgardes deemed the ecological side incompatible with the accident at the mine, only conceding to research remaining loosely joined. Namely, he wanted two separate cases. After consulting with Liz, Jack Lewis agreed to take charge of Port Letta and let Henri loose on Savage River. I was pleased with the way things fell into place and how seamlessly Vertex was once again merging with Front Shield day to day operations. Sure, covers were the thing of shadow entities, but I can't stress enough how it pleased me in our case to know how cover and shadow were kept indiscernible from each other. Vertex existed by the simple rule of placing confidence in proven methods, and since we deemed most means of communication inherently insecure, all internal correspondence was via an unbreachable closed system. But take my word for it, nothing beat a good cover—thus why Front Shield was so indispensable to us. That being said, how in hell did things get so fucked up at the mine!?

— o —

In some respect, *Branched Resources* and Vertex share a common structure; there we had a company with open books, a vision of the future, and the proverbial promise of a better world via sustainable practices as a cover, while behind, its real intentions were kept under the seal of secrecy. Although I must stress the similarities stopped at the gates of incongruity—we aimed to save the planet while they carelessly trashed it.

— o —

As the first course of action, Desgardes agreed to meet with Harold Freeman. For now, I think it's best to let the two do the talking.

"Glad we meet at last, Harold!"
"Bonjour, mon ami! Pardon my French; it's about the extent of it! Pleasure's mine; how are you fancying

your new place—is Lizzy treating you right? I heard the wedding's planned for Christmastime."

"So, you already know everything about me—good, that'll save us the agony of small talk! I read your file; it appears that you and Abraham Garner were good friends—really sorry for your loss."

"Well, I'm sure you went through the ordeal with Elizabeth, no need to revisit the old pain. But yes, I'm suing these bastards for negligence."

"Let me get to the point, Harold, I've been told you're as top as it gets in your field; so how could you not have prevented the accident from happening?"

"It's true that I could have saved everyone the unnecessary sorrow, but I was taking a dump when Abe, instead of staying in place, decided to poke behind the last line of trees when the grounds gave and he went down with the lot to the bottom of the tailings dam."

"What followed, if I may ask?"

"Well, the racket got the attention of the mining crew. When I made it down there, a few blokes had already pulled Abe's body out of the rubble and called the facility doc. I'm not sure how they got a chopper down there so fast, but they immediately airlifted him to the nearest hospital. Security then took me to their office until the arrival of the police from Queenstown who flew me out of there."

"Indeed, such a remote location judging by the topo map. What took you guys to choose packing in under such adversity; I mean, wasn't that rather extreme!?"

"Yeah, some crazy shit, but not unusual for a couple of coots bent on outdoing themselves, and to be honest, each other as well."

"I get it; men will be men, right?"

"The arrogance of the male ego, if that's what you're alluding to; but I see you're rather fit yourself, so you're not in unfamiliar territory, I reckon."

"Guilty as charged! I must admit that I enjoy a bit of the old challenge myself, and with obsessive regularity, to be frank—hiking being a good chunk of it."

"Then we must find the opportunity to indulge; trust me, I know the bestest of the least trodden paths!"

"Which in your case means what, no path at all?"

"Touché! But I can make it easy on you."

"But let's get back to our case for a sec. You understand that while suing a large corporation for grievance, you mean nothing to them, or if you do, they'll want to settle out of court. So, yes, we'll go through the motions and you'll likely get a token compensation for your troubles. The question is what makes you think our offices would be interested in the job? It's hard not to call it a mere formality, considering you have near-zero of a case. It's just that Jack Lewis thinks there's something, but I'm at a loss here. Can you please help clarify?"

"Well, it wasn't clearly accidental."

"Yes, there's rumor of it, but you're suing for negligence, remember?"

"That's why I want to go back there to sniff for clues, because the authorities sure won't do it."

"If I get it right, you want to postpone serving Branched Resources *until you get what you're after. That might be stretching things a tad, but I guess it could be considered part of building a case with real teeth."*

"Correct! I also could use a solid hiker on my side—a win-win situation since you must absolutely check our wilderness out. I promise you won't regret it. You certainly can't pass on the offer, can you?"

"I say you set me up for it, but you know for sure how to hit the soft spot. I must check with Liz and Jack though. I'll get back to you!"

"Cheers, I count on you, mate!"

— o —

As expected, Jack Lewis was delighted by the arrangement. On the other hand, it still remained a matter of convincing lovely Ms. Garner, whose scar left by the loss of her father was still fresh, especially since it involved Freeman once again. But as a member of Vertex, it was unlikely she would stalemate the opportunity of moving forward. You be the judge!

"Freeman asked you to do what?! Is he out of his mind?! You're not going, are you?"

"I'll tell him no if you think it's a crazy idea, but I could use the exercise, especially if it's tied to the case."

"I'm still a bit fragile about the whole thing; I just don't want anything to happen to you—I don't see how I could handle it if you got hurt!"

"No way, I won't do it unless you want me to go!"

"Just let me think about it; it's so sudden!"

"OK, but no pressure, right?"

"I'll keep that in mind."

— o —

As suspected, Liz couldn't afford to pass on the opportunity even if she deemed it off the charts to let Henri within Vertex jurisdiction. She called Lewis, who, in no uncertain terms, reminded her of the purpose of

Front Shield. As long as Henri didn't know anything about the deeper layers of the case, he would simply be doing his job, albeit with the unorthodoxy of trekking for clues in the remotest part of Australia.

"But Jack, we're not talking about paperwork and phone calls here; there certainly is more danger out there than behind his desk!"

"I concur, but you know just as well as I do that if your father was indeed the victim of malfeasance, no one's safe anywhere, not even in our fair city."

"Let me be frank, Jack; it has long bothered me that Harold had so little to say about the accident. For Heaven's sake, dad was gone before he even had a look at him!"

"I shouldn't have to remind you that he had to act confused for the sake of saving face. At least, even if the mine surmised Abe was nosing into their business, Harold's slow response helped dispel their suspicions. Sure, one man died, but if it looked like an accident, it must have been an accident. You're with me, right?"

"I guess... I mean, can't we send someone else?"

"Who, me? Do I look like the hiker type to you?"

"Damn, Jack, this is cruel!"

"If John Lehman says Henri's the man capable of tackling our particular problem; why not put a little faith in this new partner of ours?"

"Aw, alright; I'll tell him to enjoy his trip!"

"That's the spirit!"

Jack confessed that Liz left his office somewhat confused, as if something greater than herself, or even the firm, had been rearranging the pieces of her father's mysterious death. In truth, the last thing she had expected was to see her fiancé thrown into the moving gears of Vertex. The fact was she wasn't easily fooled and I had no doubts she questioned my motives and judgment about deeming Henri capable of moving the case forward, as well as instrumental in helping recover the documents lost during the aborted mission. Knowing Liz as I did, "instrumental" already rang of the painful truth, because, at that moment, I was certain she was unable to see how Henri wasn't being used.

I couldn't blame her for feeling that way. She knew too much not to be aware that Vertex, the group she had joined in her teens, had seen an indispensable asset in her fiancé. The matter was that our choice stood at the fulcrum edge of her personal reality, making it harder for her to navigate emotions when tensions pressed against sensitive nerves. Of course, losing her dad complicated things somewhat, but at some point, she had to concede the methodology was sound.

————— o —————

5 – DICHOTOMY

As recorded, instead of flying to the mouth of the Pieman River and catching the Arcadia II to Corinna, Henri and Harold took the Murchison Highway northbound from Hobart, switching west to the old tin mining community of Waratah, where they spent the night at the one and only sleeping place on Main Street.

After taking off for Corinna following an improvised breakfast, they dipped southwesterly across the settlement of Savage River where the six hundred *Branched Resources* employees lived. Our two travelers who qualified as late-season/last-opportunity adventurers, were of no consequence to the mine's security eyes, as long as they didn't stop. Fun fact: in the quaint fashion of Australian road mapping, Waratah Road turned to Corinna Road just prior to veering northwest at a right angle to become Norfolk Road for a short stretch, before switching to Western Explorer Road. At that point, in a way difficult to describe, it turned to Corinna Road again, though no longer as the main artery, dipping due south and soon ending at the bank of the Pieman River where the Arcadia II was moored. To many a poetic and philosophical mind, Corinna was where the world ended; the last pit stop before entering the ephemeral *au-delà*.

— o —

"Now's the time to be a tourist before the hard work, mate!" Freeman uttered on arrival.
"No thanks, maybe later with Liz!"

"I reckon she might appreciate a honeymoon in the wilderness, being kind of wild herself!"

"Don't make me regret having left her in Hobart to worry about my wellbeing, Harold; part of me isn't so sure it was the wise thing to do."

"I gather that much, but it'll be over in a few days and you'll be glad we did it."

"Alright then, let's stick to the plan!"

— o —

The plan was a repeat of the trip with Abraham, except better, since Freeman had priorly taken the necessary steps to meticulously map the way, with food, water, and shelter details tallied to their basics for the double purpose of packing less and moving faster.

One could humor that our two men splurged on a night at the Tarkine Hotel and fine dining at Tannin, which incidentally was preparing to close for the cold season, but that would greatly misrepresent the Corinna experience. They called it a night after a game of chess.

— o —

Indeed, it was fall in the Tasmanian rainforest, with winter conditions approaching rapidly; and though the weather had been holding, Henri and Harold had to be well aware a surprise storm and a swollen river could drastically hamper their progress. Was it what Henri alluded to by not being sure it was the wise thing to do? Likely not, but Harold was quick to reassure him it wasn't going to happen and that colder conditions were actually working in their favor. In his words, *Branched Resources* weren't about to expect someone crazy enough to hike their way up the Savage at that time of year, which left Henri to reflect on the soundness of the guide's reasoning in the face of the obvious contradiction; although it made some kind of sense when trading an evil for another.

To save time and hiking distance, Harold parked the rented Land Rover in the last wayside area where Norfolk Road met the river. It was hoped the vehicle was situated far enough from the mining facility to not arouse suspicion; but once again, the guide was quick to reiterate that even with worsening conditions, a few hard-boiled hikers had to squeeze at least one last trip before season's end.

Naturally, Henri's rational side was at that point beginning to wonder why backpacking with Abraham had required so much more vigilance.

"I know I've already said it, but the more we go, the lesser I understand why you chose such an elaborate route the first time around. I mean it's clear that your main objective was, for whatever reason, to get to the mine, but why the added tedium?"

"I admit we wanted to see the mine, but you're wrong in calling it our main objective; that was reserved to manning it up all the way to the top, and we did that. What followed was a monumental fuck-up!"

"I guess this time the objective is different, sorry, my bad!"

"You're the lawyer, old man; inquisition is in your blood. I'm sure you'll pester me till all of your questions are answered, right?"

"Right, the questions are here for good reasons, but placement is paramount. I'll try to remember that."

"Well, to answer your initial query, I don't even know why you keep on asking, since we've already established the bad weather is bound to arrive soon. I think you're trying to ferret something in the narrative and you're not getting to the point."

"True, there's something I can't quite put my finger on—some kind of production in the making of the first trip that is absent here. From going over the dossier, I can't reconcile the extra length that went into arranging for the Arcadia II to pick you guys up at the beach after having been dropped there by helicopter with any kind of logic. I mean, having been close to Abe myself, I would never have guessed the man capable of going through such trouble to get to a trailhead. If the hike was the objective, why the unnecessary arrangements?"

"I reckon your way of looking at it is your God-given right, but Abe always did things his way, and since I saw no wrong to it, I went along without getting my shorts in a knot. I don't ponder on that sort of detail, but then again, I'm not an investigative lawyer."

"That's what I am, a nosy bastard. But since you practically begged me to come so that you could show me the fun spots, I feel fine being a nag."

"That's the Australian way, mate, we live with our faults for all to see!"

— o —

Surely, Freeman was jesting—Henri was no fool! There were too many innuendos and artifacts of double entendre to not expose the veil. No doubt Desgardes was beginning to trust his intuitions about the trip being closer to a mission than a quest for clues!

From that point on, I understood why Henri refrained from asking any further questions, becoming the observer instead. In spite of Harold's raw cordiality, he sensed the man was on the defensive, as if threatened by the tightening of a snare he couldn't comprehend.

— o —

The fact was, Henri was moving too fast on figuring out he had been enrolled in a scheme, while Freeman lacked the quickness of mind and the finesse to dispel that notion. I should have known for working with Desgardes all these years that Harold wasn't a match for his mental acumen. But the guide was the only man for the job, and Henri the only individual capable of sorting the mess out of our diminishing options before they died.

I hate to say that, but for a multiplicity of reasons, it was too early for my friend to home on the nature of his involvement beyond Front Shield, a moniker, irony of all ironies, he wasn't even aware of! Too much was at stake—his relationship with Liz for one thing—but the level of betrayal inflicted by a group he considered his long-time friends was too cruel for words. Right then and there, I contemplated pulling the plug on the whole thing, so that he and Elizabeth could enjoy a life together.

What stopped me from doing it was the sheer direness of letting an international league of crooks perpetuate irreversible savagery on the planet—that ship had to be sunk! I said there were no tricks involved; call me a liar if you wish, but someone had to take the plunge, get the ball rolling! I had wished for a more prepared other to walk in his shoes, but Henri Desgardes was the chosen one for reasons too complex to explain. Let's just stick to trusting there were layers in play at the time that hadn't coalesced into enough of a force to turn my vision into a focused reality.

— o —

By the time Henri and Harold made it to the spot of the accident, ominous winds had begun blowing from the direction of Bass Strait, gathering the earlier patches of clouds into a mass of swirling greys and blacks. Before long, the rain moved in, turning the ground to slippery muck.

The hikers hurriedly set up their Stormbreak solo tents within a natural shelter of high bushes, a few hundred meters away from the dam.

With still plenty of daylight ahead of them, they set their hopes on inspecting the collapsed wall and a chance at stumbling onto something of significance—luck had it the rain subsided as they got there. Harold noted the road below had been graded anew, but scars and rubble still marred the side and bottom of the west wall. As Henri reported, the entirety of the tailings dam was a mess of fissures and slides, which in mining reality, as he rightfully pointed, translated into a critical mark of failed engineering, implying a wall could collapse any time of day without warning, which, as we saw it, provided the ideal environment for an accident to occur—a detail that glaringly opened the field to unspeakable opportunities.

Henri later confirmed that his private commitment to investigating the possibility of foul play was based on that observation alone, while unbeknownst to him, Freeman, by his side, was churning different matters—namely, how to recover Wu's documents.

Since the whole of the half-mile long structure of the tailings dam was visible from above, Henri noted another glaring fact: beyond it, crews were busy in open pits, carving and hauling ore, digging and blasting, but no-one tended the dam—it didn't need tending.

"Harold, you said workers saw to Abe's body before you managed to make it to the bottom; isn't that peculiar based on what we're not seeing here?"

"You read it in the report, mate, I didn't even have a chance to get to my friend before he was hauled away."

"I gather there could have been a survey crew in there at the time doing a routine job. Did anyone look into schedules?"

"I personally wouldn't know; isn't that for your firm to find out?"

"I didn't come across any mention of it in the mine's report—why I'm wondering if you overheard or observed anything out of the ordinary."

"Well, the blokes didn't look like equipment operators, more like engineers, except fitter."

"Fitter? You mean like me—fitter than your lawyer type?"

"Yeah, like you!"

"So, what you're saying is that they weren't your regular engineers. Maybe they were from Quebec, no?"

"Don't fuck with me, Henri, now's not the time!"

"Alright mate, but please, cut me some slack; I don't joke very often."

"I'm just getting impatient, plus I'm not sure what I'm looking for. Maybe you're right; this trip could be pointless after all!"

"Don't you think it's a bit late for remorse!?"

"Yeah, just saying—I'm done fucking around!"

"OK, Harold, I'm sure you hear as well as I do the general racket that comes from all around this hell; we've got blasting, conveyor belts, grinders, engines, and what have you—you get my point. Now, the report says the noise of the collapse was what attracted the attention of the crew. I find that odd, don't you?"

"Yes, that's why you're here, Henri, to comb for the fine mental details, because there sure isn't much in terms of obvious clues."

"I'm not looking for anything specific as you are, Harold, I'm just observing and picking at the inconsistencies. Now you tell me you and Abe weren't onto something? Rubbish! Anyway, I'll get to the bottom of it eventually."

"You're losing it, mate; I never said it wasn't personal, but yes, I admit that by taking you with me, I thought you might see things in ways that could help me figure out what happened—nothing more, nothing less!"

"I can't help you figure anything out if I'm not seeing the larger picture, sorry!"

— o —

I'm sure Harold was dying to know what the larger picture meant, but he refrained from digging any deeper—no doubt he had recognized the slippery edge of the impending abyss before him. Henri should never have smelled foul play in the first place—now my friend wasn't only on the defensive, but on the offensive as well, because he had suddenly realized teamwork was never part of the deal. At that point, Freeman had become both useless and dangerous—all games were off!

31

That complicated things somewhat, for all had hinged on Harold maintaining his composure, which I feared was now lost to the ages. From Vertex's perspective, the desired outcome of the trip was much more in Desgardes' findings than in trying to make up for a missed opportunity. Sure, the documents were important, but the plan was for our man to sniff out what had eluded us all—and nothing else! Sadly, Freeman had mouthed off early, not realizing Henri was on him from the onset.

— o —

From where I stood, I much doubted the trip ever was for pleasure. Henri relished the workout, but his number-one purpose was the job: to see for himself what had taken Abraham to his death. Now, he had to deal with the added complication of figuring out why Freeman had lied about having chosen the Pieman River route. He knew damn well it hardly had been Abe's wish to opt for that itinerary. According to office data, Abraham had already booked the flights to Burnie Airport with plans of driving south from there; something the guide was obviously unaware of. According to Liz, the last minute change had annoyed her father. Technically, Freeman had nothing to gain from lying about who was in charge of the details of the trip; it was just a terrible case of mental arse piss, to use one of his pedestrian terms. But that was the point; something needed to be exposed, which justified why I chose Desgardes as our main man, knowing the breadth of his investigative acumen.

Until proven otherwise, Harold was in the clear; but let me tell you that the notion of murder had taken the case on a twist for the bizarre. Henri's main responsibility had been to build traction in suing *Branched Resources* for negligence. Now, Freeman had managed to compromise himself, and the possibility of murder, not only at the hands of the mining company, but possibly of another player, had tainted the pages of Henri's findings and challenged the soundness of my personal reasoning. It made for unplanned convolutions that could only translate into slowing things down on an already thin schedule. I started to look for options when the news came in.

Liz was at the end of the line, sounding frantic. A first draft of the new lease proposed by the state for the opening of reserves and parks to mining had come through the back door. Things were moving at a faster pace than envisioned, which proved that enormous amounts of money attached to international interests were being poured into the pockets of federal and state politicians alike. It was nothing but a heist of the highest order, impervious to the catastrophic consequences that were to follow. Vertex was silently failing humanity and the planet, with the added irony that the only man on a mission to save the day didn't know the first thing about his assignment.

— o —

6 – LAYERS OF DECEIT

As it went, the bad weather ended up flushing Desgardes and Freeman out of the rainforest, but not before they got to Yang Wu's original meeting place. By then Henri had stopped engaging, surrendering to Harold's visible desperation. After all, silence spoke volumes.

Henri's notes checked the parking lot as empty, with just the orange glow of a lone sodium vapor lamp flickering in the heavy downpour. Memorized aerial photographs of the facility made quick work of the service box on which the documents had originally been slated to be left by the engineer. Nothing there naturally, but upon close inspection, Henri discovered a small, muddied plastic object lodged in a crack at the base of the cinderblock wall—a common, inexpensive thumb drive sold at local markets. He handed it to Freeman, whose facial response didn't lie.

To Henri, whatever flashed through the guide's head only enforced the fact he had been played. His angle on the case was now all too clear; he was in charge of following his own instincts and logic, intent on keeping even his fiancée and business partner, Elizabeth Garner Esq., out of it until further notice—yes, that bad!

On a softer note, he had put one foot inside Vertex without realizing it—a lot like most of us did.

—o—

I now rejoice at the thought, but at the time, I couldn't see how that trip would be of any service to us. I essentially relied on gut feelings, basking in grotesque vulnerabilities, while trying to convince myself I had chosen wisely in getting Henri involved in our affairs. I couldn't fathom my dear friend was made of a better fiber than most of us. Now, I deeply regret the arrogance that brought me to think he could be harnessed into our scheme—he couldn't, or be fooled for that matter, because he always had played by his own rules.

— o —

Back at the mine, things quickly turned for the worse when a pair of security Land Rovers appeared out of nowhere from both sides of the horseshoe lot, forcing our two intruders to seek shelter at the bottom of a flooded gully, until high beams and engine growls returned to the night. Blind and drenched, Henri and Harold skimmed the half-circle of the lot, reaching the service road that spanned a swollen branch of the Savage, to at last reenter the forest, relieved not to have been caught. From that point on, rolling rocks, mud, and a treachery of branches littered the precarious edge of their travels all the way to the lower dam, where they miraculously reunited with their tents. It was nearly three o'clock by the time they laid their wet bones inside their sleeping bags. Outside the thin shelters, the rain came down relentlessly, while in the short distance slides were heard tumbling and crashing.

— o —

Henri could simply have pocketed the flash drive and said nothing, but, as recorded, he needed to verify the

35

one thing that had been nagging at him from the moment Harold first lied to him: his true reason for the trip.

There was nothing to lose in letting go of the drive; likely it was nothing of importance. On the other hand, the reaction on the guide's face told Henri the story of a man determined to find something, anything that made up for the one reason he and Abraham breached the mine's perimeter in the first place. Call it a glimmer of hope crossing his eyes, a twitch of the lips, or a nearly unperceivable pause that only a readied observer could latch onto—it went in a flash! It was the moment Henri had waited for, the affirmation that mind and senses were on the same page. Eventually the drive's origin and contents would land on his desk, but for now Desgardes had no interest in it—it wasn't why his head lay mere inches away from the weather. On the other hand, the mine's lack of interest in addressing the structural issues of its tailings dams mattered. Perhaps *Branched Resources* didn't need to bother, even if it was well known in the industry that a ruptured dam had all the makings of hell; but then again, Desgardes was alert to the fact regulations around such structures were practically nonexistent, since a staggering only ten percent of them were known to exist around the world— negligence wasn't even a factor. The Freeman suit against *Branched Resources* had no legs. It didn't stand a chance in court—Lewis knew it, Liz knew it, and so did Harold. It all tumbled down to a pile of irrelevance that left Henri with the vague notion that the essence of truth had nothing to do with the trip, yet everything to do with it. His tired mind demanded answers, knowing too well that over-thinking was the antithesis of reasoning. He closed his eyes and slept until the noise of machinery and the raucous banter of cockatoos woke him up. The rain had subsided with steadied temperatures at a manageable fifty degrees, bringing the anticipation of a safe return within the realm of feasibility. Freeman stirred in his tent.

"You're awake, mate?" he grunted.

Yes, Desgardes was awake alright, and anxious to get back to Hobart to put his version of the case together.

Predictably, as in all things ever so close to being perfect and convenient, the rain returned with a vengeance. Water was everywhere, making progress gruesome and the prospect of locating the rental pointless. With no food, drinking water, or respectable rain gear, the spectrum of survival had critically narrowed. As obstacles increased exponentially with every added turn, a defeated Freeman declared they were lost. Henri kept to himself, plowing ahead, making the best of his compass, which more often than not acted confused because of the ore-rich subsurface. As I knew they would, they reconnected with Norfolk Road, but nowhere near their vehicle. With dead phones and no access to global positioning, they each took an ignition key and walked in opposite directions.

—— o ——

7 – JACK LEWIS

Henri asked a reluctant Freeman to drop him off at Burney Airport. The idea of spending interminable hours in the company of the guide was beyond his capacity of tolerance. He arranged for Liz to pick him upon arrival at Cambridge and drive him directly to the house.

"Two days late, no phone, I was beyond worrying! Please promise me to never do that again!"

"Next time, love, you and I will lose ourselves in the forest—Harold's company was a total downer!"

"I hope you at least gained something from it."

"Yes and no, but first I need to cleanse my body, clear my head, and get some real rest."

"I can help with the first part and then you can go lay your sleepy head on a clean pillow, no?"

"As you say, sweetie!"

With that, Henri leaned back and surrendered to exhaustion.

— o —

As mentioned, Henri was convinced the suit against *Branched Resources* was pointless. If it hadn't been for Jack Lewis insisting on moving forward with it, he'd have thought of it as a ploy to assign Freeman a companion on his quest to retrieve what he and Abraham Garner had failed to obtain. Although, it wasn't Henri's business to preoccupy himself with anything beyond the scope of negligence on the part of the mining operation, being kept in the dark about the true reasons for the trip seriously hampered his ability to find validity in his work.

Here's what was said in Lewis' office:

"Why are we doing this, Jack?"

"I believe Freeman has a case, plus we owe it to Abe and Liz."

"I don't wish to disagree, and you know how much I care for my fiancée and Abe, but based on the location and the instability of the terrain, not to mention there was trespassing involved, Branched *owes nothing to Freeman or the public at large. All we'll end up with is some barking from the media and a waste of time. Don't we have more important cases?"*

"Freeman is the plaintiff/petitioner. We, by rule, don't sue on our own behalf; you should know that."

"Didn't you just say we owe it to Abe and Liz?"

"The question is, why didn't the suit pop-up in your conversations with Harold? I believe that was the purpose of you guys getting together—to get familiarized with its details."

"It did, and it's not like Freeman is convinced either. I tried to enquire and educate myself, but have you ever known the man to be chatty beyond being incapable of not divulging what he wants to hide? The whole thing was a disgraceful fiasco!"

"I gather he's a bit heavy-footed when it comes to subtleties, but what would he lie about anyway?"

"The real reason for our trip, for example."

"I'm not saying that he didn't have reasons other than those originally stated, but I don't see why you should concern yourself with them. Did you or not find

evidence of negligence around protecting the public from failing dam walls? That's all we're after, the rest is Freeman's choice to keep to himself if he so desires."

"OK, if that's all there is to it, I'll be at my desk polishing the details. Next time, I would appreciate if you thought of me as more than just a glorified clerk."

"No worries, we just want to make it easy on you during the whetting stage. We know what you're capable of and we're honored to have you here. You'll have full reigns when your resident papers get sorted out."

"Thanks, I will also send the file to Lehman when I'm done; you're still OK with that?"

"Absolutely!"

— o —

The brilliant side of Jack Lewis lay in his ability to make difficult matters sound easy. He always sought the shortest distance between two points, never encumbering himself with the detours of emotional distractions. He had no time for them since they required energy that he would rather put to good use on more important affairs. That quality didn't go unnoticed to Henri, a man of no nonsense himself, a trait that had been instrumental in him envisioning he could one day belong to the Hobart team. That was before Abe's death, around the time things began souring up in Quebec. The two men became friends; the kind of friendship that called for two like-minded individuals to connect when it mattered. During Henri's many visits, they never socialized for the sake of entertainment, sticking instead to analyzing the fine points of business concerns, and then part with a handshake, sober and fulfilled. They were agents of purpose, rational thinkers who recognized the importance of irrationalities as the solving half of many puzzles. Together, they possessed unprecedented peripheral vision.

That was one of a handful of characterial elements—if I may be allowed to imagine a stage full of actors—that confirmed Henri was the naturally-fitting element to our mission, even more so when Abe plunged to his death. So, yes, with the senior partner gone, it opened the path to partnership for Desgardes, a scenario with all the allure of orchestrated placement. But no, Abe or no Abe, Henri was destined to join the firm, albeit at a less convenient time. All existed in the light of our then-present circumstances; had the first trip to the mine been successful, convenience would not have applied—just to prove the connectivity of all things.

Eventually, we must return to Elizabeth Garner and how she fitted in our process of bringing the wilderness leases to a halt. Circumstances dictating, I am least suited to speak about her *present-past* around Henri, compared to recounting her earlier life as she grew up on the ranch. I thus propose that the torch be passed to Desgardes as the main narrator until further notice.

— o —

PART TWO

8 – FREEMAN

It seemed strange that I came out of winter to enter fall. Even weirder was the sense it wasn't my first time around, although that may have arisen from my wish to live in Hobart with my beautiful wife-to-be, Elizabeth Garner. Paradoxically, she was the one and only reason why I found myself backpacking with Harold Freeman in the Savage River Regional Reserve.

I couldn't believe I had fallen asleep the whole length of the ride back from the airport when Liz woke me up in the driveway of her house—our house, rather.

I was torn between sharing my impression of the guide and his lies, and keeping my suspicions to myself as I had intended up at the mine. I was well aware that by hiding my thoughts I was inculpating Elizabeth and jeopardizing the trust between us, but on the other hand, I felt it would have been a mistake to move too fast.

Even though I believed I wasn't cleverly coerced into moving to Tasmania, and that my relationships with the Garners and Jack Lewis over those last three years had been genuine, I couldn't shake the notion of a subplot following its course beneath the surface of my daily life. All that because Harold Freeman had lied to me, while Jack Lewis insisted there was a case when there was nothing more than a sentimental gesture cast to the memory of Abraham Garner, and the showing of team love towards his daughter.

I considered myself rational, but my intuitions had always served me well—I was always at home when insight and method worked side by side.

Coming out of Lewis's office, I felt the split tongue of doubt travel down my spine; on one hand I was delusional, on the other I wasn't, but my closest friends weren't what they seemed all the same. If anything I was a lot like my confused compass, up by the mine. What I needed most was a long walk, alone, by River Derwent.

Gusts blew from the north, it was cold and drizzly—it felt wonderful!

— o —

It was obvious that John Lehman, the individual I considered one of my best friends in Quebec City, had intentionally prevented my promotion to senior partner from happening. Yes, I took it as an unprecedented act of sabotage towards my career, but the true hurt was in not being given a reason for it—he washed his hands of the decision in a most condescending manner by keeping a profile of disgraceful nonchalance around our inevitable interactions at meetings. From the minute he put Sackman in Marchand's place instead of me, my perception of the firm and life at large veered to the unreliable side.

I could have confronted him; it was in my court to challenge him, but I was one to take a fait accompli at face value. His decision was motivated by a personal evaluation of my professional capacities, and as unfair as it seemed, I had to accept it as some form of viable truth. I'm not saying that I surrendered to the injustice; no, I needed to think about my options. After all, it wasn't a case of having lost my job; on the contrary, I got swamped with work as a result. That fact opened my thoughts on the possibility of a fissure somewhere below my personal awareness of the self. There was something of my own making that transpired into blame towards Lehman, even though he certainly was to blame for being an asshole. At some point, I had to take responsibility for what was happening; so, short of finding direct answers, I put myself in a place where I could at least form cohesive questions by taking charge of my life and contemplating the options before me that best aligned with John's motives. It didn't require cognitive genius to realize that my one opportunity to further my relationship with Liz while gaining partnership in her father's firm was right in front of me, a below-the-table gift from an old friend who didn't want me to know where it came from, or rather, didn't wish for those at the firm to discover its existence. I could have come to him to say thank you, but I believed I was expected to play by his rules. Whether he intuited I had caught up with his intensions or not at the time was up for debate, but there was a deeper communication transcendent of all things rational, one unbothered by superficial details, that ran in the sub-layers of shared consciousness. I kept the cold front going for the sake of it being there. I guess it was a rather transparent cover, but that was all my instincts were willing to give me. Within a few days of John's decision, I called Elizabeth to tell her of my wish to move in with her.

—o—

By the time I returned from the mine, an active picture had formed in the back of my mind. As much as I objected to Liz belonging to it, I couldn't pretend she didn't exist—of course, she had to be on that stage somewhere. During my walk along River Derwent, I made the surgical decision to expulse delusion and paranoia from my psychological makeup, and rather than looking at the situation from the outside, I opted to stand as one of the actors. That automatically removed doubt and incrimination from my case research, and turned the tables from facing the dark to embracing the light.

— o —

"Where have you been, Henri; I thought we were coming home together?"

"I know; I'm sorry, but after meeting with Jack, I needed to clear my head, so I took a long walk."

"That explains why you're drenched. Why didn't you ask me to join you; I can handle a bit of rain now and then?"

"I needed to be alone to exorcise the demons that had taken possession of me, if you should know."

"Whoa, that bad, hey?"

"Fear not, it's all good now."

"Do you care sharing with the love of your life?"

"I will tell, but first, let's order some dinner!"

— o —

That was one way to commit to my new, personal dicta. I had to share my thoughts if I didn't want to lose Liz, but there were ways to go about it that flowed better than others. It came down to not offering anything that didn't belong to the subject at hand, the miracle of simplicity, so to speak—easy and uncompromising.

Neither of us liked to cook after work, so we opted for Thai delivered from our favorite place, a candle, and a pot of Sheng Pu erh to accompany the food.

We only were occasional drinkers; something that pleased me greatly about our relationship. Booze was the drama of my previous marriage where I witnessed, first hand, a human's steady fall from grace in my then-wife, Claire. No need to elaborate—it just wasn't pretty.

James, Liz's ex, was a bit of a sot himself, so we shared similar pains about love.

How comforting it was to sit across this gentle woman around noble food! I couldn't believe I had once twitched at the notion of her not wanting to live up to the standards of a successful lawyer. That night, I was grateful for the wisdom that had softened those views, because I wouldn't have wanted to be anywhere but within the warmth of a place Liz so happily called home.

— o —

"So, what's up?" she asked lovingly.

"It's all about the case Jack assigned to me—the oh-so absurd negligence suit."

"I thought it'd be perfect for an introduction, plus it's personal. I understand it's not very interesting, but believe me when I say you'll get your fill of challenging cases in no time."

"Let me rephrase that; I'm worried about Harold. I don't believe he's totally upfront with me. Jack told me I shouldn't concern myself with what he does. The way I see it, what Freeman does has a lot to do with what happened to your father, or at least, it leads me to think it has a lot to do with it."

"They were together when he died. They also were close. But I'm curious—what makes you think he isn't upfront with you?"

"For one thing, why lie about who made the travel arrangements? He told me your dad was in charge, when clearly it wasn't remotely true. It made so little sense that it forced me to doubt what I had read in the internal report."

"I see... I admit it's a bit out of character. Yes, he did make changes to dad's original plan of flying to Burney and taking off from there."

"Don't you find it outlandish for them to cruise up the Pieman? Right, it was a pleasure trip after all, but it never was in your father's style to act like a wealthy tourist. What surprises me was how easy it was for Abe to buckle under the pressure."

"I should have known you'd have the nose for the stuff most people don't notice, but since you and my dad were also close, it makes sense you should pick up on characterial inconsistencies."

"I can live with a few inconsistencies as long as they don't manifest as lies. Freeman told me that your father always did things his way, meaning it was his idea to go up the Pieman."

"I disagree with Harold's insinuation that my father was controlling; to the contrary, he was known to be rather flexible."

"Well, apparently, Freeman wasn't aware I knew your father well, otherwise I don't fathom he would have had the nerve to say that about him."

"I see what you're aiming at... So in your words Harold is hiding something both he and my father were complicit of; am I right?"

"You might look at it that way or not; I'm more inclined to think Freeman is working from an agenda going beyond suing B.R. for negligence."

"And what would that be from where you stand, my dear one?"

"Something you might have been exposed to or overheard—how would I know? Have you guys been involved with some of Branched*'s legal matters before?"*

"No, but we've been approached by a number of environmental groups seeking our services."

"About what?"

"Apparently, there are talks of opening the wilderness to mining—pretty serious stuff."

"You're not saying! How long has that been going on and how come I wasn't told?"

"I hate to put it this way—longer than it should have! The state has already drafted a proposal that, if it pleases Branched Resources, *will open the road to the full-on industrialization of our beloved island. As to the other half of your question, it was a matter of time before you'd stumble onto the info."*

"Thanks, I just have! Am I to guess the proposal is backed by wealthy countries short on materials?"

"You move on fast, mister!"

— o —

I knew it! At last we were getting somewhere, but I chose to swiftly shift the conversation to a less toxic topic, sensing that going any further was about to drag Liz to a place she didn't wish to go. I had enough on my plate to arrive at my own conclusions anyway. It was nice to learn I wasn't totally mad; yes, Freeman and Abe were in it together and something had gone awfully wrong. I sensed ominous winds coming our way—could Abraham Garner have actually been murdered, and by whom?

Of course, I suspected Harold saw more than just negligence in Abraham's tragic end, but until Liz unveiled the larger picture, it didn't quite add up. I began to believe I had been subtly coerced into joining the guide as someone who could observe from a fresh perspective. Interestingly enough, I was finding my comfort zone in the deceit, as if catching up with my true place. But who was behind putting me there—Jack? Lehman? Liz?!

— o —

I didn't think of Freeman as someone other than a big guy with so-so manners. But I was now forced to revise my impression of him. First of all, he wasn't who he claimed to be—that became clear the instant Liz shed light on *Branched Resources*'s shenanigans; and second, he had too much clout over Abraham to be a mere peon— the last minute change-order before the trip sealed that up. But why wasn't he aware I was close to Liz's father, or was he? So then, was the damn lie a calculated move to bring me where the hypothetical *they* needed me? It was difficult to see otherwise. I felt the current pulling me out of the eddy and taking me down the rapid—my river was calling! Even if the circumstances felt fabricated, they were circumstances all the same which I had to embrace.

Liz snapped me out of my thoughts.

"Time for bed, dear man, we have a long day ahead of us tomorrow!"

—— o ——

9 – NOTHING EVER TOO STRANGE

John Lehman called when I was out of the office. I had anticipated some form of feedback from the case files I'd sent to Quebec City in the early morning, but instead of the usual confirmation of delivery followed by the approved, sanitary small talk, he left the least expected of messages.

"Henri, I'm coming to Hobart; you and I must meet in private. By the way, I just spoke with Liz; glad you guys are doing great!"

No, there wasn't any surprise in John visiting Tasmania; he had been there often both on business and for pleasure, but this was different. It sounded urgent, almost desperate, and that worried me. "By the way" was Lehman's way of saying, prepare for some unexpected bullshit. I immediately wondered what he and Liz had shared that prompted the unscheduled trip. I had the gut feeling my darling fiancée had rung him with the news of how I had jolted her out of her comfort zone. What in the world did he have for me he couldn't convey in a simple phone conversation? Damn his fucking drama!

— o —

I was particularly intent on getting the inside story, so I took Liz for lunch to our favorite seafood place by the cove. Not only did she show no surprise about me having heard of the call, she was actually excited about the news of John's visit. True, they were close, which likely explained the absence of what I was unabashedly looking for in her demeanor. The fact she acted as her regular self hinted at my invalid reasons to doubt her trust. Shame on me, I was the one with the trust issue, and if she perceived any of my regression, wise of her to ignore it! Still, I pressed on.

"Henri, I understand your confusion about the call, but remember, John used to visit a couple of times a year, and more often when he could. Of course, my dad was around then, but still, we're family."

"Did you mention anything about our dinner conversation last night; I gather you called first, right?"

"I don't know if you're digging or being psychic, but yes, I reached out to him first, and yes, we spoke about you and Harold."

"Would you have told me if I hadn't asked?"

"Do you tell me everything that goes on with you, Henri? There's a time for revelations to meet the occasion, and both of us, I believe, share the same book of rules. But since we're on the topic, let me simply confess that I don't have the resources to face up to the pressures of your deductive skills concerning matters tied to both here and Quebec City. So that's why John is coming, hopefully the day after tomorrow. All I can say is brace yourself for some out-of-the-box disclosure. You now stand fully updated!"

I thanked Liz for being upfront with me, although I couldn't help feeling diminished by the elements of secrecy that kept on being heaved in and out of the narrative. It wasn't in my nature to lag behind the latest, but I admit to being confused by the mode under which I had operated since Marchand fell ill and Lehman pulled that dirty trick on me. For the sake of clarity, I ventured to ask Liz one more question.

"You don't have to answer this, but are you and Lehman onto something I should know about?"
"It's not a game, Henri, but I understand why you would see it that way. On one hand it's yes; there are things you must know, but I believe I've also been kept out of the loop in regard to your involvement in the case, or rather, how it was arranged to involve you. So, I'm just as curious as you are about what John has to say."
"Thank you, I needed to hear that."

— o —

Lehman had insisted I pick him up alone. In his words it was imperative that matters be introduced without the energy of another person around. It was a curious way of asking for privacy. In my book, either someone was there to hear or no-one was, but the "energy" of another person being in the way was new to me. John was never known for his parabolic requests; under normal conditions he would simply have asked me to come by myself. I didn't make it all the way to that point in life to not heed nuances. Basically, he didn't want Liz or Jack around, but he could just have said that. I knew the fact he didn't was yet another expression of his annoying characterial kinks.

"Nice to see you Henri; I reckon I've got some explaining to do! But first, let's take a detour; I'm not quite ready to face the welcoming party, plus, I need time

with this—hope that works for you? Please, Sorell to Richmond, and over to Dowsing Point, if you don't mind! To cut to the chase, Liz hasn't played you; she has no idea what I have in mind. And no, I didn't fuck you over by getting Sackman to fill in for Marchand—I needed you in Hobart, and since things worked out so well between you and Elizabeth, I pushed for it with the tools at my disposal. Ultimately, it was your choice, irrespective of whether you believe me or not."

"I'm free to deduce you played the matchmaker as well. You didn't just jump on an opportunity; you created one, am I wrong?"

"As usual, you're moving fast, Henri, and that's the reason why we're here. It's a good thing, a very good thing, because in some places we don't make it this far. But stay with me for now; your questions will fit much better later, and I promise they will be answered with full disclosure. As I'm trying to put across, this isn't your only time sharing a life with Liz or working on a case with Jack Lewis. It isn't a loop either; these other times exist within this very present, just a tad removed from our senses. Liz, Jack, Harold, Jean and Eric in Quebec City, and of course, Abraham and myself, among the many who attended the gatherings at Ranch Acacia, are either part of or connected to this group we call Vertex. I'll get to the technical details later, but for now, based on your impressive skills, the time is ripe to ask you to join us. Here's the gist of it: in this version of reality, we find ourselves facing the unique opportunity to make an impact in saving the planet from over-industrialization and the irreversible collapse of its ecosystem. Imagine if you will devolution on a race to the finish—that's what we have in all the versions paralleling this one. In each of

them, we pathetically fail at stopping the state from granting mining rights to Branched Resources, *which in a nutshell will lead to Asia, with China at the helm, controlling all planetary assets. In no scenario but this one are we contemplating a murder case, and consequently in neither of them do you come pick me up at the airport—in other words, this discussion isn't taking place. I hope you're following me. You were not tricked into joining us, Henri; you found us, and you're the reason for this dim light of hope flickering on the horizon. Do you want me to do the driving?"*

"I'm fine, John, I get it. I just wish I had your peripheral vision; does Liz know that?"

"To a point, like most of us at Vertex. So that you know, we all started in your shoes. It's all a matter of disabling the mental safeguards meant to protect those of a lesser personal evolution. I don't mean it in a derogatory way—we all evolve at our own God-given pace. The meetings at the ranch were for the purpose of initiation; some made it, others didn't."

"I assume those who didn't have no memory of the process."

"No, they do. For them, it was simply a fun experiment that failed—nothing more than a social game around wine and good weed."

"Was I one of those who failed?"

"No, it never came to that. Had you remained in Canada, you would have had to go through some form of briefing ahead of joining the partnership. It was on my agenda until I realized your true place was here. But before we go into the finer details, bear with me and let's round this up! Vertex has metaphorically been around since humanity's first steps. The name's a reflection of the

ages, as there was no need for one then. At the exception of an era stretching into the dark ages, its purpose has been to keep evolution sputtering along, so to speak. It didn't always work and some versions of reality just went flat, but we never came to the level of seeing ourselves on the brink of a planetary catastrophe of our own doing."

John's revelations could have hit me like a ton of bricks, or left me incredulous as to the level of bullshit cast my way; but no, as crazy as it sounded, I was drawn to it by immeasurable curiosity; even more so now that some churning of memory was being felt on the far shores of consciousness. I had never been in the car with John under any scenario; that I was sure of, but what preceded my return to Hobart after the hike with Freeman was rife with déjà-vu. In some rather odd way, I saw side roads to my past already explored, places I had visited—the same places, the same people, but disparate outcomes that all led to the same catastrophic future, give or take a decade or two. The images became more powerful as the drone of John's voice faded in the distance of my inner *recollectings*. Yes, *Branched Resources*, China, the environmental groups, Abe's accident—all there—all ending at the same place of me not challenging the faits accomplis. One could say the repetition finally brought me to the right place.

"So, Henri, are you in for the ride? Now's the time to ask questions if you have any!"
"I've got it, mate, forget the initiation!"
"You're not going to pass on it, are you!?"
"Come on, John; don't tell me you need to keep this going past its useful point. We're good, I've caught

up and I shouldn't have to tell you! It all began to make sense when you called."

"Then welcome to Vertex, Henri!"

"Are you sure I haven't been there all along."

"Of course you have."

$$— \text{o} —$$

Liz had been waiting for us, as radiant as I had ever seen her. She hugged her Uncle John, as she called him, and kissed me on the nose like she would a loved pet. It was her way of saying *I love you* when she was full of play. I didn't expect to find her in such a bubbly mood; rather I would have imagined she had all the reasons to be anxious about how I would be faring after speaking with John. But no, she acted as if nothing ever happened.

I admit that I got a bit cocky when I told my old friend that I was ready. I wasn't quite there yet, although I could see my past shifting in the form of overlapping memories, like the one of being let down by the firm in Quebec becoming overshadowed by my distinct choice of relocating to Hobart. I was moving from one plane of focus to another, on a quest for the ever-better scenario. My long practice of choosing the path of least resistance was paying off.

Liz turned to me.

"Eventually all will come into clear focus, darling. You may choose to access the memories of other life courses, or not; it'll make no difference as long as you stay as sharp as you've ever been—they'll just come to you when needed. Or you may opt to be curious and dig deeper, like John here, or my father. Me, I'm still

learning, but I gather we never stop. Based on where you're at, I suggest you go for the whole package. I'm here to help whenever it suits you."

Jack Lewis joined us later with a celebratory joint of the finest Hawaiian. With a head full of smoke, I began to settle in my new self, one not too different from the old one, just a bit sharper, a bit more optimistic, and distinctly more open to loving the love of his life. One look at Liz, and I instantly knew we shared one thought: we couldn't wait for the guests to leave—we were both on fire!

— o —

10 – TOTAL REBOOT

Harold Freeman entered my office as I was preparing to work on the larger *Branched* case. Jack had informed me earlier that my papers were in order and to expect my permanent resident permit to be issued within a matter of days. I guessed being a high-level lawyer on the way to marrying another was worth a lot of points in the Australian immigration rating system—a good thing they knew nothing of the business I had embarked on. Of course, that would have been wrongly assuming the Australian Border Force Commissioner approved of systemic corruption within the state of Tasmania!

Harold looked awake and fit like a man that had already visited the gym. He was gracious in all of his roughness and I was glad to see him.

"So, ready to go over what we covered at the mine?"

"Yes Sir, did you get the flash drive?"

"Brilliant! Who would have thought Wu had the prescience to foresee someone eventually picking up where you guys left off and finding his marker, and a clever one at that? I know it isn't much, but it's a step in the right direction. You'll be working on it, I gather?"

"Correct, my man's on it as we speak."

"OK, I still need clarification on why you changed your approach plans for your trip with Abe; any specific reason?"

"Yeah, I got wind of someone snooping around—Burney no longer felt right or safe. I immediately

contacted Abe and we decided to make new plans. He wasn't too happy but we had no choice."

"What were your sources' concerns, anything concrete?"

"Well, it's been their conclusion that something leaked out of one of the environmental outfits anxious to get your firm's attention. Someone within Branched must have eavesdropped on a conversation, because we've been on their radar since those groups first made contact, but you already guessed that, I reckon."

"Indeed, but here's where we're at: going after these guys for negligence of public safety, while suspecting them of having orchestrated the accident is a bit of a dilemma. We found nothing at the mine that supports foul play, except for the presence of a crew that technically wasn't needed. I'm still awaiting a work sheet through the back door, which as you know isn't totally reliable, but I keep hoping something will show up."

"That certainly would add weight to the package. I've got to confess that I'm no longer keen on suing for negligence—it'll just undermine what we're after. A murder case is bound to impact the momentum of their shady business with the state, but I also understand that we're short on time any which way we shake it. We know we can proceed immediately with the grievance case, but is it worth it?

"Hey, I'm with you, Harold, but you need to tell Jack; otherwise I'm ready when you are. Why don't the four of us meet tomorrow same time before we proceed; does that work for you?"

"Sure, I'll be there."

"Oh, I almost forgot; thanks for the birthday present; that was a nice surprise!"

"Think nothing of it, mate, it's been a pleasure working with you. We're glad to have you in these parts!"

— o —

And just like that, Harold and I went from foes to friends—the type of transitional process I wouldn't have been aware of from the standpoint of a few days ago.

The beauty of Vertex was in being connected to a source of knowledge not previously available. According to Liz, I was a rare case of seamless adaptation. I guessed, and ignoring John's wheeling and dealing, I was mostly there by nature, at least in terms of amenability. It was a rather comforting feeling to find myself around people just as odd as me. But "odd" might be a tad harsh for staying the course of clarity. Persistence was key; it paid off the minute I forgot about the notion of being owed a modicum of justice. Justice had nothing to do with it; thrust, on the contrary, was the ticket to a lot of learning in the shortest amount of time. From the moment that wheel made its first revolution, the laws of exponentiality kicked in and I was on my way.

It wasn't as if Harold Freeman's lies were gone; rather, they had become absorbed by a haze of miscues, like causes whose effects were lost in a dreamlike past. They stood as ghost memories, only vaguely connected to the vivid present. I imagined that for minds of lesser focus, parallel realities and their pasts were blocked from view, as they were from me until recently. It took the trigger of those very lies to bring me to the gates of my own inner workings and help me realize the futility of life as a linear concept. Possibilities begged to be explored, as the self no longer wished for the constraining circle of its illusionary tethering post. As such, Harold became a new man whose lies and secrecy were replaced by a genuine desire to share; he too opted for the path of least resistance, choices that instead of stifling the larger picture, gave it a chance to spread into further possibilities. Ultimately, those changes came because I yearned for them. I was taken into a world of my own making whose players had made similar choices about theirs—we merged into a common element of synchronicity, as one of combined individuality and togetherness.

Under that new light I observed the glaring ineffectuality of suing *Branched* for negligence. Win or lose, the end results would simply bar the way to going after the more serious charges of premeditated murder. If we really meant to put the brakes on the momentum gained by business and politics, we had to strike an exposed area. Without the grenade of a murder case we had no chance of creating a big enough wave—going for the jugular in one quick move was the ticket—then may the doors open wide for the environmentalists to pour in!

Naturally, we didn't quite have a murder case, only the hypothesis that Abraham Garner wasn't dumb enough to fall to his death when he should have been waiting for Harold to finish relieving himself. It was up to me and Freeman to go after the clues, which categorically excluded a third visit to Savage River. We had to assume everything we needed was within reach, obvious or not; for now, not so much, but trust was the given in finding the unfindable of desperation. Somewhere out of the two trips, and perchance with what Harold extracted out of Yang Wu's flash drive, was the path to building a slammer of a suit against *Branched Resources* and a devastatingly negative public opinion of the company.

But first I had to convince the partners and win their support, which likely meant monopolizing our entire resources and some. But I had ideas, which I sensed may not have been strictly my own.

— o —

As anticipated, everyone, including John Lehman, was there on time, except for Jack who had been put in charge of coffee and pastries. He came in with a cartful worthy of a hungry crowd—his way of setting the tone in keeping all of us in the best of moods.

I opened.

"We're ready to file a motion against Branched Resources, *but I'm not convinced it's the right way to go as per what Harold and I shared yesterday. I propose we take a close look at our options before reaching a consensus."*

Liz: *"The premise of the suit was to get Henri on board in hopes he and Harold would come up with more useable material than that consolidated from the various police reports and* Branched Resources*'s internal inquiry. Although the fact that nothing striking has come of yet doesn't imply such material doesn't exist. It's my opinion that we should invest our means into activating phase two of the plan."*

Me: *"Phase two of the plan?"*

John Lehman: *"Phase one started when you chose to move in with Liz and ended yesterday when you made your mind about the irrelevance of filing for negligence. Phase two commences today with the murder case. You get the chronology of it, Henri, don't you?"*

Me: *"Yeah, alright, John, I do..."*

Jack Lewis: *"There isn't an option for consensus when we all already are in agreement. It's obvious that much of our resources with be needed, but John and the rest of Quebec are joining us for a one-two punch assault. There also are firms in the U.S. and Brazil that might connect at the appropriate times. For now, we need to move swiftly with the murder package.*

Harold Freeman: *"Glad we're getting on with the program. Thanks for what you did, Henri; now we can start the real work!"*

— o —

Talk about being caught in the throes of radical changes—I yearned to quickly regain a sense of balance. Nothing like struggling with my further education, while digging into the derma of our collected material!

We needed both the mine worksheets and what Harold's man, Uri Dudko, was after up north. In the meantime, we had extractive work on the slate demanding surgical separation of intuitions from wishful thinking into a clear exposition of facts.

Until we could put our hands on those dreaded timesheets, we had no way of delegitimizing the presence of a crew at the dam. But nothing stopped us from working with what the odds had brought to the tangible: the chances of a crew of structural engineers being there to respond with such unprecedented efficiency as to load Abraham's body onto a helicopter before Harold could make it to the bottom were in the realm of one to the million. Pending the contrary, preparedness had to have been a factor in such a smooth operation!

From there on, a new field of speculation opened to lively possibilities, the wildest of which, a smoke screen concealing a disappearing act. This is how it went:

Harold: *"Mate, what if Abe had been snatched at the top and the rest was just an act? Say, they grabbed him, blew the face of the wall, put one of their own on a gurney and declared him dead on arrival! All I saw was a mess of flesh and crushed bones the next day at the morgue—his body was unrecognizable from the injuries. Liz had a look and fainted!"*

"Yes, everybody assumes Abraham's body was properly identified, but I must admit it crossed my mind that something could have been overlooked or rushed at the hospital for the possibility of error in confirming his identity to occur. Now you're saying he might never have made it to North West Regional—what a concept! So, you're inherently telling me that all stones are still left unturned, if I read you right?"

"You can say that's the type of shit that keeps me up at night, starting with that dreadful day!"

"Now you understand we're looking at an insider, someone so close that they knew everything about your trip. In other words you'd been followed, which also means your informant was jeopardized. Tell me, Harold, on what do you base your assumption Yang Wu was there as planned? He could just as well have placed the thumb drive at your rendezvous spot at an earlier time, as a last ditch effort to warn you."

"I dig the way you think, mate; you know how to put some meat on a bleached bone!"

"Colorful! But yes, I admit it's quite the plausible scenario, and within the reach of organized crime. At the

end of the day we must ask ourselves, are we there? Is Branched Resources *that sort of villain? Where else can we go with it, any idea?"*

"Well, it gives us the hope that Abe might still be alive; that's something worth looking into. It also gives us the motivation to forge ahead, which at this conjuncture is the boost we've been waiting for. I'd go with it and not look back!"

"It's a start; but who's our dead man then?"

"Umm, presently pondering on it... That couldn't be Wu, he's working at Southdown, plus he's Chinese; that would have showed through the injuries. One thing for sure, our dead bloke wasn't a friend of those miners."

"That either leaves a nosy environmentalist, or one of Wu's sources as our top candidate."

"That demands checking into who's missing among the groups, or who died at the mine around that time. If nothing shows up, we'll go down the ladder."

"I'm on it, Henri!"

— o —

With his kind of no-nonsense approach in unearthing possibilities, Harold missed his vocation as an investigator. We were on a path to something, but first I had to check in with Liz, even though the hope of her father still being alive was at the risk of swaying her opinion to the side of invested interests—the cost was high, but she couldn't be left in the dark.

"Listen, Henri, it's not that I haven't thought about it; we all have. It's just that we can't back-engineer that kind of scenario without a form of compromise at

some vital level—we simply can't afford it! As much as I want to see my father alive, I'm not going to bargain our one chance at slowing down the ongoing negotiations between B.R., the state, and heavy international interests. We must pursue the murder case because it's the only element of tangibility on our table, now, tomorrow, and every day until the jury returns with a guilty verdict!"

"Liz, one man died! It makes no difference to the court who did or didn't. Officially, Abe is the victim and we'll stick to that scenario, but looking into a broader level of criminal sophistication might benefit our options. It's a simple addendum to what we're already working on."

"I get it, Henri, but it's a bit too close for comfort. Sorry about raising my voice."

"I understand, love."

— o —

When Harold called two days later, I had an odd feeling something went wrong. I picked up, bracing for the worst. He was frantic.

"We must meet, Henri—now!"

I hurried to the coffee shop around the corner, on Elizabeth Street, where I found Freeman at the back waving at me.

"Mate, bad news, we lost Uri in Launceston. Last I heard of him, he was meeting with one of the connections listed on Wu's drive. He had caught up with a live trail to the documents we're after. His mobile is down; I wonder what the fuck could have gone wrong!"

"OK, Harold, calm down! How long has it been since you two connected?"

"Three days ago. He claimed he would have something for me by yesterday, but he went cold. As I said, his mobile is no longer active; I checked with his provider."

"Well, I've got news; it sounds like you and I are going to Launceston. Liz is going to kill me!"

— o —

Liz didn't kill me. She was coming too and there was nothing I could say that would make her change her mind.

"Consider it that trip you promised me, darling. I'm sure we can arrange for some private time away from business!"

I had no choice but to surrender.

——— o ———

11 – LAUNCESTON TRAIL

We were now warned that a modicum of vigilance was required. Liz and I flew to Launceston Airport, while Harold drove the hundred miles in a rental. For the sake of staying apart, we also booked rooms at different hotels. Just like Uri Dudko did, we memorized the data from the thumb drive. It wasn't much; just a one-page text document with a list of random numbers accompanied by names, and the one instruction, *Follow chronologically*, typed at the bottom. In all likeliness, the names weren't real—it read like a code meant to be deciphered by Vertex recipients. Harold confirmed that Uri was working on the second item, number twenty-one, when he last heard of him. It turned out, according to Liz, that Launceston was the twenty-first largest urban area in Australia, while Hobart was the thirteenth and first on the list. There were two names under twenty-one, James King and Val Dosne, neither of which rang a bell.

Uri never recorded the steps of his findings, something Harold didn't expect him to do. His role was to first get to an item of importance before reporting. Last he called from Launceston, he sounded emotional—he had, according to Freeman, caught up with a live trail.

For Dudko to have been stopped in his tracks before turning in his first report was alarmingly indicative someone had been following him from the get-go. Harold was at the helm of a leaky boat, becoming painfully aware that either *Branched* or one of any hypothetical villains was keeping a close watch on his operation. Incidentally, it meant that Vertex had been jeopardized the minute Garner,

Garner & Lewis hired his skills, which as it turned out were those of an investigator under the unofficial cover of wilderness consultant. One more instance of me being behind the facts despite having correctly intuited earlier about the nature of his true calling. But what else was new!

— o —

I deemed it safer to break up the team, with Harold going solo, leaving Liz and me as twin sleuths. That meant no more meetings in person, and only the encrypted line to communicate our findings with each other. While we didn't think more than one set of followers would be after us, there was a chance I had been spotted in Harold's company at the café on Elizabeth Street, notwithstanding what happened with mine security when they came barging in from both ends of the lot as if we had been expected! No need to pretend Liz and I weren't compromised. But we both wondered why Harold was making his move without proper protection. It looked like negligence, or maybe he gathered that staying out in the open, being loud, was his best camouflage—kind of weird, if you ask me...

— o —

Two names begged for different directions. Checking the phone directory led nowhere. Yes, there were a few James Kings that popped up through identity search, but that pretty much self-explained the futility of that route. It meant the names weren't as they seemed, if they were people at all! It took Liz's lateral thinking to circle an answer. The plural of King, Kings, connected her sonically to King's Bridge, and it didn't take her long to link Val Dosne to Val D'Osne, the cast iron fountain in Prince's Square built by the art foundry Barbezat & Cie in Osne-de-Val, France, also commonly known as Barbezat Fountain.

"Someone's been doing her homework; you sound downright encyclopedic!"

"I told you, my schooling was rather rigid, plus I studied in France, taking the opportunity to visit places of interest. As it turned out, I rode with friends to the site of the old foundry, a museum now, to connect with the origin of our cherished Launceston landmark and the casting methods that went into it. There's a funny story about it; according to one myth, the statue was meant to travel to Launceston, Cornwall, but instead was shipped to Launceston in 'Cornwall Shire,' Tasmania. Due to the high cost of shipping, the statue couldn't be returned, and the council, not knowing what to do with it, placed it in the freshly built St-John's Square, now Prince's. But you can't always trust a myth, can you, Henri?"

I felt like asking her to marry me on the spot! I could have made love to her right there and then, hadn't we been in plain sight of passer bys. But that didn't stop Liz from pinning me against the door of a recessed entrance and pressing her knee against my groin.

"You're not safe tonight, Henri!"

That was all I needed to hear to find myself in my comfort zone. I loved her, adored her; I elevated her like the Goddess she was, knowing quite well in all of my bones that the sentiment was reciprocated. What a magical time it was—love, suspense, danger, et al!

— o —

Harold went to the bridge, while we, lovers, lolled around the square. Although, it wasn't the best time of year to act like insouciant tourists, we were impervious to the chill and the steady drizzle that threatened to turn to rain any minute.

We circled the fountain, looking for clues, watching for potential onlookers, spies, villains crouching in the shadows; drawing lines and angles from Moreau's Acis, Galatea, Amphitrite, and Neptune to trees and surrounding structures. We leaned against the fountain's circular edge, kissing like students high on hormones and weed; letting ourselves be soaked by the waters above and the beneath-currents of knowledge. We were one, Elizabeth Garner and Henri Desgardes, in the perfect moment, in a place so indefectible that nothing, yet everything mattered, neglecting the mechanicals of protection against the unknowns of greater realities for the open of pastures. If it was what Vertex did to you, I was a convinced buyer. Liz and I had no idea what Uri Dudko had been up against, or how he got to interpret the list on the drive, but we were certain he didn't see what we saw and feel what flowed through our beings.

— o —

What we saw and felt was the rise of a force whose roots plunged deep into the pool waters of potentiality to which multiple versions of our present reality were already plumbed. It was vibrant with purpose, aware of itself, and intent on realizing its vision into accomplishments. We both liked our new path, and somewhere by King's Bridge we hoped Harold had found his as well.

But how to explain what went on when words were too short on meaning to extricate something that didn't belong to the common language? For the sake of corniness, it was an immersion into some developmental humus that knew not of the physical because it didn't comprehend it, but because it didn't seek its association. In all certainty though, Liz and I stood firm on the clear understanding that it had everything to do with love.

— o —

That metaphorical path was our new direction. Astray from it, we were doomed to failure, and it wasn't about to show itself without Liz at my side and the renewed vitality of our love for each other acting as catalyst. If what stood before us lacked in concreteness, it certainly wasn't short on magnetism. As I said before, we aimed for the path of least resistance, the one along which all the elements of reality coalesced into an unbroken flow. So, it was no surprise to find that what we came for had been around us all along—water! Water from the fountain, water under the bridge—plain old fucking water! As we checked each item on the list, all the names, when switched to places, led to water, the blood of physical life!

Harold called shortly after our stunning discovery, stating that all he saw was a river below the bridge and rain running in gullies. He had his answer, but he wasn't looking at it. I simply told him that we didn't need to check any of the numbers on the list, the answer was the list. It didn't mean that Uri hadn't been followed, or that his disappearance was a false negative—we still had to look for him. Unfathomably, it appeared that his hot trail was a trap, but set by whom? It was time to confer with Harold on whether to get the authorities involved or not.

We didn't have to; an hour later, Uri Dudko's body was found floating in the South Esk River.

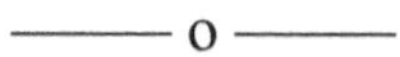

It looked like *Branched* had now two murders that needed explaining. Harold was devastated by the news, but most importantly he realized that his own life and those of anyone found nosing around the company's affairs were in danger. It naturally included the law firm and the environmental groups. It was time to maintain a low profile and keep Freeman from visiting the office.

— o —

In spite of the commotion, it didn't stop Liz from acting on her promise. After a lovely dinner followed by some dancing, we returned to our hotel room and had the best sex of our lives. We also discovered that we were exquisitely suited for teamwork. The best was still to come!

— o —

PART THREE

12 – THE MEANING OF WATER

The water enigma was yet to be cracked. A mix of intuition and logic dictated that the toxic documents sought by Abraham Garner had a connection with it. But water existed aplenty in and around Tasmania, and the chance of locating where that particular water pooled or flowed, was left to the contents of the thumb drive to tell.

The instruction said, "Follow chronologically." Did it mean that the last item, Perth, or number four, was where those papers would be found? It was also close to Southdown Prospect, another *Branched* facility, where Yang Wu had been transferred. But that sounded both too good and tedious to be true. Liz and I doubted the engineer sought to meet. No, this was a diversion, the kind that didn't bode well, a corruption in other words.

As if she read my thoughts, Liz entered my office.

"Henri, I'm practically sure the thumb drive was placed by Branched*'s men, even if Yang uploaded the text onto it originally. The minute you retrieved it, they got their signal. Here's how I see it: they understood the number code but couldn't decipher the names, and then added the instruction as a means to trace Harold and his associate. They also knew first hand that he and my father had planned to backpack into the wilderness to reach the mine. I'm almost certain Yang Wu had been compromised by then. By killing Uri, they're expecting Freeman to pick up the trail at the fourth item, number forty-six, or Devonport. He mustn't go there; I believe they are seeking to eliminate anyone following that list. Trust me*

when I say it was never meant to be a chronological search, which may explain why Wu chose cities by urban population as opposed to that of their greater areas. I swear the instruction is the corrupt item; it screams of 'do not follow chronologically!'"

"I fully agree; the same scenario has been gnawing at me since we returned. I guess now's the time to figure out the meaning of water!"

"An anagram, perhaps; the only one in English is 'tawer' for white leather maker. Henri, can you look for a tawer reference on your laptop?"

"From what I can see online, there's nothing, except for that guy in Devonport who makes high-end whips—Devonport again!"

"Odd, but that's got to be a false positive, if it's any positive at all—too vague!"

"Rivers, lakes, bays, frog ponds, tailings dams..."

"No hike to the mine, mister; not without me!"

"In all seriousness, would you go if asked?"

"Earth to Liz, you walked into it, girl! But in all seriousness, Henri, I hope we don't have to!"

— o —

I couldn't get my own mention of the tailings dam out of my head. It was like a bad song that kept on playing. Seriously, where in the world could the engineer have hidden a set of documents by a dam, waterproof case and what not? It was a crazy idea, period! But the more I thought about it, the more I comprehended that Wu couldn't have walked out of there with the papers. They had to be at Savage River, or if they were gone, they went a different route. At any rate, the very existence of the thumb drive indicated mine management didn't get to them. Meanwhile, the coded list was proving to be both pointer and diversion, depending on who read it and how to interpret its recommendation. Suddenly, the whole thing became over-complicated; something the metaphorical fork in the road created by two lovers at the Val D'Osne Fountain wanted nothing of.

— o —

The minutes of our findings and speculations were recorded, encrypted, and then sent by Jack Lewis to Lehman, Leduc & Marchand for evaluation and backup. The connection with the Canadian firm was kept at its lowest level as part of new protocol. I didn't expect to hear from John unless he had something important to add to the pot. But "important" being a figure of speech, the short text that landed on Liz's mobile simply said, "I see more than one water on that list~~ xo."

"It's Waters, Henri, not water!"

"I get it; but take a pick: name or place?"

"You're right, another fold in the plot; at any rate, the only choice we have is to look into it."

"Too many people named Waters—it's got to be a place or a placement reference! Let's see... here we go, two hotels, one in Swansea another in Orford, and a café in Glenorchy."

"Wow, it turns out James and I stayed at the Freycinet Waters in Swansea on a few occasions, and Lips Waters Café is a hit at the Garners; dad and I used to eat there regularly."

"Which one is it going to be, darling?"

79

"Both, Henri, let's have lunch at the Café then drive to Swansea and book a room at the hotel for a bit of romance; what d'you say?"

"Definitely in my line of work, partner!"

"We're both serious, right?"

"Absolutely!"

— o —

Some made play feel like work, others like Liz made work feel like play, keeping the joy of existence front and center. The path of least resistance was naturally effortless; it flowed, allowing for an unobstructed line of sight. Focus remained steady and sharp, the mind clear and alert. Said effortlessness translated into unparalled efficiency. True that kissing and playing with each other's bodies caused much distraction to staying vigilant, but it didn't mean the senses weren't tuned in to the task. As a matter of fact, due to Abe's frequent presence at Lips Waters, instinct leaned in favor of someone having information they might or not have recognized—same for the hotel in Swansea, another favorite among close friends, namely Jack Lewis as well as quite a few at Front Shield.

Miracle had it that the minute we entered the café, the manager, Irene, handed a locker key over to Liz.

"Your dad left it for me to give to you in person. It was a while back, but he insisted that you had to come in first. Sorry if I misunderstood him."

"Thanks, Irene, any idea when that was?"

"About a month ago."

"Thanks again! Any recommendations today?"

80

"The calamari is always a favorite, but you can't go wrong with the Nasi Goreng. Take your time."

"Thank you!"

— o —

"Wow, Liz, thanks for not saying 'Are you sure!?' That was fucking intense!"

"That's for sure! The key belongs to one of the lockers facing the conference room. Let's swing by there on our way out; but first we've got to make sure no-one's presently keeping a tag on us."

"Right, and let's get out of here as soon as we're done with eating; we can always talk details in the car."

— o —

Sure enough, the attaché case left in the locker was one of Abraham's. It contained a single envelope addressed to Liz.

Dearest, Use your unique skills to figure out your place in these family matters; it will soon make sense. Hope your drive to Swansea goes uneventfully. Please return the case to the office; it belongs there. My love to Henri, Dad

That was, in no uncertain terms, extra-odd. Liz looked at me clearly befuddled. Apparently the man was alive—the case and the handwriting couldn't lie. Irene, the front of the house manager, couldn't have mistaken such a flamboyant regular renown for his charm and excellent culinary knowledge for someone else!

On our way to Swansea, we both agreed that Abe's note didn't change the fact the man was officially dead—the suit would stand as planned. Notwithstanding that with Dudko found floating in the South Esk, the fundamentals of the case remained the same: *Branched Resources* looked bad, whichever way you shook it. The overall feeling, though, was one of inversion, an instance of the plot taking us back to a different beginning.

"Why would dad do something like that? I feel so betrayed. How can I ever forgive him?"

"I don't think forgiveness can be factored in such a situation; only a last recourse option could push anyone with any love for their close ones to make that kind of a choice—it's an inhuman demand. There's something below it that feels swampy, and frankly, I wouldn't want to gamble all of my chips on this one play."

"Are you saying you don't believe dad is alive?"

"No, I just don't trust he's alone in this. We're trudging the murky waters of a monumental hoax. If anything, he's in danger and so are we."

"So the note is dubious?"

"Could be, love—we must approach what's ahead with renewed caution."

"I'm with you, but why is he asking us to return the attaché case to the office; don't you think it's odd?"

"Liz, you genius you; forget Swansea, it's a trap! The list is a trap—we're being played as we go along; that why we're getting nowhere!"

"Man, you've got to be right; this is ridiculous! Someone knows way too much about us. Let's turn around and think this over; it's obvious we're just wasting precious time. Of course, that's their plan to stall

us—the whole thing is a sinister setup of Machiavellian proportions!"

"If so then Yang Wu is a poser for Branched Resources, *a cut-out figure. What do we have on him, and who's our dead man at the mine?"*

"I wasn't briefed on Wu, but Jack has access to his record. I've always assumed he was Vertex."

"It's my fault; he should have been my first concern; but to my credit, I didn't quite anticipate ending up here, in this kind of investigative clusterfuck."

"It's not like you didn't ask for it, darling, but now isn't the time for self-flagellation. Get over it!"

— o —

Jack returned with the info on Wu, a printout he insisted we shred after memorizing it. He was Vertex, based on the nearly indiscernible watermark in the paper stock, but he wasn't Chinese—his wife was, and the likely reason why he changed his identity. He was born Dominic Vaughn, in Newcastle, England. His family migrated to Australia when he was four and settled in the Melbourne area before crossing over to Tasmania. He married after majoring in mine engineering at Curtin Perth, getting hired shortly thereafter by *Branched Resources*. Last but not least, he was a physical match for Abraham Garner. The odds that Yang Wu, né Dominic Vaughn, was still alive were practically zero...

— o —

Before sending the latest to Quebec, Liz, Jack, and I reconvened around our options, which didn't amount to much beyond questions in need of answers. Without a doubt, we had to realign our logic and catch up with *le temps perdu*, the time lost on a wild goose chase. But Liz, who wasn't so ready to abandon our gathered information, valid or not, came forward with a recap.

"Wu's death implies he was holding potent information regarding the deal between Branched *and the state. Let's imagine he was uncovered and taken, but not before placing the thumb drive at the rendezvous spot, which was found, manipulated, and used to take Uri and the rest of us on a path of deceit. What doesn't stick though is for anyone to have arrived at the same conclusion as we did. There isn't another path to water, Waters, and then Lips Waters Café where we found the attaché case, unless someone read our minds. Since Harold was out of the loop when we took off for Swansea, it only leaves John Lehman, who suggested Waters as an option. I don't think the idea here is to fall for a game of division within Vertex, unless an insider crafty enough to be a step ahead of our affairs is invested in undoing the organization. That leaves a mystery character walking in the shadows of this very room, or bugs everywhere we go. Talking of bugs, Jack, I trust they're not a fixture of these offices?"*

Jack: *"No chance of it, Liz."*

Liz: *"So, we have a body that doesn't want to settle on a specific victim, another found floating in the South Esk, no proof of shady backroom negotiations between* Branched *and state politicians, and a bunch of environmental noisemakers insisting that we sue for no pay—that's for the one end. On the other, we're in charge of saving humanity and the planet. Anyone feeling the burn yet? Henri, darling, aren't you the guy who's supposed to put this train wreck back on its tracks? Is Lehman's golden boy a total bust, an overrated underachiever? That's what I would ask if I didn't know any better! Sorry, love, nothing personal! I'm done!"*

Me: "No offense taken, sweetie, your better side far eclipses your good one! But for the record, the slate has been wiped clean and it's our one opportunity to start afresh. We still have a murder case against them, except that they won't expect us to switch bodies on them. We shall sue them for the wrongful death of Yang Wu. Someone interested in calling his wife? And of course, at some point, we'll need to find some incriminating documents. But first things first!"

———— o ————

13 – THE SHADOW MEN

Ehuang Wu lived on Westfield Street in Seville Grove, one of the Perth southeastern suburbs. She hadn't seen her husband in ages, but knowing the demands of his job, she resigned herself to long stretches of silence between phone calls and visits. She didn't try to hide how it pained her to not have a real family, though she refrained from saying that their union was a mistake. In her report, Liz mentioned picking up on broken hopes and a loveless life. Yang's paychecks were deposited directly in a shared account, but since she had her own, Ehuang claimed she hadn't kept track. As incredulous as it sounded, besides lamenting over the lack of cell coverage at the mine, she saw nothing wrong in her husband's absence. They did email each other, sharing news once or twice a month, but nothing more. Although Liz wasn't at liberty to tell her Yang might be dead, she made it clear that his whereabouts were unknown, suggesting that Ehuang try reaching out. The woman remained emotionless, but something had awakened inside her judging by the sudden changes in her aura, a detail that couldn't escape my partner's acute sense of perception. She took Liz's card, receptive to the recommendation to call us if in need of anything. Now we waited.

— o —

Getting a positive identification from ash was tricky business; bone fragments needed to be present for DNA testing to be effective. Liz and I had spoken of scattering Abe's ashes after our honeymoon, never imagining that the thoughtful delay could one day be a case solver. Abraham Garner was followed by a medical record containing all the information necessary to pit any outside testing against it. All of it, including DNA data, had been downloaded and kept in Vertex storage, while a physical copy was stashed in Liz's office safe.

It didn't take long to identify Abe's ashes as those of another body. In the meantime a desperate Ehuang Wu had called Liz for help. She was flown to Hobart, while her husband's medical files were wired to Macquarie Street, courtesy Vertex's proverbial back corridors of power and an ever-accommodating John Lehman.

With DNA test results as evidence, a motion was filed against *Branched Resources* for Yang Wu's murder and the kidnapping of Abraham Elliot Garner, a powerful and highly respected Australian attorney. The local news, timid at first, but under pressure from forces they couldn't control, were eventually all over it. Of course, the mining company apologized for its bad seeds, promising to do all they could to assist the authorities—meanwhile the corrupt state officials involved in the leases played dead.

Still, no news from Abe.

— o —

In spite of a successful first step, Liz, Jack, John Lehman, and I believed that *Branched* didn't act alone. The company was a machine dumbed down by its own monstrous weight. They had the power to want, but no skills of execution; the finesse was in the hands of more crafty players, the professionals of the dark with a profound understanding of the psychology of the open—the fearless ones—those who delivered while sweeping their tracks with the finest bristle. Most importantly, their motto operandi was self-protection, even if it meant turning against the client, and logic dictated the day would come when the money stopped flowing.

From that scenario's standpoint, it wasn't a reassuring thought, because if Abraham was still alive, he was soon to become useless, notwithstanding he knew too much. Discomfortingly, the time of his execution balanced on dynamics still unknown to us.

— o —

There were ramifications to Abraham's kidnapping that hid beyond the face of an accidental death; otherwise, why not kill him outright! I expected bargaining chips in play for both *Branched* and their "outside consultants," and perhaps, the idea of a ransom wasn't too far-fetched, just in case the client failed to pay in full. Also, *Branched Resources* had all to gain from an outsider making Abe reappear amid court proceedings—a catastrophic outcome for anyone invested in bringing the lease negotiations to a halt. In other words, there was still hope of getting Abe back in one piece. As my mind spiraled down the rabbit hole of unfathomable scenarios, Liz's voice brought me back to reality.

"So, what about the attaché case and the note, not to mention how they arranged to read our minds?"

"Did they? I don't believe they deciphered anything; they just followed Harold and Uri because they had tags on them. Freeman and your dad were the original targets, the first to be set up. I wasn't factored in

their plans, which is why John thought—because of our relationship—of lining me up for duty here. Finding the common theme to the list of names wasn't quantum science. Arriving at "water," and with a little push, Waters, was relatively easy. I deem it a simple puzzle entry with a two-layer clue that repeats itself throughout the list, irrespective of the order."

"Henri, allow me to remind you that not everyone is a genius; at least admit that it wasn't obvious!"

"Obvious or not, we found the entry, no?"

"Actually the entry should have been Waters, and if it hadn't been for John pointing to said obvious, we wouldn't be here talking about it. So, genius boy, what have you got to say?"

"If I recall, you solved it and I was too slow-witted to compliment you for it. Perhaps we should get back to the main topic, Liz, ma cherie?"

"Right on! So, a month or so ago, dad showed up at Lips Waters with his case and handed the key to Irene for her to give to me, at which point we discovered that the best way to not be followed was to return the case to the office as advised by his note. Based on my brain flashing on multiple hypotheses, the mundanity of his warning was what made it actual. He knew we were going to meet with trouble in Swansea—but how, and why Swansea—we were going there, remember?!"

"Yeah, say he was being watched and perhaps, his hand was forced; so what could he have written other than what they told him to write and some benign stuff about Swansea? But you and I know Abe would never waste anyone's time with banalities—there's nothing innocent in mentioning the town; he was both telling us we were on the right track and warning us about

ambushes. The clue, besides returning the attaché case, was his use of 'uneventfully.' There's got to be something still awaiting us in Swansea!"

"I hope you understand how futile this all is, Henri; you can't possibly believe Wu's documents landed in a resort town?"

"The thumb drive led to the attaché case proving Abe was alive and Yang to be the actual victim. If it said, go to Swansea, and your dad's note, as ambivalent as it was, also mentioned driving to Swansea, then there's got to be something there, documents or what have you!"

"What about our bad guys? If those documents are still floating around, Branched Resources *will want them at all cost. Here's a theory—say we find those papers and the kidnappers know we have them, what do you think their bargaining chip will be? Of course, that's got to be it!"*

"So, in a nutshell, they won't kill your father until we hand the files over to them, and then they'll off us too!"

"Something like that."

"OK, there's a detail that has been nagging at me for some time—didn't Irene at Lips Waters know your father was dead?"

"I agree, it doesn't quite add up; she must follow the news like most of us do—of course she knew!"

— o —

As usual, the obvious wasn't always so. The human mind was full of vacant spots, or maybe, holes through which memories disappeared when the collective makeup required them to go, and reemerged when needed again. What were the rules, the method, the logic by which right places, right times, right circumstances were defined? And what was right versus wrong? In a wiser world, said mind had no need to map the human experience with biased markers rooted in existential angst. Likely, there were no wrongs, only a series of linear, and maybe curvy, or even, multidirectional sequences of rights on their evolutionary paths. This was where I wandered when Liz and I bounced ideas, observations, or speculations about the unknown we had deliciously unveiled. The dangers weren't a bad thing; they represented intensity, which in perspective firmed up our skills of resilience and invigorated the courage within our hearts. There was so much love between us that we practically felt invincible. Simply imagine two bodies in the throes of a sexual act amid fire and brimstone and you get the picture! We built strength on fearless forays into possibilities, knowing that even losing ourselves on a dubious path would eventually take us to the most resonant of outcomes. If patches of doubt clouded our minds during moments of difficulty, they were seen as intellectual and emotional weather patterns that would assuredly make room for clarity as they passed—trust was ever on our side, or at least that was where we insisted it should be.

———— o ————

14 – HYDRA OF DESTINY

Liz Garner here! I guess the metaphorical torch passed onto Henri by John is now in my possession.

After slamming *B.R.* with the Yang Wu murder, my dearest partner and I had found ourselves at the midpoint of our Vertex assignment. With the mining company at its most vulnerable, and the wilderness lease negotiations at a standstill, the time was ripe for digging into the dry rot of state corruption, and bringing the dirty laundry out in the open. The problem was, we couldn't endanger my kidnapped father now that we had a chance at getting him out alive.

Harold would have been the perfect lad to help in dealing with the *shadow men*, but after Launceston and Uri's murder, he had been in hiding, and no-one, at the exception of Vertex, had any idea where he had holed up. He was due to testify as the main witness, but until then, he had no reason to be seen in public. Once again, it was left to Henri and me to take care of ground work, thus why we were traveling along the Tasman Highway onward to Swansea to awaken the hydra of destiny.

"Tell me, Henri, have you ever fired a handgun?"

"No, it's not common practice to shoot people in Canada."

"Would you consider owning one if you knew you were in danger?"

"I'd be lying if I said it never crossed my mind, but so far, I haven't had the urge. Any reason why you should mention weapons?"

"I can think of one—bad guys with guns ahead."

"Honestly I wouldn't know the first thing about using one. It may sound counterintuitive in my case as a field investigative lawyer, but again Canada isn't the U.S."

"Before Port Arthur, there were lots of guns in Tasmania, but the National Firearms Agreement of ninety-six and the government buyback put a heavy damper on ownership. Now you've got to have serious reasons to carry a gun, and self-defense isn't one of them."

"Liz, you never told me that you possessed a firearm!"

"I never did; how did you guess?"

"Puleeze, you've walked me into it. Don't tell me you brought a gun to the fight!"

"Man, it's fully registered and I'm good at it. I grew up on a ranch, remember!"

"And your reason to carry is?"

"Being an investigative lawyer, my darling!"

— o —

That was the thing I adored about Henri—his boundless innocence. While some may have considered it a weakness, it was, on the contrary, a strength of unique properties. It acted like a shield on him. It made him invisible because adults were supposed to have lost their childhood virtues. Metaphorically speaking, he didn't need a gun because bullets went right through him. It was a notion that actually was a lot more effective than assertive protection. As a result, I felt safe around him, like being inside a golden bubble.

The drive along the coast would have been delightful if it hadn't been raining ropes. Like Henri said in his delicious use of French, *Il pleut des cordes*. I imagined ropes dangling from cardboard clouds above a sea of papier mâché, a children production from the top down, free of adult rules and control—the stuff I was deprived of in my youth from being surrounded by so many grownups. Henri was a single child too. He told me that as a youngster bosomed by parental love, play never seemed to end, and that even later, during his years of studies, it colored everything around him like stardust. I can hardly imagine he ended up marrying someone who had no play in her bones. I guess we all craved for a taste of the other side, like me and gambler James, a man who never took life seriously, to the point of hurting his loved ones. But in his case, it was adult play, like extramarital sex, all-nighters, fast cars, a perpetual case of midlife crisis years ahead of midlife, and likely, years beyond. But not Henri with his heart of gold and a mind built to dream the simple things that made life so rich. After having sampled what the other side had to offer, we both returned to our roots and met across the vast distances of land and sea. I was so blessed to have him next to me as we made our way through *les cordes d'eau*—the water ropes.

The thing that attracted me to Henri was the harmony between his feminine and masculine sides. Me, I was a tomboy, practically destined to become a lesbian, or have it both ways. Somehow, I wasn't drawn to it, but not for the lack of trying. By the time I studied at *les Hautes Études Appliquées du Droit*, I had found my balance, which leaned a wee tad to the female side—subtle make-up; calculated, savage hairstyle; a bit of leather here and there; and the customary tattoo to boot. Henri, nada, not one dot of ink on his body, and believe me when I say leather wasn't made for him. The man looked too sexy in a suit to spoil his image with a pretence of toughness—he was, and very much is, too strong and toned to bother.

— o —

We booked a room at the *Freycinet Waters*, standing warned that the hotel was operating with a skeleton crew that time of year. It didn't mean much to us—it wasn't our honeymoon yet, and talking of honeymoon, the wedding date, because of the present upheavals, was put on hold until further notice. We didn't care fundamentally, but immigration wanted us wed by the end of the year. Worst case scenario, all we needed was a witness, and surely, Jack would oblige.

The rain had relented by the time we got to Swansea. No more *cordes d'eau*. We checked into our room, one overlooking the grayness of Great Oyster Bay. The hotel wasn't known for its spectacular view, but it was popular, enough so that said skeleton crew was kept very busy. We eyed each other, wondering what to do first: having sex or conducting business? It was an unbalanced match from the start—we guiltlessly messed up the bed and everything around it!

Business came as we sat at a café table a block away across Franklin.

Me: *"So now, what d'we do, love?"*

"Just as we've said all along, wait and see. I trust we remember the class on existing in the best case scenario, and if memory serves, it also stated that everything was meant to be as planned. So, in three, two..."

Our order arrived at exactly zero, with a note from a client who, according to the waitress, had just left.

It said:

Punctuality is always appreciated. Thank you.

I wasn't the slightest surprised. It appeared my sensitivity to the unexpected had diminished from the early days of the case, which barely were two months ago. Henri wasn't either because he actually did the countdown, but was he faking? I doubted it. When that close, coincidence lost its edge. The man had a foot in the miasmic ambience of malfeasance courting everything *Branched Resources*. The note commending our virtues of exactitude was nothing more than a reminder that we were forever watched and in the vicinity of danger. Had it been written by my father's hand, it would have come with an element of reassurance, but not this one; it stank of obliquity.

"What do you make of it, Henri?"
"Good timing, if anything."
"Don't be so smug; I've lost my sense of humor."
"Les jeux sont fait; can't undo at this point."
"I'm talking about the danger element here!"
"If you want my advice, tensing up isn't going to work to our advantage. We didn't make it all the way here to come unraveled. This calls for trust and countenance."
"OK, Henri, just a reflex. Sometimes we don't always know how we're gonna fare until we get there. I thought I was prepared, but I guess I still have to firm up on my resolve. Have faith, I'm almost there!"
"Don't ever think I don't trust you!"

"Thanks, I already feel much better!"
"Bon appétit, by the way!"
"Cheers!"

— o —

Following lunch, I sent encrypted texts to both Jack and John Lehman confirming linkage with the *shadow men*. It had been Vertex's recommendation to stay updated in case the back corridors of power needed to be consulted.

There was nothing remotely exciting going on in Swansea or in most places on the island for that matter—it was winter. The action was in the politics of resource exploitation against environmental concerns. Loggers, as in most forested countries, acted their usual disgruntled selves when confronted by "university scumbags," outsiders with the effrontery of telling natives how to run their lives, even when said scumbags were natives themselves. The same went with miners and farmers. Actually, now that I had said it, Tasmania was a pressure cooker about to explode. But I was talking about tourists, those who would return to their lands with sanitized memories of my beloved island. Tasmania had been hurting for too long at the hands of profiteers barking the false rhetorics of sustainable harvest and practices. Tell that to the real natives, the endangered fauna and flora, and the extinct species! The thought sickened me. But still, nothing was going on in Swansea, except for a tension between two attorneys and a bunch of bad men—nothing visible or even remotely palpable, but something nonetheless. It wasn't until well into the evening that the second sign made its entrance. There was a knock at the door, but as Henri asked who that was, only silence ensued. Actually there was no-one outside, just a thing left in the hall. I say a thing because the object in question was inside a paper sack identical to the one that carried our leftovers from the café across the street; greasy stains et al. Henri couldn't resist jumping on the opportunity to test my humor.

"Your fish and chips dinner has arrived, dear!"
"I don't want it in here, what is it?!"

Henri emptied the contents of the bag on the floor.

"The usual, a mobile and a locker key!"
"I see—are they going to dick us around with their instructions and demands, just to take the humanity out of it so that they can kill us with a clean conscience, or is it merely a farce?"
"What's the difference? Let's wait for the call."

— o —

The call came at midnight just as we shut off the last of the lights. Henri picked up.

"Yeah, go ahead!"
"You have a package at the post office, use the key and follow the instructions inside. Goodnight!"

That was all she wrote. Henri was about to ask about my father when the man hung up on him. How classic! It was like being locked inside one of those

British gangster flicks, light on plot, heavy on clichés, one that dragged its knuckles on the broken concrete of some decommissioned hangar. Frankly, we were getting tired of the amateurish nonsense.

— o —

The wind and a hard-hitting rain woke us up at six, two full hours before the alarm. It was still pitch black outside and the swollen bay waters could be heard pelting the sands of Waterloo Beach. While Henri showered, I ran things in my head, trying to comprehend the sequenced elements that had brought us to Swansea all the way from the Val D'Osne fountain in Launceston. The road was littered with false negatives turned positives and back again. To call it a rollercoaster would have been akin to breathing life into a corpse, rather, it felt like the trudging was calculated, meant to impose the kind of dull fatigue that turned momentum into a heaviness of being. It was aimless, devoid of the essential quality of "somethingness," vicious in the way viciousness might be interpreted from the comfortably numb standpoint of a stoned junkie. It sickened me. Who were these *shadow men*? Were they truly *Branched Resources*'s henchmen, or were they outsiders doing it for the fun of psychological gamesmanship? And where was dad?!

Henri came out of the shower naked, slightly erect, the point that triggered a subtle arousal within me. But like two souls connected to the last tendril, it didn't take long before all subtlety left the room. We remained embraced until the alarm snatched us from Heaven for a hard landing into reality. It was daylight, both wind and rain had relented, making room for a palette of monotonal grays. We had time before post office hours. We showered together, got dressed, and walked up a block for coffee. We didn't say much, for there wasn't much in terms of feeling talkative. A slight apprehension was mounting from the lower levels. I took Henri's hand and squeezed it.

— o —

The package contained a large stamped envelope addressed to a box in Wynyard. The only instructions consisted of putting both the documents—when we found them—and our personal mobiles in it. Upon arrival of the mail, a call would direct us to Abraham's location. We were not to return to Hobart or make contact with the office the minute the envelope got mailed. Until then, we were free to do as we wished. We had one week to comply—"no negotiations, no money offers, only the documents and the phones. Good luck!"

— o —

It was the end of the road—one more probability going nowhere! I swore, the planet didn't want to be saved, or if it did, the odds against saving it were too high, all hopes having been lost somewhere in the seventies when the opportunities to act led to viable outcomes. We missed the turns in the road despite the science and the eloquence of commonsense. Sure, we stalled the negotiations, but for how long? The *shadow men* operated as if nothing happened, while the authorities hadn't made one single arrest. Meanwhile, the media was losing interest, indicating a shift in public

100

awareness. Hopefully the trial would refocus the news, but that wasn't enough. Without a proper villain it was unlikely the court would go for an appeal. Parties would settle, allowing backroom talks to resume between state and industry, promising jobs and fortunes while swaying opinions to the dark side of reason.

In spite of all we knew through our Vertex education, the forays into the unknown and all that jazz, we were faced with an immutable reality and no clear window into alternatives.

The stamped envelope was nothing but a joke. What did they think we do with the documents when we found them, not make copies or send PDF-ready pix to the office? I mean, what about our phones, turn to stone without them? Plus, we'd still have theirs! We were back to contemplating a sick prank; there was no Abraham Garner at the end of the deal—my dad was either dead or wasn't abducted in the first place, and that was all it came down to. It was time to return to Hobart and prepare for our next move, internal documents or not.

——— o ———

15 – WYNYARD

Following the Swansea snafu, as Henri and I prepared to drive back the way we came, it occurred to me that Wynyard was the closest major town to the mine's processing plant and port. Although the ride to it from Swansea was insanely long, especially at that time of year when snow could likely impair our travels on Lake Leake Road, I felt an urge to visit the town's post office and investigate whose name lurked behind that box. Engaging the authorities came to mind, but frankly, we didn't trust them. Nobody had friends in the system when money could buy state and justice, and believe me when I tell you we were well-placed to know it!

In spite of the rain, we made excellent time on Lake Leake Road, with just the odd bit of wet snow at the highest elevation. Technically, we were good to go all the way to Wynyard, but first and foremost we much wanted to spend the rest of the day lazing in Launceston and stay the night at our favorite hotel.

By commonwealth standards, Launceston was an old city with history's ghosts going in and out the through-walls of time. Henry and I could feel the traffic brushing by, native hunters and gatherers, prospectors, missionaries, loggers, shipmen; gentlemen in top hats arm in arm with their laced and *chiffoned* ladies; world war soldiers, last frontier drinkers, brigands and profiteers, specters minding their own businesses; each and every one of them nescient of the layers. They flickered like old film actors streaked by the wear of memory, one by one marching on into impending oblivion. Such was the nature of the in-between.

There was a quality to Launceston that triggered my inner-thought process, the same way the mid-sized cities of the world, caught between times, maintained their focus on history. Not so for the large ones whose paces made it impossible for the soul to pause for a snapshot into the *has been*, and remarkably, the *will be* as well. Similarly to when Henri and I visited Barbezat Fountain last we were here; the town conveyed a sense of possibilities yet to be explored. Maybe we missed something then, the plausibility of yet another fork in the road. I felt it in my core, unresolved, reaching for air and light, neither a hope nor an omen, but the owned intuition this was indeed the right track, always had been. Swansea was all geared up to be the reminder of what it was to err from the call. The *shadow men* were nothing but a metaphor for the messengers of misguidance. The stamped envelope never truly existed other than as a reminder of the absurd. We lived an illusory version of existence, just like the ghosts of Launceston. Interesting how life loses its substance when walking against the grain, and more so when we don't notice. We fight our battles never questioning the nature of personal conflict, and when we finally awaken, we ponder on the reason why it ever happened. Funny bunch we are!

The fact was—Swansea was a dead end and Launceston the hub of possibilities, and for a time, our center of gravity and fulcrum of balance. I knew it, Henri knew it, and the rest of our Vertex team recognized it as well; not as established knowledge, but as an amendment to it. In other words, we had, with nary a second left, veered from critical error.

It wasn't like the stamped envelope miraculously disappeared, or that the address in Wynyard ceased to exist; rather, purposes shifted from one foreseeable development to another. It was a matter of looking at the seemingly unconditional elements of the demand as an interpretation instead of an immutable instance of causality. We had exhausted all options out of the Swansea deal; whichever way we shook it, we were royally screwed. At that point, there were only two paths to choose from: the one of defeat back to Hobart, and the one of empowerment by forging ahead into action. It was surrender versus recklessness, but the latter had the kind of snap that sent ripples down our common spine.

Were we followed out of Swansea? I doubted it! The sixty or so miles of practically empty road, from the east coast to Campbell Town, left no indication of it. The tables turned the second we made the decision to hit west, seeing to the unraveling of a poorly put together reality. What lay ahead was made of a much stronger cloth—we were now back in focus, with our Vertex gloves on.

— o —

Nothing important needed reporting on the hundred mile plus stretch between Launceston and Wynyard. It was gray and rainy most of the time, with the occasional flooded area requiring the annoying stop-and-go of traffic occasioned by mental lapses, rubbernecking, and various distractions of dubious validity. By the time we arrived, Jack Lewis had identified the owner of the post office box as Samuel O'Reilly, a trauma surgeon at North West Regional Hospital in Burnie, and the man likely to have examined my dad's body, or should I say the remains of Yang Wu, aka Dominic Vaughn? That sounded like the kind of information we had been dying for, a name attached to a fiasco of the first order. Even though it was likely the authorities had already questioned him in regard to the mix-up, we had no reason to trust the outcome of it. We intended on cross-examining the man in or outside the court, so letting him off the hook was out of question. Now, we had reason to inculpate him for wrongdoing and drag him in for questioning. No doubt we would be hearing from his lawyer soon.

— o —

Henri and I went around the island, caught between states of disquietude and elation, steadily feeding the case with our discoveries and extrapolations. Quebec and Hobart Front Shields churned the info into coalescent and comprehensive judicial data, but with only the two of us as their prime investigative team, John politely advised we seek reinforcement as needed. We concurred—it was time to give the thought serious consideration.

On Vertex's recommendation, Upton Clay, a private investigator out of Devonport—unsurprisingly our third town on the list—joined us the next morning to go over what we had. I knew Upton from the days of Ranch Acacia as one of the few who steadily attended through the years, and for being a good friend of dad's. I was happy to have him by our side. He, like my father, was extremely fit and good-looking, with age working as an asset to wisdom and dignity. Nothing escaped him.

Upton: *"I'm glad we're on the subject of intuition, because I value instinct over the individual interpretation of facts. I can't realistically rely on the old staple of establishing veracity from memory; it's too arbitrary."*

Henri: *"Case in point, over-thinking nearly made us miss the turn; although the risks are unchanged."*

Me: *"While we may consider our 'shadow men' to be a metaphor for some non-existent villain, the fact remains that Wu and Dudko were assassinated."*

Upton: *"An appropriate term for non-entities. I'm sure they'd appreciate, but I wouldn't cross them out yet. Don't, for one second, doubt these blokes will catch up with you—O'Reilly is either one of them or a peon. I'm not saying they're placing you where they want you, but it won't take long before they realize you didn't buy their bluff—we have to move fast! For now, let me do the dirty work of connecting with the doc and make him talk. You just stay put until I call, hopefully sooner than later!"*

How anticlimactic! Sitting around waiting wasn't exactly my forte. But since Henri and I were still new at prolonged, close intimacy, there was nothing like full immersion in the rose-scented bathwaters of novelty to see how we would come out at the other end; a metaphor whose descriptive was as much open to heavenly sweetness as it was to brutal cruelty. But I doubted Henri would fall prey to darker instincts and spoil the romance.

In the meantime, the facets of the major suit against *Branched* and the state needed congealing into a mass before hardening. Upton's arrival brought forth momentum, the confidence that came with added positions along the perimeter of the operational field. My mind might have been a window into a cut-to-fit view of the case, but it was far from not heeding my female intuitive. As I said before, the tomboy in me wasn't enough to tip the balance to the side of rigid logic; there were lots of greens and vibrant crimsons and pumpkin oranges scattered in free splashes and bold brushes across the broken glass and the twisted metal. Doc O'Reilly was about to meet with a particularly unique way of thinking; nothing his field of contradictions was used to. I wasn't passing judgment on his skills as a surgeon—it wasn't my habit to rate the unknown—but his equivocal presence at the end of that stamped envelope had me riled up. Sure, I didn't ignore the potentiality of him having been acting under the ills of a gun barrel to his head, but puleeze, innocence wasn't the first word that came to mind at that vivid moment. The man was *louche*, as Henri would say, shady as in suspicious with that *je ne sais quoi* of suspense. My only concern was for Upton's safety; I was getting weary of the dead bodies playing musical chairs, and believe me, the idea of cardboard cutouts of skeletons walking the waters of a seesawing sea of papier mâché wasn't far from my hyper-imaginative mind.

Henri too was lost in his own thinking. I couldn't pretend to read what was going on in his sweet head, but energies didn't lie—his preoccupations were aligned with mine in ways likely less chaotic but surely just as intense.

"Any idea where we're going with this, Henri darling?"

"I'm thinking of the many ways we can bust that lowlife. I presume Upton has the leverage to officialize his status as both witness and suspect."

"It goes without saying his office is already on it; the man is thorough to a fault. It's likely a full profile on O'Reilly will be available by tomorrow morning."

"Good, that's progress! Are you feeling the way I do, because I'm walking on red ants right now. I sure could use something to distract me. Wanna see a movie?"

"I already looked, the Metro in Burnie has a nice room with a curved screen; might be worth checking. It's playing the latest Samuel Jackson—any takers?"

"Action, right? I could use some!"

"We could have some right here, right now, or we could save it for later."

"It's a toss, baby, but I propose dinner, a flick, and putting the unused energy to good use after that!"

"You speak my language, dear man!"

— o —

The call from Upton came as we were on our way out. He had located and approached Samuel O'Reilly, who refused to answer any questions on the premise he didn't have to, but not before he slipped that his biggest supplier of broken bones and ghastly wounds was the Savage River operation. In other words, the company had an account at West Regional and our doc was the main scalpel, which in legalese translated as a lot of confidentiality wrapped up in fringe benefits and protection. It was likely that, this time, Vertex would have to visit the global department of the back corridors of power to find the right lever, although a dose of good old local persuasion was known to save time. Talking of time, the moment was ripe to consider rehiring the services of Harold Freeman, who probably knew just the right guy to shake down the tree.

— o —

Henri immediately called Jack letting him know we wanted Harold back on the job. Amazingly enough,

Freeman was already on it since he had been staying in Devonport within a stone's throw of Upton's office. Perhaps I should have been paying closer attention to internals. Sure I had guessed he would eventually follow the items on the list, but I missed on the nuance that two Vertex-linked investigators living in the same town couldn't simply ignore each other. My first reaction was one of dismay at Jack's lack of disclosure, but the omission made sense as soon as it was revealed Freeman had been watching our backs from a distance—still...

Harold called as we got back to our hotel room; he was on his way.

— o —

We met the following morning at an out-of-sight café. Henri and I had just reviewed the freshly uploaded file on O'Reilly. I couldn't help noticing how Harold was energized by rejoining us—you just didn't keep such a man captive for too long, even for his own protection; he wasn't built that way. Men of his kind died of prolonged inactivity; they dwindled to nothing when deprived of purpose. He had brought with him Aleksei Yegorov, another Russian expat immune to fear. The plan wasn't exactly subtle, but hard times called for hard measures. The agent would corner the doc and question him the old-fashion way, preferably tied to a chair. Of course, there were limits; the design was to test his melting point, not torture him, and hopefully he would talk just enough to shed some light on his side gig.

After Yuri Dudko was found in the South Esk with a bullet hole in the back of his head—a detail of sub-investigation tied to the case—Harold, on a Vertex recommendation forwarded by John Lehman, went into hiding in Devonport. Far from staying inactive, he connected with Upton Clay with the aim of picking up an odd job until hearing from us. Well, as it turned out, the apple never fell far from the tree, as the job in question was the same as the one he wasn't supposed to be on in the first place; but then again, stranger things happened. In simple terms, Harold didn't heed John's advice, but we didn't exactly expect him to do so. It wasn't in Vertex's interests to enforce suggestions, for Vertex was the glue to individual talents and refined skills. Where and whenever any of us stood was always the right place and time. That alone was the main power behind the group, its *vi naturalis* or *force naturelle*, as Henri would say; the coalescent strength that tied each of us to a common core of knowledge and foresight.

When drilled by Upton on what exactly the fresh trail Uri had been sniffing in Launceston was, Harold showed a frustrated look that oh too well expressed his regret for not having done the job himself.

Henri: *"I mean, mate, how could you have done it more safely, Uri certainly wasn't a novice?"*

"I know, but we wouldn't be talking about his dead ass today if I had taken his place."

Me: *"No, but we would be taking about yours!"*

"Maybe or maybe not; we all have our angles with their strengths and weaknesses. I probably would have sensed danger before it hit me."

Henri: *"So, why are you sending Aleksei after the doc if you're going to show such remorse?"*

"Aleksei is in a league of his own. Actually Jack recommended I connect with him about the job."

Henri: *"I thought he was one of your men?"*

"No, neither was Uri. We have worked together before, so he's on my mental call list, but he and his team are independent contractors operating under the system's radars. He technically doesn't exist. It's unlikely his face will show up in any database."

Henri: *"Impressive, so you believe he's going to get the job done?"*

"I don't only 'believe' it; I guarantee it!"

— o —

I wasn't there, but here's what happened: Aleksei Yegorov drove to the hospital, parked his rented Mitsubishi too close to the driver's side of O'Reilly's sedan and waited. It took a while, but the agent knew how to make quality time out of waiting. He opened the hardcover novel purchased for the occasion and immersed himself into reading.

When the doc knocked at the glass, it was night. Yegorov put on the face of someone snapped out of his reverie, opened his window, letting the rain fall in, and squinting his eyes as to see the man in focus, asked:

"Yes?"

"You're blocking my door, can you move!?"

"Sorry, I'm waiting for assistance. I left my lights on—dead battery—use another door."

"You're shitting me?!"

"I'm sorry."

Aleksei got out, pretending to have a look at the inconvenience. Stealthy as a cat, he expertly knocked the doc cold with a hit to his lower skull, swiftly gathering and plopping his limp mass into the back of the SUV. The two were soon on their way to a country barn off Petersons Lane in Elliott, south of Somerset, a town west of Burnie. What ensued was taken from the recording.

"Are you not recognizing the symptoms, doc?"

"You fucking hit me, asshole!"

"Mind your language, Sir; we're between men of manners here."

"What the fuck are you talking about?!"

"OK, I can see you're a tough guy; manners might not apply after all."

"Get me out of here!"

"Oh man, this is going to take time... For one thing, your rights of entitlement have been revoked indefinitely, so you'll get out of here when I say you do, or maybe you won't; it all depends on the way you answer my questions. So, let's get this going, will we? There is protocol around identification guidelines I believe you didn't follow when you received the body of a certain Abraham Elliot Garner flown out of Savage River, back over a year ago. Why was that?"

"It's confidential information, so piss off!"

"Not as confidential as you may think, since it's now popular knowledge the body wasn't Garner's."

"The process of passing a corpse through each step of the administrative system of identification can be prone to error in certain circumstances."

"OK, I'm all ears, what circumstances?"

"Severe disfiguration, or in that case, complete savagery of the body—I had never seen anything like it."

"So, if I understand, he came with a name tag?"

"Glad you get it, now let me go!"

"Not so fast! Who put that tag on?"

"The mine doctor, the victim was with a friend; a no-brainer."

"Did you by any chance catch the name of the friend?"

"Yeah, he came to the morgue; Freeman I recall. He was accompanied by the deceased's daughter."

"So, you're saying that this Freeman saw him die, yet came with the daughter to identify the body?"

"What's so strange about it?"

"For one thing, it was the wrong body, if that rings a bell. Don't you find that strange? How could the friend have mistaken a mine employee for his buddy? It takes some serious practice to put on such a performance. Now, I want the name of the fake medic that brought the body over, because since you know the real one and you put his name in the report, I'm seriously curious about the kind of circumstantial identity error you referred to a minute ago. As a fair warning, you are in no position to bullshit me, so what's his name?"

"Go fuck yourself!"

"I appreciate your admittance of guilt, tough guy, but let me put it this way; since the presence of a lawyer is optional here, talking will save you a lot of trouble."

"Nothing like what awaits me if I talk."

"Ha, we're going somewhere! So, you're not part of them, the bad guys, I mean?"

"Who are you anyway, and why should I trust you? As far as I know, you could be one of them!"

"And you'd be in serious shit. I see your point, but I'm not your psychologist, so, the name...?"

"What the hell—Gerald Harrison."

"Can you be more specific?"

"We met at the University of Sydney. He contacted me a couple of years ago after nearly two decades since I last saw him. He said he was freelancing for the mining industry as an environmental consultant. Just before the accident, he called me for a favor. I didn't know what it was, but he assured me it would be a mere technicality. So, when he arrived with the body, I assumed he had been put in charge based on his background in medicine, but when I saw Paul's name on the admission form, I pulled him to the side for an explanation. All he said was, 'Remember the favor I asked of you? Now, if you keep this to yourself, you and your family will be fine!' That's all I have for you; now let me go."

O'Reilly sounded defeated. Aleksei drove him back to his car without a single word exchanged. I felt sorry for him. I wasn't sure what made him crack—perhaps his conscience, or something the agent said in some calculated, subliminal way. That was what skilled operatives did—persuasion through the back door of the mind.

In spite of having moved a step closer, we were still a long way from inflicting critical damage to the mother ship. But Henri and I felt confident we were at last on the right track.

— o —

In recap, driving across the island to Wynyard led us to identify the owner of the postal box as the doc who admitted Yang Wu's body at North West Regional. Whether we were expected there or not didn't distract from the fact we were onto something—it felt like the right track to us. Now I was dying to explore how deeply O'Reilly had been duped by his old friend, if that was even true. But since the lead to the box automatically inculpated him, I had no reason to doubt his words. It remained that we still were expected in Wynyard, otherwise why would the note ask of us to not return to Hobart? Somehow it felt as if the whole thing was tailored to specific characterial traits—ours. But in the end and the way I saw it, it didn't matter what the game was, as long at it arrived at the desired end. Out of the blue, a hazy picture of the *shadow men* crossed my mind. Who were those guys and why did they seem to operate against the grain of commonsense? And then I envisioned another group, the *bad guys*—who were not the *shadow men*.

My brain started to hurt.

— o —

The concept of two disparate groups resonated with Henri as well. Using that train of thought, it was apparent the *B-guys* were never far behind the trickery of the *S-men*. Case in point, "Waters" led to identifying Wu as the victim, and then the self-addressed envelope brought us to O'Reilly and Harrison. That quasi-associative mental process conjured a unique dimension to the picture—one I was familiar with—prompting me to ponder on the possibility that dad was directly involved. Predictably, I came to a major head-on dilemma—if my father had arranged his own travesty, he couldn't have been one of the *shadow men*, since his connection with Harrison and O'Reilly, the bad guys, would have been inevitable; hence, I was left to contemplate that one group played both sides of the same coin. That was twisted! It was as if clarity and confusion had found an agreeable commonality in the filthy room of a shady outback motel. On the one hand I could have opted to lose my mind, but I chose to convince Henri to have sex instead and leave the sinuous mental process to work itself out. After all, what was a girl supposed to do with a plot filled with items moving in and out of meaning?! There was a lesson in there, no doubt, but not just for me alone; the entire Vertex was taking a course in humility. I gathered that, due to the direness of the global circumstances, and the lateness at which we, as a race, had arrived at recognizing our glorious evils, it was to be expected that solutions would require the utmost in imagination and originality. For now, I was ready to put my brain in a jar and affix a "do not disturb" label to it.

— o —

Having said that, sex being a visceral, now-thing to me, its aftermath, given that period of peaceful release, tended to perk me up into a solution-seeking monster. The two-gang hypothesis had me front and center of a clusterfuck doing and undoing itself. My inner eye couldn't find its focus. I then decided that I was looking at it all wrong again, once more losing the metaphor I had created in my mind. *Shadow men* and *bad guys* were nothing more than personalized characters in the light of the trauma of having lost my father. My hopes of finding him alive, when things settled, was throwing my compass out of alignment—one moment he was the victim, the next, the master puppeteer. Yet, I wasn't the only one operating from within the smokescreen; Henri, Harold,

Jack, John Lehman were all, to various degrees, affected by a sense of contextural powerlessness. Our moves, crisp one minute, were reduced to a crawl the next. It was, in the eyes of Vertex, the recurring theme of all versions in the process of failing; each ushered towards irresolvable conditions. Henri's arrival saw us leap ahead of our adjacent struggles, but we were now barely squeezing by, each side alley getting narrower and shorter, all of it because of a fundamental, perceptual dilemma. We needed fresh thinking and Henri was the one slotted for the job; yet, to my dismay, I realized I had taken that away from him by assuming center stage. Not that I thought I did, but Jack, through a polite reminder of where my place was, brought me to face the music. I was built that way, to take charge, create assignments, but this wasn't Front Shield, and my role wasn't that of investigating. I just wanted to be with Henri because I loved him and I feared for his life. No, I wasn't going to mope in a corner—I was aware it was time to let the man resume with his work and for me to assist him to the best of my abilities.

PART FOUR

16 – SHADOW MAN (Henri)

Following Liz's return to Hobart, it felt as if a part of me had left with her. I longed for her presence, her body, her witty and colorful mind. Her metaphorical way of thinking conveyed so many pictures that an evaluation of my own thought process left me begging for those colors. It pained me to hear that she felt her presence was overpowering my work. It wasn't that at all. The truth was I enjoyed her so much that my prime desire was to walk into the sunset with her. So, yes, one could have said that she distracted me, but I wanted that distraction from the bottom of my heart—I craved it!

I resumed working with Harold and Aleksei on the logistics of our next move. We needed more out of the doc, but his role as witness in the murder case was so primordial that pushing him was bound to affect our chances of winning in court. His lawyers had met with Jack—it was confirmed that their client would testify. It was all that mattered at the moment.

We were left with a number of unanswered issues, namely, finding *Branched*'s incriminating documents and figuring out whether or not the same guy murdered Uri and Yang, and kidnapped Abe. Of course, we weren't ignoring the threat of not following through with mailing the envelope, but we deemed it an item of no consequence, since we had to find what they asked for first; notwithstanding that we were approaching deadline. After all, what would O'Reilly do, since he was the receiver— did he even know about it? Liz's notion that the envelope was a metaphorical representation of the absurd made sense. The task of fulfilling the demand appeared too outlandish to be anything but a bluff or a pointer. Vertex, in dealing with overlapping realities had left a few doors open for possibilities to collide. It was what I saw in the presence of paradoxes, bleed-throughs, artifacts of redundancy that confounded logic. It was best to recognize the present as the meeting point of randomness, while using vision as the road to follow. In simpler words, facts were to be picked and chosen based on the nature of the quest; alone, they were too unreliable to provide a solid foundation. We were not even sure how Yang Wu ended up dead; it was all presumptive. In actuality, we counted on court proceedings to uncork a few truths—a risqué game of chance at best. An instance of malfeasance within *Branched* didn't make the company complicit of wrongdoing. For that to materialize, someone had to testify, or conclusive exhibits had to surface. For now, we had stilled the momentum of the leases and scared a few sheepish peons—nothing more, nothing less.

— o —

It was obvious Aleksei Yegorov couldn't wait to put his hands on Uri's killers, but his dignity prevailed over his lower instincts. Although Dudko had worked off the same list Liz and I had decoded, there wasn't a doubt he went after names rather than places, consequently either being served a hefty slice of irony or inadvertently knocking off an unrelated hornet's nest. The names in question were James King and Val Dosne, with the latter absent from our database. Unsurprisingly, out of the many Kings listed in the Launceston phone book, none of them went by James. But leave it to Vertex to come up with the list of a few with past connections to the area, one with the coincidental particularity of working at the Savage River operation around the time of the accident. The discovery brought me face to face with yet another dichotomy plaguing the case: two tracks simultaneously branching out, names one way, places the other. The list, in all of its presumed simplicity, was intrinsically a revolving enigma that played as much on time as it did on space. Whoever had put it together was either a riddle-maker or a wicked probability mathematician. It sufficed to say that Aleksei was on his way to meet with James King, last spotted—according to John Lehman's information—at a market in Stanley, sixteen miles northwest of *Branched Resources*'s smelter on Sawyer Bay.

— o —

I began to witness the flexing of Vertex's muscle. Its ability to trace someone like King in such a remote area spoke of a reach uncommon to most law firms. It was the kind of resources that belonged to the realm of intelligence, thus putting new meaning to our allegorical *back corridors of power.* I realized then there was much to learn—or remember—about my new family and my role within it. Although some of the cognitive elements leading to my present position came in waves, my immersion into the case dictated that I stay within distinct parameters not conducive to inner exploration. It was possible that I hadn't fully surrendered to the reality of already being within that exploratory field, but again, there were many distractions that obscured my personal evaluation of the self. That being said, I trusted my place in time with utter conviction, which was all that mattered.

While Aleksei Yegorov went after James King, Harold kept an eye on O'Reilly. The doc had been busy meeting in out-of-the-way places with a number of characters including Gerald Harrison, whose face was familiar to Freeman from meeting at the bottom of the tailings dam on the day of the accident. It proved the doc was a bigger fish than what came out of the interrogation and that his association with the usurping mine medic was much deeper than confessed. After all, O'Reilly was the official surgeon in charge of receiving mine casualties. It didn't take much cleverness to visualize the arrangement as beneficial to *Branched* in the light of their impeccable safety record and much-lauded work standard awareness. If one could swap bodies, one could manage to hide a few as well—after all, mines, throughout history, had been known to bury the dead with their past.

— o —

It had become evident Harrison was the principal character behind most of the evils strewn our way—an environmental consultant on the surface, but one of the devil's own below. He was *Branched*'s primo henchman, the Swiss army knife of its backroom wheelings and dealings—the man we needed to frame. His real name— of course we couldn't take the doc's confession at face value—was Alec Gilbert, another bit of datum cast our way from Quebec that showed up after cross-referencing mnemonic imaging made from Harold Freeman's memory with University of Sydney records. The man was indeed a shadow, likely moving in and out of identities, Gilbert being no other than the mask of the time. The thing was O'Reilly lied, which made him more dangerous than first thought. His stance of deflation following the confession was nothing but an act, one good enough to fool Aleksei, which spoke loudly of his skills of deceit!

—o—

It seemed at first peculiar that James King would be seen in Stanley, a community best known for its quaint shops and the peninsular rock rising above it. But then again, the *Branched* smelter and loading dock was a mere eight miles in a straight line across the bay, and no other towns in the area offered much in terms of convenience. The fact King no longer worked at the mine didn't mean he wasn't involved in its shady business, and following Harold's view of Stanley as the perfect off-season rendezvous spot with its many hotels, restaurants, and few eyes, the arrival of fresh suspects was highly expected, if they weren't already there.

The suspicion was soon confirmed when Liz rang with the news that calls had been made from a Stanley payphone to O'Reilly and Harrison's cells. Once again, Lehman had been hard at work, which meant Vertex's global gears were meshing into irreversible motion. It showed that the trickle of data provided by our skeleton crew was being put to good use; and with Liz as input coordinator, we couldn't ask for a better arrangement.

—o—

Aleksei had just arrived in Stanley. Harold briefed him on the latest, urging him to tighten his cover and refrain from cornering King at the cost of ending up the prey. Best was to tally numbers and monitor movement.

Although the Russian didn't need enforcement, Freeman was on his way to assist him. In the meantime I opted to move my operation from Wynyard to Smithton, the largest community west of Stanley. I booked a room at the Sheer Pleasure, longing for Liz's presence, while knowing oh too well that work and focus were calling. I was so certain she would have loved the place and the view of Duck Bay, especially on this rare, clear winter day.

— o —

I was concerned about Harold being seen in Stanley. The town was too small for his footprint, especially with Harrison in it; not to mention O'Reilly knew Aleksei as well—a single faux pas and it was all over. But I had to put my trust in these men and their skills, even if Freeman had more than once tested the limits of what I deemed subtle.

The first pictures to arrive on my laptop were of King and Harrison fist-bumping outside the doc's car; then of O'Reilly stepping out, apparently being introduced to King; and last, of the three standing and looking in a direction pointed by Harrison. It was likely they had seen others arrive, those we knew very little or nothing about. The importance of not blowing it at that point was immeasurable.

The photos were simultaneously sent to Hobart and Quebec City to be inputted to the case.

The second set showed two more individuals, a man and woman, whose demeanor immediately identified them as attorneys, likely O'Reilly's. There was something foreboding about their presence, simply by the fact we were witnessing the making of an ad hoc defense committee intent on circumvallating us by all permissible means and destroying our progress. The meeting of criminals and lawyers for the purpose of business was never in the best interest of the competition, which in our instance amounted to the use of just about any method in the book qualifying as justified, as long as it followed a specific path defined by spurious legalese, such as murder turned self-defense, etcetera. That was enough for the moment as far as Vertex was concerned. Lehman advised Harold and Aleksei to meet me in Smithton. But before they did, a series of shots showing our suspects passing the security gates of a wooded property was sent to my laptop.

— o —

I was on my way down from my room to the self-service breakfast counter when I passed a face I had seen before. We didn't make eye contact, but the man's energy alerted my senses. He was someone I had crossed in the last month, a pedestrian, the proverbial face in the crowd, most certainly an unknown, but my mind refused to let go of the notion he was important to my work. And then it came to me in a flash; he was that one exiting customer holding the door as Liz and I entered the café in Swansea, just ahead of the waitress handing the stamped envelope over to us. I had a visual on my first *shadow man*!

I had been followed by what I had already deemed an abstraction—crazy! These guys knew where I would be ahead of me making the choices. As unprecedented as it sounded, I couldn't think of a saner possibility. The presence of the entity pointed in the direction of bleed-throughs between *present points* along the timelines of multiple, related realities. As we already mentioned,

Vertex had left some gates open between probabilities, allowing for access into the memory data of variables. I began to believe that our *shadow men* were not of this world or even of this present. It didn't take me long to come to the conclusion that the man in question didn't manifest in the stairwell by accident—he wished to communicate!

— o —

His name was Jeremiah Jones.

"And so, Henri, here at last! I was wondering how long it would take before you remembered where we first met. It's OK to call me J.J.; I'm used to it. There are no others, so feel free to refer to me as 'Shadow Man.'

As you should know, I am responsible for the thumb drive and the list. It didn't matter what path you chose to follow—I was always ahead of you, prepared to be exactly where you ended up going. The list was designed to keep you moving as to prevent a predictable outcome, such as those enacted in other versions of your present reality. Figuratively-speaking, you have come a long way from them, as you are now able to foresee beyond the scope of linear thinking. This discussion is happening within a fractal of your focused reality—others cannot see us, for we have literally stepped aside. It is only possible because of your acceptance of the greater purpose of your work and your place within the advanced consciousness that is Vertex. I am what you may call a 'super-agent' of the group, a personality that doesn't strictly exist in one dimension or the next. Rather, I am adept at taking many roles across realities and timelines.

Or, you may refer to me as a more evolved version of yourself, the one from which you find your inspiration and powers. One way or the other, I am satisfied with your creative way of connecting—it suits the intrigue of your case.

The two principal items of your focus, the so-called documents and Abraham Garner's whereabouts, are still to be located by you and you only, for I am not permitted to tell you or those involved in your work how to proceed. If it sounds like a test, it's because it is fundamentally one, albeit one of endurance, as it is through resilience only that your chances at saving the human experiment will stay alive. I have guided you thus far with the help of a few concealed innuendos, and I shall continue to do so in the following meetings. One of them I give you now: as long as you and I find ourselves on the same plane of reality, consider it being an accurate compass reading to your progress, as well as the safest path. Stay firm and choose your allies carefully.

Until next time!"

———— o ————

17 – NEW FRIENDS

The meeting with Jones left me unsettled, as in inadequate, or poorly equipped for the task of freeing an entire planet from the clutches of greed and simultaneously saving the greedy from themselves. That sounded like an insane prospect, and yet, the *super agent* was serious. Although I still had much to learn about Vertex, I fundamentally understood the layers involved in the making of multiversal realities and the quantum consciousness within which they existed. But I needed trust at the base of all that I endeavored to harness and push forth. It didn't matter how much cognitive sense I had in forming my reality if I didn't believe I existed within the best case scenario at all times. A lack of trust was akin to throwing a monkey wrench at the mechanics of forward-motion; it simply brought progress to a halt. Whereas trust was the uncontestable base of conception, faith was the transitive element to accomplishment. It accepted no distractions, no counter-arguments; it was the missionary of trust, providing it knew its proper place. That was essentially what stemmed out of meeting with Jeremiah Jones—the order of importance, with trust as the stepping stone to faith, and faith as the master of vision.

— o —

John Lehman was first to connect after my last report, with Liz and Jack Lewis joining the conversation shortly thereafter. Nothing about the sequence surprised me; as a matter of fact, I had anticipated it as being the past of a close future. My present had broadened into a zone of impulse-based connectivity, positioned between variable outcomes and their respective relations to the past—in other words, a place in the making, with a wider view of its mechanics. It was the super agent's gift to me—a glimpse into my own soul.

John Lehman: *"Delighted by the news, Henri; that's a remarkable achievement."*

"Thanks, John, it surprised me how fast I figured out Jones wanted to meet; although, 'meeting' in our case is very much a figure of speech. But I enjoyed the set-up as much as the next guy in the room."

"Figuratively, of course, as you are I'm sure aware that it happened outside conventional settings."

"Yes, but near-enough the conventional settings to provide that homey, je ne sais quoi sense of comfort, candle light included."

"Ha, you understand, it's a green light given to your work and I'm proud of you, man. I must also thank you for honoring my vision of choosing you for the task in spite of its numerous parallel failures; although I have to say that you come close to making it happen with each of them, and I sense nothing will stop you here. We are of course one hundred per cent behind you!"

Liz: *"I knew it, darling; although it looks like our wedding date may become hypothetical as a result, but I'm sure you understand it's worth the price!"*

"Brilliant! As a token of my appreciation, I'll let you pick the reality of your choice for the ceremony!"

"I'm hoping to stay in this one for a while; it's got the kind of glue conducive to a strong marriage. I'm happy to leave the drama of another bad relationship elsewhere."

Jack: *"Hey, keep my brother out of this, lady, he's OK! Well, perhaps you're right; he's a bit of a loser after all. Back to the point: Henry, it's a rare privilege to work alongside you, and of course, it's nice to feel we're actually moving forward. The meeting in Stanley is crucial to our investigation; if everything works as hoped, it will fan the flames under Branched's ass. The jury likes it when the defense lawyers turn out to be part of the bad guys, not to mention the journalists."*

John: *"Jolly good! Let's keep up with the pace and hopefully, we'll see to the end of this nightmare."*

That was all, brief and concise. I wished I had been granted the privacy to have Liz to myself for a while, but distraction was distraction, whichever way you shook it, and Vertex, so it seemed, had put a clamp on it. I connected with Harold, who confirmed he and Aleksei were on their way with important information.

— o —

"Choose your allies carefully," sounded like the beginning of a cautionary tale. Aside from trusted ones, Jeremiah must have meant those in the making, like Harold and Aleksei, or perhaps Upton Clay, who was now assisting Liz down in Hobart. The three of them were Vertex go-to operatives, as solid as they came. Surely *Shadow Man* didn't insinuate the presence of a traitor amid them; it had to be yet another innuendo cast my way to keep me alert. When short on certainty it was always best to heed the warnings and pay attention to details; thus, I opted for vigilance and a revision of my loose definition of "friends." In the meantime, Freeman,

Yegorov, and I had arranged to meet up for lunch at a seafood restaurant on West Esplanade, along the Duck River. The men had spent the night at a different hotel as advised by Liz—a critical suggestion that sat squarely with my encounter with Jeremiah Jones. That detail was to strictly remain within the tight perimeter of the case. In other words, Harold and Aleksei were not to be entrusted with the knowledge of that meeting.

The important information mentioned by Freeman consisted, among other things, of the property's address where the gathering took place, which when crossed-referenced with Vertex database showed as belonging to Xing Liu, a Chinese entrepreneur based in Canberra, whose title merely concealed his real function as middle man for the Chinese steel industry. Further scrutiny exposed him as a major *Branched Resources* shareholder with a seat on the company's board. And that explained while we needed Quebec City involved as part of a massive one-two punch class action suit against the firm.

Naturally, proof of wrongdoing was required before moving forward, something tangible, written, recorded, or otherwise. But as material steadily trickled in, I perceived a coalescent hardening of our plan of attack. Most importantly, we were gaining confidence in the strength of its foundation; we knew we could build on it without a chance of the edifice falling flat on its face.

All the thinking in the world couldn't make up for nailing King, Harrison, and O'Reilly. The first scheduled court appearance was in five weeks and Jack Lewis needed all we could harvest for a chance at rattling their defense. No doubt all kinds of alibis would be handed out like free samples at a market, muddying the waters to the point of casting enough doubt amid the jury to throw the prosecution out of balance—in other words, the typical drama of justice. What we needed most was a rank defector, a remorseful actor present during the murder of Yang Wu, or the handling of his dead body at the tailings dam. I pressed Liz to put the heat on *Branched Resources* for the complete task schedule and worksheet for that day. The excuse of administrative incompetence, not to mention the feigned interest on the part of the authorities had tested my limits. I wanted that info—now!

Meanwhile, Freeman and Yegorov were antsy to return to work, by which they meant bugging Liu's mansion. I wanted Lehman's go-ahead before approving the move; not that I needed it, but Liz protested on the basis of insanity. She simply didn't want to see anyone hurt, well knowing her objection was tied to much direr consequences. Of course, John was OK with it.

— o —

I was no drinker, but seconds following Freeman and Yegorov leaving, a squat and well dressed Chinese man entered the restaurant and sat at a nearby table. I ordered a glass of Port to accompany an impromptu dessert in the hopes of striking a conversation.

"On business?" I asked nonchalantly.
"How did you guess? But yes—you as well?"
"Precisely, Henri Hartman, Metals Canada."
"Oh, the deep sea node-mining company, most excellent! Xing Xu, Taiyuan Steel. A pleasure to meet you Mister Hartman!"
"You may call me Henri."
"Same here, Xing, I prefer casual among family.

So, Henri, how do you go around all the environmental fuss about protecting sea life?"

"We keep on plowing ahead, convincing the I.S.A. one member at a time. After all, don't environmentalists need tellurium for their solar panels and cobalt for their EV batteries?"

"We live through hypocritical times, Henri, but those guys are pushing hard. You're aware cobalt is on its way out in battery manufacturing?"

"I am, Xing, but NFA is still at its experimental stage, and if nickel proves to be a suitable replacement to cobalt, we'll have the densest and purest form of it ready to ship! I mean, you guys are in the lead, so you know what I'm saying?"

"Exactly, fuck the environmentalists, right? But sorry, Henri, I've got to go; I'm expected at a meeting. Nice chatting with you! You'll be here tomorrow? Let's have lunch; maybe we can work together!"

— o —

No doubts I had just spoken with Xing Liu, one of the main men behind *Branched Resources*, the lever that pried the weakness box of local government, and the wrecking ball that demolished environmental protection acts. He was the parlous friend Jeremiah referred to when he advised me to choose wisely. Likely, he would be checking for a Henri Hartman at *Metals* while expecting me to do the same at *Taiyuan Steel*. It wasn't uncommon for important individuals to conceal their names on first meeting; hence, he presumptively didn't expect to find me in his database right away. Still, *les jeux etaient fait*, and danger had notched his way closer to my person.

Whereas a saner individual would have gone to great lengths to avoid the proximity of such a person, I was drawn to Liu under the time-tested reasoning that gains were made with just the right amount of risk-taking. Against Liz's desperate warning, I made up my mind to meet for lunch the next day.

— o —

The lone security guard highlighted the fact the property was rife with hidden cameras, necessitating utmost scrutiny on the way to the house. Fortunately, the deck-side sliding doors were kept open, leaving the inside alarm system disabled. As it turned out, someone was in using the upstairs shower, but with the operation requesting only minutes for the concealment of the device, Freeman and Yegorov were in and out without a hitch. Our boys were gone by the time the visitors made their way into Xing Liu's mansion.

Liz called to inform me Upton Clay was up our way to assist us—her decision. She was right in knowing we needed all the bodies we could get, as I intuited things were going to escalate rapidly from that moment on. Meanwhile, I crossed my fingers about the listening device, hoping nothing would fuck up. All I asked for was a modicum of luck and enough incriminating material to tip the scales in our favor.

— o —

While Harold, Aleksei, and I listened on the exchange, encrypted streams went Liz and Lehman's ways. The beginning sounded distant and undecipherable.

For one second we feared the bug had been placed in the wrong room, but thank God for small favors, the guests soon approached in the expected cacophony of cheap talk before settling in. What we heard was shocking.

Xing Liu: *"That Quebecois motherfucker, Henri Desgardes, is in town, passing as a hotshot Metals Canada executive—I could spot him a mile away! There's no doubt he isn't alone; most likely that rhino, Freeman, and some of his Russian sidekicks are sniffing around Stanley. We know they're after you Sam, and ditto with you, Ger! So, Jimmy, you know what to do, and this time, no bodies floating in the bay. Take them to the smelter and make them disappear!"*

Male lawyer: *"If I were you, I would scale down on the dead bodies; the board is particularly sensitive to the kind of drama surrounding the kidnapping of Abraham Garner and the alleged murder of Yang Wu. Our clients are already the focus of public scrutiny, so let's take it easy."*

Liu: *"The board can eat shit; we can't afford a whooping from Desgardes and his cronies! You guys figure out the legal angle; you're being paid amply to make things look normal."*

Female lawyer: *"Your actions will end up incriminating the company; it's a risk we cannot afford to take."*

Liu: *"Who asked you, Emma, do you see women in this room? So, shut the fuck up!"*

Sounded like James King: *"Yeah, zip it, bitch!"*

Liu: *"And you too, Jimmy, shut up!"*

O'Reilly: *"I'm for restraint as well; I'm already in enough trouble. Can't we just slow those guys down?"*

Harrison: *"Oh, come on Sam; don't start acting like a crybaby. I've seen you cut into those bodies—you're nothing but a fucking butcher, remember? You love that stuff; it turns you on. You don't have to pretend anymore; you've got lawyers covering your ass!"*

Liu: *"It stands as I say; Jimmy you go find those two fuckers, I'll take care of Desgardes personally! As to you two, Justin and Emma, start working on an alibi for Jimmy here!"*

That wasn't exactly subtle. I had a hard time imagining Xing Liu exposing himself in such a crude manner. Something was up and I couldn't put my finger on it. Yes, we were uncovered, but that wasn't the reason. The whole thing was as if Liu had been expecting us to listen on the conversation. The absurdity of it was too obvious—a clue had to be hiding somewhere!

— o —

I didn't pick up when Liz called. My mind was too busy circling a variety of sinuous scenarios. I just couldn't shake the notion there was a greater evil involved. Was I crazy to think Liu sounded the alarm by serving James King to Harold and Aleksei on a platter? In no way could I ignore my instincts—I absolutely needed to see the Chinese businessman over lunch the next day. Hopefully, it wouldn't be too late.

I rang Liz back while Freeman and Yegorov prepped James King's snare—she was beyond herself. But as soon as I told her my version of the story, she saw right through the stratagem. Of course Liu had acted the part! "Oh my!" was all she said before wishing me luck.

When Lehman called, it was to enforce the importance of figuring out Xing Liu's role. In his usual style, he showed no sign of being alarmed, admitting instead to finding the conversation rather entertaining; especially how it incriminated those poor lawyers. Vertex already knew how deeply O'Reilly was compromised, but now that Harrison had showed the face of a hardened criminal, a warrant for his arrest had been issued. We would simply wait for the arraignment to expose the lawyers for complicity, although, it was unlikely they would be prosecuted for it. It would come down to their ambitions backfiring; but then again, the money would largely make up for it.

— o —

At last, mine schedules and worksheets for the two months preceding and following the accident were released and forwarded to my laptop. On the day Wu's body was flown to Wynyard, Doctor Paul Desmond was on duty. He signed the discharge form and remained at the mine while Harrison flew with the deceased. But according to the sequence of events, the accident could only have happened after the paperwork had already been filled, exposing the glaring truth about Abe being the target. Harold confirmed Gerald Harrison was the medic present at the bottom of the dam; the other four men being structural engineers finishing a routine check of the west retaining wall before part of it came down.

Although Yang Wu wasn't scheduled for work, he was on emergency call, meaning he could have been on top of the wall, finalizing the placement of the explosive charge needed to bring the fissured section down. It was a theory that rang so strongly of plausibility that my mind could not un-think it. A premature detonation and Wu would vanish amid a race of boulders, while Abraham Garner was taken away! Although Freeman couldn't confirm whether he heard a detonation or not, his words were clear: *"It made a fucking racket!"*

My thoughts leaned to the side of a choreographed maneuver involving people on top and bottom of the dam. I was told the four engineers were longtime employees, but one, William Dorset, had since then retired. Vertex database found him living in Somerset, east of Wynyard. He was the man I needed to speak with, and for once, I didn't have to cross the island to get to him; the town was only sixty miles away from Smithton—a return trip I could easily manage in half a day.

— o —

While driving to Somerset, I pondered on Paul Desmond's role under the longer shadow of the case. My take was that he had been blackmailed by Harrison, just like O'Reilly, but truth and lies sat too close to the line for me to not heed the warnings. The doc only signed a form after all, so what kept him from coming forward? Another nagging question was, "Who was in charge of direct-depositing a dead Yang Wu's wages?" The payroll accountant, Harriet Donovan, was a senior employee slated for retirement. The thing was she didn't work at the mine—someone at ground zero sent her the info—leaving head of engineering, Johnathon Weisman, as suspect number one, since he also had scheduled the crew for night work at the tailings dam. I was counting on Dorset to illuminate me on the details.

I had left early, hoping to make it back for lunch with Xing Liu. I reckoned I was taking a chance on Dorset, but I didn't want to call him at the risk of getting him scared. Surprise was the mother of confession, albeit generally accompanied by a plethora of hazards, the nature of which I couldn't gauge. Nonetheless, my intuitions carried the easiness of things in their right places—I convinced myself he would be home.

— o —

William Dorset was a man of confidence, tall, with thick white hair poking out from all around a heavy wool cap. Upon hearing the reasons of my visit, he opened the door wide to let me in.

"Yes, indeed, the accident—that was one of the scariest moments of my life. And believe me when I say I saw it all!"

"I trust you are aware Branched Resources *is embroiled in a murder case concerning the body recovered that night, that of Yang Wu, one of the mechanical engineers working at Savage River."*

"It was a shock, when all the time we thought it was the body of a hiker!"

"What did you make of Wu's disappearance; was he working on top of the retaining wall?"

"There were a few men up there, setting up a charge, but I didn't know whether or not Yang was one of them. Now, thinking of it, he must have been."

"Was Johnathon Weisman the head engineer in charge of scheduling the work?"

"Yeah, I never understood why he did that."

"What do you mean?"

"We never worked the dam at night unless it was an emergency. Some of us protested but he insisted it had to be done while no crew worked below. The thing was no crew was scheduled to work below for at least a week."

"So, what do you make of it?"

"Since nothing about it made any sense then, I resigned myself to not ponder on it. With time, my thought process has been engaged into believing there was purpose behind it. I don't want to sound like a conspiracy theorist, but now, with the news of the body swap and the kidnapping, I believe Jonathon Weisman knew something I generally prefer not to dwell on. But since you're here, I don't see why I should keep it to myself. Would you like a cup of tea?"

"Yes, thank you!"

I followed Dorset to the kitchen.

"We were aware the west wall had suffered damage from heavy rains, but we also knew that being on the upslope, there was little chance of the dam breaking—what we're watching for in engineering. On a danger scale of one to ten, that one's a big zero; there's never enough water in it to put pressure on the walls to start with. So, the excuse of emergency maintenance, especially at night, doesn't hold water—pardon the pun."

"What did you make of Gerald Harrison taking Paul Desmond's place in the helicopter?"

"I never knew his name—I assume you're talking about the emergency doc?

"Precisely, didn't the thought occur that there was something unusual going on?"

"Well, it's a tough question; the fact a man was killed in the collapse was rather unexpected. But yes, in the back of my mind I wondered who he was."

"There's something that has been bugging me about the crew above the dam: why was the charge detonated before Yang Wu had a chance to get to safety, and who did it?"

"Technically, nothing is done until everyone has exited the red zone. If Yang was the last man to step back, he was in charge of telling his crew chief, the mate responsible for the OK signal."

"So, the way you see it, there was no premature detonation?"

"That was my original take, but with Yang dead, it makes one wonder."

"What if I told you that Wu wasn't scheduled for work that night?"

William Dorset remained silent, as if stricken by a sudden revelation. When he looked back, handing me my tea, his face was ashen and there was a shake in his hand.

"Are you actually saying that he was already dead before coming down?!"

"Dead or persuaded to remain in the red zone. Does the name James King ring a bell?"

"Yeah, there was that punk who liked to call himself King James, a jittery sort that worked as a mechanic. Now, thinking of it, I believe his name was mentioned over the radio right before the detonation."

"Any idea how long he'd been working at the mine?"

"Not long, a couple of months perhaps."

"Would I be wrong if I said he wasn't seen after the accident?"

"Matter of fact is I never saw him afterwards, so no, you're definitely right."

"Warrants have been issued for King and Harrison's arrests; would you testify in court if asked?"

"Branched Resources has been good to me; I'm afraid I must decline."

"Well, you understand I had to at least ask, William, but if you change your mind, you know where to get me. Thank you for your time and the tea; I must be on my way!"

"My pleasure, and good luck!"

It was definitely worth the drive, but without William Dorset's testimony, indicting Harrison and King was going to be tough—we really needed him in order to bolster our chances of putting those two behind bars and remove the imminent danger that they posed.

—— o ——

18 – XING LIU

I made it back just in time to meet with Xing Liu. Same as the first time, he was dressed in an impeccably tailored suit that looked expensive. The man, in spite of his roundness of shape, moved his body with ease, all the while emanating stateliness. It was hard to imagine he was the same person heard on the recording.

"You look like you've been busy, Henri. Is it too impolite to ask which company you've been courting?"

"Not at all, Branched Resources; I'm preparing my visit to their operation at Savage River."

"Of course, I guess you'll be meeting with Jonathon Weisman, their head engineer."

"Not sure who they'll be assigning to show me around, but if you say so, he'll be the one. I guess you've been there."

"More than I care to remember. We buy a lot of pellets from them, but competition is wreaking havoc to their finances. Their production costs are too high, and their Southdown Prospect is operating at only seventy per cent, which puts a lot of strain on Savage River. But tell me, why is Metals Canada interested in their iron; don't you have your own?"

"You may call it Commonwealth allegiance; in reality I'm here for the same reasons as you are—to make sure they'll be operational in the near to medium future. That's why they need to strike the deal with the state in order to mine the wilderness. That's their one chance at remaining competitive."

"Indeed, but I didn't know a young, green company such as yours would be interested in supporting the exploitation of the last of the Tasmanian rainforest; what's your angle, Henri?"

"Between you and me, being green doesn't mean we work for nothing, or that we necessarily care for the ecology of the planet, as long as the consumer of solar panels and batteries believe we are. We're not the villain, hypocrisy is. So yes, we're scooping the bottom of the ocean for ultra rare metals, while destroying the fragile ecosystem that took billions of years to form, taking with it species nobody knows exist. That's the point; if you don't see it and you don't know it's there, you live in green bliss, driving your green vehicles, and running your house on green energy. Green is nothing but a slogan that bars the mind from seeing the elephant in the room: rampant consumerism by a population that has exceeded its number quota."

"OK, Henri, I get your bullshit and you got mine. Perhaps the time has come to air our dirty laundry. How is good old William Dorset doing?"

"Ha, and how's the board of directors faring?"

"You see, that wasn't too hard!"

Xing and I regrouped our thoughts, as our order was brought to the table.

"Then, I must thank you for giving us Jimmy King and exposing Harrison and the lawyers for what they are. That voice couldn't be that of the man I am speaking with right now. What do you get out of it, Xing?

"Branched Resources has nothing to do with these brigands—I'm who's in charge of damage control."

"So, you're their internal investigator and we're here to strike a deal."

"Not exactly an investigator like yourself, but you're right about the deal. I want the company exonerated from the murder charges. My job is to purge the bad seeds out of it."

"If I get it right, what you're saying, Xing, is that there's a villain greater than Branched, like what, China?"

"I wish it were that simple, but China has nothing to do with it either."

"Who then would be invested in eliminating the obstacles to leasing the wilderness, if not Branched and its main buyer?"

"You may have to look somewhat deeper than mere financial reasons. You're certainly aware there are multiple layers in play, Henri. I believe you've met with a certain Jeremiah Jones, who advised you to choose your friends carefully. I'm here to remind you that there is nuance to the word 'friend.' You may add me to your list, even though I might also be the enemy. I trust you understand exactly what I mean."

— o —

I guessed what Liu and Jones meant was for me to read my friends properly, and in line with the specificity of my work. I agreed that "friend," in of itself, amounted to nothing but a subjective item of appreciation and depreciation within a volatile mental and emotional environment. In other words, I had no true friends save for Liz. The others were of the one-way, conditional type with no anchors in the terra firma of trust, which hardly worried me since I had long trusted to not trust the fickleness of friends. Their influence was far from being as important as personal integrity. That having been said, it left me with evaluating the nature of my recent contacts with William Dorset, Jeremiah Jones, and Xing Liu himself, as well as the narrative borne of those meetings. Oddly enough, the engineer was the tricky one of the three. In spite of his cordiality and openness, his energy was conflicted. He spoke like a man who had been anticipating an official visit. Needless to say I didn't buy the bit about his allegiance to the mining company. There was an air of vacuity to his claim of not knowing Wu was working atop the dam wall. My intuitions were screaming that he already knew the man was dead, and if so, he bold-facedly lied about James King, the likely assassin. His story about Weisman was too inculpating to not have been exaggerated, or downright fabricated. Contrarily to the appearance, William Dorset was protecting his boss. At that point, nothing prevented me from suspecting the entire crew of acting as a close unit. That left the mine doc, Paul Desmond, as the wild card.

— o —

As it turned out, Paul Desmond was also a University of Sydney student that graduated the same year Samuel O'Reilly and Gerald Harrison, aka Alec Gilbert, did. Liz matter-of-factly hypothesized that the three must have been close friends before going separate ways, with O'Reilly and Desmond reconnecting through their work when the former gained employment at North West Regional after a decade-long stint at Fairfield Hospital in Sydney. I wholeheartedly embraced her point.

A lot less clear was the nature of Harrison's work at Savage River and how he ended up covering for Desmond, who, according to schedule, was on infirmary duty that evening. Incredibly, the impostor wasn't listed anywhere, although the fact he was an independent contractor partially justified the omission.

According to Liz's search, Paul Desmond was presently on a health-related leave of absence dating back to a week after the accident. Vertex database showed him residing in the Maranoa Heights neighborhood of Kingston, south of Hobart.

The time was ripe for dear Elizabeth to get back to field action; you just couldn't keep a wild thing locked in an office for too long, no matter the reason! Personally, I was invested in seeing us back on the trail together, even if it meant operating a distance away from each other. Knowing she was part of the moving and shaking on a shared assignment was the next best thing to intimacy. And since going after Paul Desmond was our one ticket to handing some serious baddies over to the clutches of justice and further impeding *Branched Resources*'s momentum in reaching the wilderness, all the better!

— o —

By the time Xing Liu and I parted, Freeman and Yegorov had captured King and taken him to the barn in Elliott. The criminal, impervious to the sophistication of critical timing, was easily fooled into following Aleksei's Mitsubishi to a preset location, where Upton Clay, who had just rejoined the team, startled him from behind. As King turned around reaching for his handgun, Harold and Aleksei sprung out of their hiding places, pinning him to the ground, his wrists and ankles swiftly locked with heavy zip ties. The aim was to make him talk before turning him over to the authorities. The recording of the interrogation was then sent to the usual places.

Clay: *"So, James, or if you prefer, Jimmy, like the Chinese boss calls you, we heard you were after Harry and Alex to off them, right?"*

"Piss off, poofter!"

"You can say that again after a few days at Risdon when shitting becomes your worst nightmare, King James!"

Yegorov: *"So you ended up being the arse that shot my mate Uri and threw his dead body in the river down in Launceston, am I right?"*

"So what if I did; I kill Russians for sport!"

"Hey, I admire your directness of sentiment towards my kin; honesty goes a long way in my trade. But let's get to the point—who's your boss exactly, the Chinaman or Harrison?"

"I don't work for chinks!"

"Are you sure? Because when he tells you to shut the fuck up, you're rather quick to abide! But I get it; Gerald's the man who ordered you to off me and Harry."

"Ger's got nothing to do with it!"

Freeman: *"But since he's the one who asked you to kill Yang Wu at the mine, he's obviously the boss."*

"That was different; the bloke went commie on his own heritage!"

"What Harrison told you—and just like that you killed the man for changing his name to a Chinese one?"

"You bet I did!"

Clay: *"No other reasons, are you sure?"*

"You, I don't speak to; sod off!"

"A man of preferences—suit yourself!"

Freeman: *"Let's wrap this up! If only his boss could be as cooperative."*

King: *"He'll have you cunts for breakfast!"*

Yegorov: *"How do we shut this fucker up?!"*

— o —

John Lehman extended his congratulations to the team. Now, the authorities had to get to Gerald Harrison before he slithered his way out of the country. He was the key to bigger fish, such as Jonathon Weisman and those whose names hid behind the power of fortunes. Of course, there still was much to understand about Xing Liu's aim behind helping us. There wasn't a doubt in any of our minds that he sliced out of both sides of his wielded blade, but we deemed him untouchable in ways difficult to explain. Perhaps it was the manner by which he straddled philosophical concepts that made him invincible. Honestly though, we weren't ready to tackle his kind of might, although we were confident he would one day join us at the bargaining table.

—— o ——

PART FIVE

19 – PAUL DESMOND (Liz)

The case played like musical chairs on a slippery slope. I was back in the field, on my way to Kingston to meet with Doctor Paul Desmond, who was gracious enough to accept my visit and subsequent questioning about what had happened at the mine. I missed Henri very much, in spite of us speaking daily, if not hourly, primarily about work, but also about pleasure in the form, dare I say, of sexual innuendos. Even though it had been merely two months since my darling man became an active member of the Garner group, it was as if a year had passed, while I wondered if our wedding plans would fare any better than those, I imagined, in parallel attempts at beating *Branched Resources* to the midnight clock.

I had been kept very busy at the office, acting as the in-between for Henri and John Lehman. Jack Lewis and the Front Shield crew were in charge of assembling the case while dealing with court schedule and the myriad details that defined the main components of the lawsuit. It was a complex mixture of state and international matters that needed to fit snuggly under the auspices of varied levels of administrative competence. Needless to say that frustration and downright aggravation often set the mood of the day, but we prevailed as we trudged through the heavy muck of the system. In all fairness, we, lawyers, had a lot to do with the beast, for it was in big part our own creation. Still, I needed to vent.

Kingston was only a ten kilometer drive from the office on Macquarie. Paul and I had agreed to meet at a restaurant on Blackman Bay. River Derwent looked gray and choppy, as ominous clouds pushed by heavy gusts threatened to send the few pedestrians scurrying for shelter. The doc was already seated when I breezed in the place, and though I didn't know how he looked aside from a blurry picture of a younger self, I could read his energy from across the busy room. I made a beeline to his table, introducing myself—he didn't appear surprised by the assuredness of my move. His face was that of a man who had seen, felt, and heard too much. I sensed he was there to comply with a private contract, to bring matters to an end and walk free, regardless of the outcome. We made short work of the customary items of politeness and food details, going straight to the point.

"Let's please get started, Liz."

"As you wish, Paul. It's my understanding that Gerald Harrison, or Alec Gilbert, one of your friends at Sydney, replaced you on the evening a man thought to be a hiker died in a slide at the Savage River mine. Can you recall the circumstances that led to the switch, since schedule showed you being on duty that night?"

"Let's take it from the beginning, if you don't mind. Because my health was in decline at the time, I requested that the company employ a temporary assistant, a nurse to help with my work. They refused on the premise the accounting office did not budget for two meds. A week later, the mine hired my old friend Alec as a consultant. I couldn't believe the coincidence, since Sam O'Reilly, our trauma surgeon in Burney, was part of what we called ourselves 'the Mighty Triumvirs.' But things didn't turn out so well; Alec had changed in many ways, the least of which being his new name. The lively banter and dash of the early years were gone; he was hardened,

joyless, and intimidating. Frankly, his energy had moved to the dark side in a scary way. When he heard I was in need of assistance, he quickly offered his services 'whenever his other tasks permitted.' Of course, I declined, but he insisted, simply saying that I didn't have a choice. He made it his habit to swing by the infirmary daily, practically drilling me on everything related to my work. Although he was cordial in appearance, I couldn't pretend to not feel the heaviness that marked his questions. I found his presence oppressive, not to say manipulative. When I called Samuel, I heard Alec had paid him a visit. By then, I had the sense that things didn't bode well between the two, but I was in no place to let it bother me. I took it we all had changed through lives that didn't bear the fruit of their promises."

"Did he ever ask for favors?"

"It's hard to tell with someone so overbearing; I think he just helped himself by assuming some of my work."

"Like on the night of the accident, for instance?"

"Before we get to it, something disturbing happened. Every time he came to the infirmary, he brought tea from his office. It took me a while to realize that it wasn't just poor health weakening me, but something he routinely put in my drinks. I felt exhausted most of the time, to the point of thinking about early retirement; in the meantime, I was diagnosed with chronic fatigue."

"You did say that you fell ill before he was hired; wasn't that chronic fatigue too?"

"No, I had just lost my daughter to a horrid car accident—the trauma left me psychologically ruined, affecting my health adversely."

"So sorry, Paul, such unspeakable tragedy!"

"I'm partially over it, Liz—my health has improved since then—but thank you! As to the night of the tailings dam accident, Alec came to me earlier in the day requesting I sign a release form for the body of Abraham Garner, your father, but I categorically refused. I wanted him to explain himself, tell me who the man was! Part of me felt like capitulating—I was too tired for arguments, still, I kept on insisting. Then he said, 'you already lost a daughter, why would you want to jeopardize another family member?' I understood he meant it, so I signed the damn form. And then the accident happened! Three days later, I was taken to North West Regional and diagnosed with advanced stomach ulceration. Samuel wasn't there to admit me and I never saw Alec again."

"You are of course aware of the murder of Yang Wu, one of the mechanical engineers, and of what appears to be the kidnapping of my father?"

"I'm deeply sorry about it, Liz. Yes, I am aware of the ensuing denouement; it's one of the main reasons why I accepted to speak with you. Of course, I am ready to testify."

"I cannot say strongly enough how much this is appreciated, Paul, but I must warn you about the implications; Harrison is still on the loose, meaning that your life is possibly in danger, at least until we can protect you."

"I'm aware of it; that's why, since you are recording this conversation, I insist that you ask all the questions you must ask, just in case I am incapable of making it to the witness stand."

"I certainly hope it never comes to it, but yes, I have questions concerning the group of engineers

working at the site that evening. Do you think Johnathon Weisman, the crew chief, was working with Harrison?"

"Yes, of course, they had to be working together— they must all have known Yang Wu was already dead and who the murderer was."

"What makes you say that?"

"With Alec at the infirmary, he took in visitors from various departments. That was when I saw Weisman and the not-so-smart kid who worked with Yang at the shop, King James was the name; he seemed to be following Alec around quite a bit."

"Yes, James King; he was arrested yesterday for the murder of Yang Wu and one of the men working for us. He's presently being questioned by the authorities."

"He definitely carried the energy of a bad seed, but so did Weisman and most of his crew. One thing that may be of interest to you is that the four were transferred at the same time as part of a switch of personnel between Southdown Prospect and Savage River."

"How interesting! Is that customary, and who was in charge of making the decision, Weisman?"

"I haven't the foggiest idea; the question is who paid for it? The company that doesn't want to spend money on a temporary nurse, doesn't mind splurging on moving crews around? That's one enigma I've been dying to solve for some time!"

"This sounds rather unusual, and considering the circumstances, litigious as well. It looks like I've got a lot of work ahead of me!"

"Before you leave, I assume you have all the names you need?"

"I do, Paul, thank you so much! I shall keep you posted on our progress. You do understand that on *occasion I will need to reach you if something calls for clarification."*

"Anytime, Liz, I'm at your disposal!"

"I will arrange for witness protection, but until that gets worked out, I beg you to stay vigilant. Don't hesitate to call the authorities should you notice something out of place, and I mean anything, including intuitions."

"Thank you; I will do that—Goodbye!"

As part of protocol, copies of the recording were sent to Henri and John Lehman's office.

— o —

I sensed we were at a median, a place so central that a slight jarring of the wheel could shift the angle of the case, its trajectory, and the fragile landscape before it. I couldn't attest whether that'd be a good thing or not, but my mood wasn't particularly set on welcoming more complications at the time. All I wanted was for King, Harrison, and eventually, Weisman to start talking and expose the masterminds.

Naturally, Xing Liu and Jeremiah Jones remained our mystery men, with Liu substantially more compromised than our so-called *Shadow Man*, his name egregiously flirting with the title of main puppeteer. Based on my version of his psychological profile, he possessed the raw ability to render the best of us uselessly confused. As to Jones, he benefited from having led us the back way to our present advancements, which wasn't necessarily a good thing if one took the time factor into consideration. Nonetheless, both were playing on the particle/wave principal of being there one minute, and existing on multiple planes the next. They appeared as they wished, and vanished with riddles in their wakes, apparently immune to the mundane concerns of the living. There wasn't a doubt in my mind that Vertex was the object of their interests; and so, who they were, and where they came from was probably worth being sorted out—the sooner the better.

— o —

While Henri and the gang were busy up north dealing with villains, Jack and I kept the ship afloat in Hobart. I cannot stress enough how John Lehman's Front Shield came of great help to our own, to the point of the two practically becoming their own gestalt. John never seemed to sleep and I can't recall a time when he wasn't a step ahead of us. A lot like my dear father or those at Vertex who stopped aging beyond their point of acquired wisdom, he transcended the needs of common mortals. There was something supernatural about these men and women, something that not only went beyond the limitations of the physical, but the reach of the greater collective consciousness as well. They effortlessly and timelessly traveled on borrowed energy rather than spending their own. They were those Henri and I wished to become, as we sought to catch up with their evolutionary momentum.

— o —

I had barely returned to my office from lunch, when my assistant, Owen, announced the arrival of an

157

unscheduled visitor. I wasn't in any mood to welcome an interloper at a moment when my mind was spindling the fine, crimped fleece of the enigmatic, but it turned out that the name Jeremiah Jones was befit of the exception— I had Owen call him in.

"Hello, Mister Jones, a pleasure to finally meet in person. Henri shared much about you. How may I be of help, or should I ask what it is you have for me?"

"The pleasure is mine, Ms. Garner, but please feel free to call me J.J., while you may allow me to call you Liz—I cherish the more casual settings. The point of my visit is to highlight some of the dynamics present in your case and hopefully unballast some of the mystery of my involvement in seemingly muddying your progress. I am uninterested in the outer mechanics of your investigative work. Although, I am aware of the failures that exist on concurrent probable lines, they do not concern me, as their outcomes are fixed. There is an exceptional development in this version of reality that provokes elements of curiosity within my realm of consciousness. Succinctly put, I am akin to an agent sent by my peers to ensure that Vertex stays true to its greater purpose of preparing the grounds for the arrival of a third coming, foreseen, in your terms, as the entry of your race into an evolutionary phase of great vitality. For that to happen, the planet must be freed from the grip of greed and allowed to retain its balance; so, it is primordial that you should succeed in your endeavors. Contrarily to what you may think, the content of the thumb drive found at the mine did not hamper your progress, and neither did it speed it up. It simply put the case in a state of accelerated activity, vital to energizing its reason of being. As I told

Henri, it didn't matter which direction you chose from deciphering the list—it was a riddle that found its strength in a classic paradox, the same exact one that keeps your reality vibrant. I have no doubt that some of what I am saying isn't news to you, but there is much in terms of underlayment that operates on nuance rather than hard facts. The importance of your case cannot be diminished, yet its significance, in scope of what it is meant to protect, is negligible—but then again the reverse also proves to be true. Such is the nature of the paradox I speak of. You must at all cost immerse your entire intuitive self into your higher calling, that of being instrumental to that incarnate 'third coming,' which, I assure you, won't have anything to do with Christianity, or, for that matter, any religion in the usual sense."

"Well, the anticlimactic response to your information, J.J., is that I have already intuited most of it. So, yes, I know quite well what lies ahead and the main reason for my unrelenting involvement in this case. But I appreciate the reminder; and now that you are here, I have ascertained that I am on the right track and will continue with my work, supported by that knowledge. I shall refrain from begging for answers regarding my father's fate—somehow I don't believe he is exactly powerless in all of this—but if you happen to see him, please say hello for me."

"Delighted, Liz, you just proved my visit was well worth it! I shall honor your request as permitted."

Jeremiah Jones was gone, almost as if he had been in my thoughts rather than physically present.

I immediately called Henri and John about the surprise visit, going over each detail, but what I wanted to enquire most about was what Vertex knew about him. What was he, really? John's response didn't surprise me; J.J. was the equivalent of an agent belonging to the family of consciousness that conceived Vertex. He was as much an ancient entity as he was one from the deep future, in other words, the evolution of one of our members, either living or not, or even deeper, the evolution of Vertex as seen from the standpoint of a single entity, which practically meant that *Shadow Man* was an advanced version of each of us at Vertex. In Lehman's words, I had figured Jones out, but I was still far from feeling the urge to brag about the merits of being a woman of intuition!

— o —

Besides William Dorset, the other three engineers present on the night of the accident were Donald Weber, Thomas Landry, and Mervin Saunders, all working under Johnathon Weisman. The crew on top of the wall consisted of foreman Tony Sanchez, with Gabriel Turner and James King as charge placers, all of whom had to be aware of Yang Wu's presence, dead or alive, before the collapse. I found it extraordinary that no-one enquired about schedules and that questioning yielded no arrests. Was it merely assumed Wu failed to clear of the red zone after checking the placers' job? What a fiasco! The only thing left unsolved according to the coppers in charge of investigation, was the mysterious disappearance of my father, which balanced on Paul Desmond's testimony and King's confession of having murdered Yang Wu before the accident. Actually, the whole case precariously balanced on those two men being able to face and address the Crown. That was how the judicial gears were due to start their meshing, and cautiously move in the larger direction of *Branched Resources*. But with the arrest of James King as the principal offender, the authorities had no choice but to return to those they had questioned. Subsequently, Tony Sanchez and Gabriel Turner were in turn arrested as accused for the offense of being accessories after the fact. As to the men at the bottom, including their supervisor, Jonathon Weisman, none were deemed suspect of wrongdoing. Only Gerald Harrison was left to respond to charges of fraud, and possibly, of being an accessory before the fact to the murders of Yang Wu and Uri Dudko. Somehow, we still had to air the rest of the crew's dirty laundry and find the stain leading to Weisman's incrimination. Those were my intuitions speaking, and I wasn't going to let go until I saw that man's motives laid bare under the sun.

— o —

Now, my main preoccupation was for the safety of Paul Desmond, Samuel O'Reilly, and James King. It would have been foolish to count out Harrison's ability to hire contract killers as he wished. I spoke with Emma Swenson, who assured me the surgeon was covered by round-the-clock security and that James King was under protective custody, but somehow I didn't trust either her or her husband Justin, who had too much to lose with a simpleton like King easily running at the mouth unwarranted. As far as I knew, he was as good as dead. It wasn't going to be easy to arrange for a transfer, but Vertex had much leverage in the domain of powers behind the scene. John Lehman, who shared my thoughts, promised to take care of the situation.

That left Paul Desmond in the open, which didn't please me the least. I understood too well how things languished when the system felt pressured; it practically was a given item of reflexivity on the part of those whose job was to protect, to inexplicably resist. Liken it, if you wish, to cubicle pathology manifested into an undecipherable sense of entitlement, as if to say, "Fuck you for the nine to five nightmare!"

Under the weight of a mounting pang, I called the doc to offer him my house until I could secure his protection. I was relieved he accepted, since I prophesied disaster at the outcome of his demise.

— o —

Also, there was an item of perplexity in Samuel O'Reilly putting on the face of victimization. It was clear that by his participation in the meeting at the Xing Liu estate he was now an official member of the bad guys, but I saw the opacity thicken around his accusation that Harrison had coerced him into doing it. In fact, the same happened with Dorset towards Weisman. It was as if the masters had told the apprentices to go ahead and blame them for all the fuckups; they could take it because they had ways around the system. Somehow my instincts told me I wasn't too far off the truth. As a lawyer, I found it somewhat entertaining that Emma and Justin Swenson should be embroiled in that taped meeting. As far as I knew, they were O'Reilly and, likely, Harrison's attorneys, but then, they acted on the broader scale of representing *Branched Resources* itself, though I doubted the company would limit their defense to just the two. The case didn't permit us to accuse the couple of wrongdoing; after all, there was a modicum of etiquette that came with the trade, but my sympathies stopped short of approving of their game. Why they chose to latch onto something above their skills, I couldn't comprehend. From my understanding of protocol, they stood way too close to the fire, and I'd go as far as saying that they already had poked at the embers. I felt sorry for them.

— o —

On my way to picking up Paul Desmond, Harold informed me that he would be putting one of his men, Dimitri Osminin, in Maranoa Heights to keep an eye on the doc's residence. One could say that our investigator had a fondness for Russians, and even if they didn't work under him, it turned out that they too enjoyed working with Harold, a man they likened to a lone wolf operating under the radar. It was also why my father loved him and trusted him like a brother. I understood that the offer also meant another Russian would be assigned to a post across my house, but Harold naturally made no mention of it.

— o —

20 – TRACKS & TRACES (Henri)

Liz called for a mix of work and play, teasing that distraction was a necessary evil in precise doses. I had no objection since my mind was in dire need of a well-deserved apartness from the hustle and bustle of the last few days. I was relieved to hear Paul Desmond had moved into our house, which Liz still called hers out of forgivable habit. I hadn't realized the doctor lived alone. I learned he had made the mine his life after a nasty divorce, while his daughter, that poor soul who died in the crash, took care of the property in Kingston. It sounded like an existence pounded into submission by the hammer of blunt trauma. No wonder he almost died of an ulcer.

But the weather of the call was set to sunny and warm, and so we played until all the naughtiness was drained out of our minds. It wasn't quite the real thing, but it came next with its unique palette of kinks. When we hung up, the world had become a much better place.

— o —

Harrison and his men left Stanley the day of King's arrest. When, on an impulse, I later visited Xing Liu's estate, I was met by a lovely Asian Goddess, who claimed to be the caretaker, while confessing that the owner hadn't been around in months. Of course, she shamelessly lied, but the fact was the tracks were now cold. I remembered Harold mentioning another person in the house, why he and Aleksei hurried to set up the bug. And so, there she stood, out of that same shower as if time was no factor in her existence, her hair still wet, a hard nipple poking from under the upper fold of her robe. I could only blame the raging hormones of youth for the indecency, but suffice to say there was also a trap concealed within it that was far from being borne of innocence. I profusely apologized for the inconvenience, thanking her for relaying the news of my visit to Xing. She flashed a furtive corner smile before swiftly shutting the door. I intuited I had been expected.

— o —

If someone had asked, I would have said that James King's arrest was the distraction Harrison and O'Reilly needed to squeeze past our guards undetected. By the time we were done, the action had moved eastbound to Wynyard, Burney, and Devonport. I worried Harrison had boarded a plane to Melbourne, possibly the same one Xing Liu left the island on. I called John Lehman to see what he had on schedules and names out of Burney Airport. Indeed Liu was bound to Canberra, while a certain Alec Gilbert had booked a flight to Melbourne but hadn't boarded yet. His plane's ETD was set for five fifteen, giving us plenty of time to make it before he slipped away.

It was unlikely O'Reilly would want to escape, since he was still in position to fabricate his way out of trouble, but his future was plagued with ghosts seeking to materialize. The taped remark by Harrison, stating that the surgeon was nothing short of a sadistic butcher, was bound to follow him in the form of further questioning. Perhaps, not all injured bodies admitted to North West Regional were meant to die.

Beyond wondering why Harrison and Liu didn't board the same plane, since the flight to Canberra required a stopover in Melbourne, it occurred to me that there was unfinished business in Tasmania that required attention, the kind that might have included Johnathon Weisman, as well as fresh recruits in charge of erasing the tracks. It was becoming evident James King, Paul Desmond, and maybe, just maybe, William Dorset had become inconvenient obstacles to clearing a path to a quick settlement with Ehuang Wu, Yang's widow, and resuming with the leases, regardless of what happened to Liz's father. The kidnapping would likely be thrown out of court if nothing showed up to prove it; he simply got lost in the wilderness and died there—his bones would eventually surface. So, it wasn't difficult to foresee what awaited us; King would conveniently die in prison, either of suicide or from an act of violence at the hands of a cellmate, Desmond, from a lost battle with whatever "health issue," and Dorset, in a fishing accident, say— three seemingly unrelated deaths that couldn't plausibly spill over the obituary page of local dailies.

It was why Vertex was there, to make sure that kind of scenario had zero chance to take root. James King was transferred to an undisclosed location only his court-appointed attorney knew of; Desmond, according to the latest, was under the heavy watch of the Russian team; and as to Dorset, he was left as the wild card, unprotected for the simple reason he declined to testify. Consequently, his fate would reveal whether or not he was one of the bad guys—life could be cruel.

But there was something that had been poking its head on and off for the longest time and almost had crawled back into forgetfulness: Yang Wu's wages, deposited for months after his murder. In fact, he wasn't "yet dead" by the time it was discovered his body was the one found in the rubble. Harriet Sullivan, the woman who wrote the checks, claimed that wage remittance was dependent on what came to her from mine management computers, both at Southdown Prospect and Savage River. We hadn't been able to verify who the sender was, having speculated earlier that Weisman had to be the one, but for mysterious reasons, the item kept on slipping out of perception, as if in its elusiveness, it was designed to prevent any anticipatory assumption of wrongdoing on the part of the head engineer. At first thought, the concept threw me off balance, but intuition saw something else in it: too early a focus on Weisman would have sent the case into insolvability, something whose details I couldn't quite grasp, but as in all intuitions, it wasn't necessarily meant to be explained—it sufficed to simply know. Within miles of Burney Airport, I called the accountant whose number I had listed in my contacts from the time Liz visited Yang Wu's widow in Perth.

"Yes, Mister Desgardes, how can I help you?"

"Good day, Harriet, I'm looking into who's sending you the time cards from Savage River. I understand the authorities may already have asked you, but I hope it isn't too inconvenient for you to provide that information now, rather than having my office subpoena your department."

"You say you're enquiring on behalf of Garner, Lewis & Desgardes; is that correct?"

"Yes, Harriet, please call me Henri."

"OK, Henri, I'm retiring in a few weeks; am I going to be in trouble for providing the information?"

"I very much doubt it if you haven't been in trouble by now, dear."

"That's funny, but to answer your question, no-one is; it's all computerized."

"Thank you, Harriet, that's all I needed to know. You have a great day!"

Somehow, I should have guessed someone had been clocking in and out for Wu instead of sending time cards to accounting—of course, it was all computerized!

— o —

An hour before reaching the airport, Harold called the authorities with the information that Gerald Harrison, using his former name, was about to leave Tasmania. As we arrived, we were briefed by the plain clothes in charge that the suspect wouldn't be able to board—all was in place for his arrest. Harrison was apprehended, handcuffed, and taken to Devonport just as he got to the luggage check-in desk. The data came in shortly thereafter that Emma and Justin Swenson would be representing him before the Crown.

— o —

While Harold, Upton, and Aleksei were off to Devonport, I decided to drive to Launceston and stay there for a few days to put order to my thoughts. Some of the details didn't add up—there were too many suspects muddying up the waters—clarity was de rigueur. The fact that the case was playing on more than one plane of reality made it arduous to connect the elements to each other. Because we had a number of failing probabilities whose events overlapped my present focus in scenes of inexplicable elusiveness, I became concerned with the thought that some of the players may not have been of this realm. Individuals like Weisman, Harrison, and to a larger extent, Xing Liu, were demonstrating, through total detachment from what awaited them, that they had exit doors through which they could vanish. Of course, I realized the colorfulness of my thoughts had no validity in the context of the judicial system, but they comforted me in the midst of an absence of clues. *Branched Resources* still could brush the whole thing with the back of the hand and resume with negotiations.

— o —

My fondness for Launceston was mainly due to its sense of history on an island where most structures appeared to have been built in the last half century. Blame it on my poor sense of aesthetics for thinking Tasmania had a craving for unimaginative modernism. Each small town was its own version of suburbia, spreading in rows of cookie-cutter architecture, fanning out into parcels of prime real estate fitted with plywood mansions crowned with rooflines that lost themselves in overdone hips and valleys. Steel tops and fibro-cement siding was the name of the game all the way into the farmland. My guess was that anything erected in suburban and rural areas before the existence of building codes either went to rot or wasn't worth keeping.

Launceston was also the place where Liz and I forged our relationship on my first visit—where we made love for the first time and discovered there was more to it

169

than quenching the desires and passions of the flesh. It was where we found our combined love of being, our inner child, alive within the solemness of adulthood. We found kinship amid the vast field of our differences, meshed opposites into wholes, and grew to embrace the sublimity of love and the infinite journey that opened before us. Although we hadn't yet performed the ritual of marriage, we were wed as two souls of a common birth, immutable in our spiritual vows, strengthened by a silent awareness of our mutual purpose—that of building on vision to its fullest, unimpeded by distraction, judgment, and lust.

— o —

Launceston was also where Uri Dudko met his end at the hand of James King, where he saw something we were yet to discover. There was a lost track begging to be found, a few steps resilient to the passage of time, or just traces left amid rain rivulets. When Liz and I visited the Val D'Osne fountain, we were in pursuit of the toxic documents that had found their way into Yang Wu's hands before disappearing into the aftermath of his murder. Uri's search, following a lead provided by the same thumb drive that took us there, had also ended up in Launceston, where he died never accomplishing his mission. No doubt he had come too close to someone or something that didn't want to be found. The question remained, why would these forsaken papers be floating around? In the back of my mind, as I sat in the comfort of my hotel room, the memory of Jones's words, "the so-called documents," rang of a dissonant truth: there was purpose to them, but not necessarily to their contents. The thought opened the scented field of nuances. If those documents were in the possession of a cabal intent on playing by their own rules, whose game was it? It took me mere seconds before homing on one of the more extreme environmental groups aiming at inflicting maximum damage on multiple fronts, fanatics that loathed the judicial system as much as they did corporate reality; those that saw into challenging the credibility of the case the one-two punch necessary to annihilate the enemy. My mind swirled momentarily before regaining its balance. Yes, the concept was far from implausible; as a matter of fact it began to gain traction rapidly. The first thing was to locate our villains: anarchists, agitators, tree huggers, deranged conspiracy theorists, malcontents, counter-insurrectionists passing as greens to discredit their works, or the plethora of contenders in the panoply of today's psychologically insoluble reasons.

I rang Liz and John to confer on possibilities. They agreed to help narrow the list of bad seeds to a manageable number. Meanwhile, Harold and Aleksei were on their way to turn Launceston into their next zone of decontamination.

— o —

A wild scenario commenced its insane build within my mind, intuition adding insight and speed. James King, as one of the crazies in some hypothetical group, infiltrated *Branched Resources* in order to sabotage mine equipment. Gerald Harrison, upon realizing the youth was an easily manipulated and willing cretin, persuaded him that Yang Wu, a traitor who had sold his soul to communism, needed to be eliminated. Upon murdering Wu on the evening the engineer was scheduled to connect with Abraham and Harold, King got hold of the documents, hid them, and subsequently handed them over to his group. A year later, I found *Shadow Man*'s thumb drive in the rear of the building where the original rendezvous had been set to take place. Uri Dudko, aided by the list from the drive, came too close and was spotted. James King killed him and threw his body in the river—the rest was history.

Of course, the elements had to calcify, especially Jeremiah Jones's presence at the facility, but it made for tactile plausibility. Things seemed to want to fall into place with King as the wild card. The assassin never was integral to the Harrison/Weisman clan; in fact, his fate appeared to be of no consequence to them; although I doubted they wanted him locked up under protective custody. That left him without an attorney; since the Swensons, apparently, didn't want to touch him; yet he was in dire need of a solid defense. Liz called around for an able lawyer not connected to the office, for we were on the wrong side of the hostilities to represent him. It turned out that Upton Clay knew just the right man for the job, Leopold 'Lelo' Eisenberg, a rotund defense attorney from Devonport with a heavy drinking habit, whose sins didn't impair his ability to work the most tedious of cases, especially when it involved the underdog. He took the job without even questioning for details; the mention of multiple murders was all he required for the go ahead. Jack Lewis took care of forwarding all pertinent data to him.

— o —

There was a fringe environmental group in Launceston, the *Ambassadors of the Wild*, which was known to take responsibility for the minor sabotage of logging equipment and tree spiking. They claimed to model themselves after *Earth First*, in spite of being far less viral and efficient. Actually, the authorities didn't believe they committed any of the crimes they bragged about—they were thought to seek the exposure for the thrill and nothing more. *AOW* was hardly the environment of assassins, but a few loose screws, as Liz put it, could send the ship adrift into darker waters. So, when Harold and Aleksei arrived, they immediately took to the task of locating their whereabouts, which no database was able to do. Of course, asking King would have been the easy way, if only we had access to him or what his lawyer and interrogators would be willing to share; meanwhile, time was of the essence.

— o —

As more data poured out of the Savage River daily operation, it didn't surprise me to learn that the Southdown Prospect crewmen had returned to their original posts. In other words, Donald Weber, Thomas Landry, and Mervin Saunders were no longer within easy reach for questioning, in the wake of which Jonathon Weisman remained the only known suspect still at the mine. If the unscheduled scattering of the engineers failed to lighten the weight of culpability, it certainly wreaked havoc on case logistics. It meant that we had to assign Front Shield to the task of sniffing for tracks somewhere in Southwest Australia. But since William Dorset was living in Somerset way before the days of Gerald Harrison, plus the fact he omitted to mention his time at Southdown Prospect, made the whole story around the

173

switch all the more fantastic. Was I to incriminate Paul Desmond for inventing a tale? Once again the plot threatened to bury itself into impotence at the caprice of each stone turned. It was the signal that pointed towards moving in lieu of over-thinking. I had to speak with Dorset before someone else did. I called Upton for backup, for I sensed I had missed something critical on my previous visit to Somerset.

— o —

Dorset didn't pick up and neither did he return my messages. Upton stopped by his place to find it vacant. Our man had seemingly vanished, leaving no clue as to his whereabouts or fate. I had failed to consider that he too could have been under threat. I reasoned he was part of a crew that had known each other for years, whether at Southdown or Savage River. I was now confronted by my own failings at broadening my scope in evaluating possibilities; I had missed the one that set him, William Dorset, apart from the other three. Yes, he did say he was allegiant to the mine, but it was clear by his words that he wasn't so fond of Jonathon Weisman, although I had doubted him. I missed on exploring his relationship with the rest of the crew, neglecting to ask what he thought of his workmates. Of course, Paul Desmond could confirm whether Dorset was or wasn't part of the men transferred from Southdown Prospect. As I said previously, he had put himself at the center of a dilemma, neither by misjudgment nor guilt, but by being a victim of circumstances. It was in essence hardly a choice, but the simple fact that he had consciously opted to work for *Branched* was enough to set the course of his destiny.

While Upton Clay, now officially hired by Garner, Lewis & Desgardes, was busy looking for the missing engineer, and with Harold and Aleksei on the *Ambassadors of the Wild's* tail, it was up to Liz and I to make sure nothing would happen to both the doc and James King.

— o —

Although I was quick to conclude Dorset had met a bitter fate, the possibility he had bluffed all along remained highly conceivable. Meanwhile, Liz contacted Paul Desmond to ask him if he knew whether the engineer was one of Savage River's old hand or part of the crew that came from Southdown Prospect.

He did know. Dorset started working there much before Weisman's hiring. As the doctor recalled, there was some controversy regarding him not being promoted to head of engineering instead.

In spite of all the back and forth, the fact remained that no connections could be made between any of the engineers and the crime. I knew Jonathon Weisman was up to no good, but nothing wanted to stick. So far, he couldn't be touched, at least not until he was proven guilty of clocking for Yang Wu. I didn't have to remind myself that we were still a long way from home.

— o —

Harold and Aleksei managed to trace the *Ambassadors of the Wild's* digs to a decommissioned warehouse outside Launceston. A half-dozen of the youth were gathered around a butane heater in a make-up room littered with old pamphlets and stained paper plates, two

175

of them scrambling at the sight of the investigators, while the rest pretended to act menacing with a chorus of vulgarities. The one who did the mistake of pulling a handgun out from under his bag found himself pinned to a wall by the Russian, his feet off the ground, his face purple from the clamp to his neck.

Aleksei: *"Whew, I smell alcohol! So, that's how you treat your guests in Launceston, mate? I'd say you must be the leader of the pack, judging by your smarts. Did you graduate to a firearm when you reached drinking age or did your folks put one in your crib?"*

Harold: *"I want everyone's name as well as those of the two who flew out of here! Now, you in the back, let's start with the bloke my friend's choking to death there—what's his name?!"*

Teenager in the back: *"That's Bruce B. Bruce— what we call him."*

"What about a real name?"

"Bruce Martens."

"And what's yours?"

"Danny Woods."

"The other two by the heater?"

"Kate Schmitt and Derek Kline."

"What about the ones that fled?"

"Mickey Stanley and Moe Weiner."

"And who among you is friends with James King?"

Kate Schmitt: *"Bruce is."*

"Who would have thought? OK Aleksei, you can let go of that pisshead before he shits himself. Actually, he's coming with us. We'll be seeing you, people—in the meantime, don't think of doing something irrational."

Aleksei: *"We'll know where to find you, even if you try to hide. You heard my friend here—we'll be back until we get what we want out of your lot!"*

I couldn't say it was standard procedure, or even legal, but we had no fear of the group calling the authorities, that would have been too below them. On some level, there was something real and alive about those kids, the kind of honesty that couldn't hide behind the posturing and the angst.

— o —

Back in Hobart, Dimitri Osminin had nabbed an individual in the process of putting Paul Desmond's house on fire in the dead of night. The pyromaniac, Stan Markalay, was an ex-crewman at Savage River, someone the doctor knew for having worked under Yang Wu. He too was hired around the time James King joined the mine—the two were apparently close friends. Our work was paying off, as we were now in the vicinity of two men who could inflict damage to the core of the operation. On the downside, the arsonist wasn't as talkative as King, willing instead to take a punishing for the glory of martyrdom. The little he let out confirmed he was familiar with Bruce Martens. So, yes, it was clear the *Ambassadors of the Wild* were in deep trouble, although their eclectic, collective lifestyle was a deterrent to harvesting coherent information out of them. Rather than turning our captive to the authorities, we kept him as a potential witness, someone we hoped to bargain with in exchange for our silence about his crime. It was seriously time to stack the deck in regard to the approaching trial.

Aleksei and Harold took Martens to an undisclosed area for questioning—the recording was sent to my laptop, which I forwarded to John Lehman as well as Jack and Liz's offices.

Harold Freeman: *"Bruce, you're of course aware James killed a man at the Savage River mine. Can you enlighten us on why the Ambassadors didn't take responsibility for it, because that's what you people do, even if you don't commit those crimes; why is it different this time around?"*

Martens: *"We don't advertise murder; that's why!"*

Harold: *"So, you admit to it; that's good! Now, you said you would answer our questions if we'd let you off the hook about the gun incident and the fact you're illegally holing up at the old warehouse; you're not going to lie to us, right?"*

"I keep my word."

Aleksei Yegorov: *"Uri Dudko was my friend and James threw his dead body in the river, so I'm still a bit sore about it. If I sense you're fucking with us, I won't hesitate to kill you; understood?"*

"But if I tell the truth, you will anyway, right?"

"I'm fighting the desire to kill you right now, but I can keep my word too."

Harold: *"What did you do with the documents James King recovered from Savage River?"*

"I kept them at the warehouse until a bloke who said he was from the mine came to collect them. When James heard about it, he went crackers."

"You wouldn't happen to remember the name of that particular individual, would you?"

"No, but he said his boss, Wise Man, needed the papers back."

"Yeah, Weisman, but what about the collector; does Gerald Harrison ring a bell, or Alec Gilbert?"

"Maybe."

"And why would James be mad about that, since Harrison's the bloke who ordered him to kill the mine engineer?"

"Because, supposedly, the papers were for us to keep, but nobody told me!"

"So, let me ask, why would James follow orders from a man he didn't seem to like much?"

"Because he didn't want to blow his cover; he was there to sabotage machinery."

"I see. In other words, he was pressured into it, if I get it right, correct?"

"That would be my guess."

"But now, James also killed Aleksei's friend, Uri; what do you make of that?"

"Your friend must have scared the shit out of him. I don't think Jimmy meant to kill him, but he should have known better than to be snooping around the shed."

Aleksei: *"You people are a bit too trigger-happy for your own good; what makes you so nervous?"*

"If that Harrison bloke hadn't put a gun to my head, we might have been a bit less concerned about unannounced visitors; hope you know what I'm talking about?"

Harold: *"Am I to assume Harrison also put a gun to James's head and said, 'Go kill the engineer!'?"*

"I wouldn't be surprised if he did."

"So, it's your opinion that James had no business killing him if it hadn't been for Harrison?"

"Fuck opinions; Jimmy had no business killing anyone in the first place, period! Why he was never the same after the murder."

"Can you clarify?"

"He became more and more irrational as he got more deeply involved with that Harrison bruce. Maybe he couldn't come free of that group. But about the papers, I heard he got them back, although I don't know where he keeps them. Last I saw him, he said to wait till he was done with business."

"When was that?"

"Right after he shot that Uri bloke."

Aleksei: *"Hey!"*

Harold: *"We just got wind that Stan Markalay is a friend or yours; is it true?"*

"No, I wouldn't say me and Stan have been friends, but we got along alright. He and Jimmy were hired at Savage River together, but he hasn't been seen at the shed in a long time."

"What happened?"

"He left for Albany, in Southwest mainland."

"What's in Albany?"

"According to Jimmy, that bloke, Harrison, has his crew over there."

"You're sure you heard that right?"

"Yeah, I'm sure."

"Any names popping in your mind?"

"Just the one, Landry, Jimmy hated him from the time he met him at the mine. He wanted him crushed and sent through the pipeline to the smelter."

Aleksei: *"Sounds like love to me."*

Harold: *"Thomas Landry, one of the engineers working for Weisman; am I correct?"*

"I'm not sure, but it sounds about right."

"Would you say Weisman is working for Harrison, or is that the other way round?"

"Don't take my word for it, but I'd say Weisman's Harrison's boss."

Aleksei: *"Since your memory is coming back to you, do you remember any of those guys visiting the shed besides Harrison?"*

"No, but Katy caught two blokes outside the building, who said they were looking for Jimmy. She said they acted like cops, the bad sort."

"I guess we need to talk with her, right?"

"I reckon."

Martens's confession made it clear the engineers working under Weisman were nothing but trouble. If anything, it was paramount that Vertex kept James King under heavy protection, whichever way their back corridors of power allowed them to. We also were pressed to share our findings with his attorney, Lelo Eisenberg, who needed a convincing defense.

Jack Lewis was on it.

It was also time to get to the waters where the bigger fish swam; where the players that entered and exited freely through the revolving door of interconnected realities lived. But first, we had to get to Weisman.

— o —

Kate Schmitt's portrayal of the two men that came to the shed was consistent with Mervin Saunders and Donald Weber's mug shots taken from Vertex database. We now had near evidence that three out of the four engineers on duty the evening the dam wall collapsed were complicit in the murder of Yang Wu, while operating under the authorities of Jonathon Weisman and Gerald Harrison. Somehow, aside from Bruce Martens's opinion that the latter worked under Jonathon Weisman, nothing seemed to stick to the man who was hired to take William Dorset's legitimate place as head engineer—Weisman was an obvious bad guy, yet he shed guilt like water on a seal. The lingering question was, who did the hiring against internal promotion protocol?

With Stan Markalay's testimony of Gerald Harrison contacting him from prison to entrust him with the task of torching Paul Desmond's house, preferably with the doctor inside, the *Branched Resources* consultant, or should we say, henchman, was looking at a guilty verdict and a long time behind bars, unless the Swenson team could perform miracles. Talking of the Swensons, we heard through the back door that Samuel O'Reilly, also represented by the two attorneys, had begun spreading the blame on Harrison for the mischief of misnaming the dead body admitted to North West Regional. I was far from feeling sorry for the surgeon, but I couldn't see how the accusation would work in his favor. There were too many unaccounted villains awaiting an order to erase whatever tracks, for us, at the office, to ignore the obvious outcome. I very much doubted his services were deemed of importance at that point in the game; so when the news came that he had perished in a car crash on Bass Highway, along *Hellyer Beach*, just a few kilometers off the *Branched Resources* smelter and loading port, it came as no surprise. All in all, he was a despicable and loveless character that lived in the shameless corner of moral bankruptcy. I hated to say that his death was a welcome convenience to both sides of the court, not unlike the removal of a ubiquitous item of distraction. In the end, it was a sad thing to see the sum of a man's life reduced to nothing more than a hindrance amid factions in dispute, but we all created our own reality and I respected his choice of parting with the world, bereft of dignity. It was a case where nobody cared about digging for foul play. As far as the report went, he fell asleep at the wheel.

— o —

It had been weeks since Liz and I parted, and in spite of the daily calls, it felt as if our relationship had cloaked itself in a veil barring all substance from radiating through. The case was the antithesis of love, the unfertile soil where all emotions attached to the natural withered and died. The forces of its vortex were such that the mind found no strength or will to connect with the heart. Although it wasn't in my nature to lose track of my core self, I couldn't help feeling that love had to take a backseat for the mind to stay focused on the task at hand. In spite of all, the voice of caution grew louder, begging me to distance myself from projected items of importance and reconnect emotionally with my partner. I was at the opposite end of keeping the distraction of love at bay—work had become the distraction. So, at the time at which a sane man would have doubled down on his work, I pressed for the reinstatement of balance within and outside the self by offering Liz the option of spending a few days away from the madness, hiking the trails of the Tasmanian wilderness, praising the merits of the cold rain that would, in all certainty, impair our steps.

My ex-wife, Claire, would have found the concept utterly absurd, but not Liz, who deemed the idea brilliant, as long as there would be a cozy place to return to at the end of the day.

There was the suggestion of driving to Corinna and hiking to the mouth of the Savage River, and perhaps, weather permitting, boating down the Pieman River all the way to the ocean, but we were quick to spot the trickery of the case seeking to attach itself to everything aimed at distancing ourselves from it. In the end, we opted for a ride along lonely Gordon River Road through Maydena, to Lake Pedder, and all the way to its end past Strathgordon. It couldn't have been more perfect, with a break from the rain and sceneries stretching ad infinitum. We almost forgot the case until its pull announced the end of the trip. There was plenty of time to recollect our working thoughts on the long way back to Hobart, where I was to momentarily reconnect with my office, before once again aiming north for Launceston.

———— o ————

PART SIX

21 – UNDERSTANDING VERTEX

John Lehman here.

I was glad Henri gained traction that time around; time, of course, being a figure of speech when realities overlap. As mentioned earlier, it wasn't his only one go at moving to Hobart to take on the case, and though he hadn't yet immersed himself in the multifaceted aspect of his work, he was closest to assessing its wingspan. The nature of consciousness is elusive, in that a lack of it may not necessarily indicate a true void—often it is a trick of the mind, a play of masks to suit a variety of causes. In the context of probabilities, the ego is a one-way traveler, incapable of imagining the nature of incipient or active realities involving other versions of itself. Yet, as part of a larger consciousness, it is never fully disengaged from its source, unless, through a barrage of beliefs, it makes the distinct choice of staying blind to the greater picture. That goes for the majority of the race, those that live under the spell and who never wish to contemplate the powers of the inner world. Individuals like Henri, Jack, Liz, and the partners in Quebec City were transients, entities overflowing the boundaries of their egos to lesser or greater degrees depending on the probability within which their focus existed. In the instance of the *Branched Resources* case, as it stood in this recollection, the egos in questions were at the apex of integration with their inner beings. What it essentially meant was that the severing from core consciousness, so prevalent in average humans, was fused anew for the unobstructed passage of information. At that conjuncture, it was unthinkable to revert, for the process of devolution was strictly a construct of the mind adrift amid the material flotsam. Vertex is the convergence of all souls weary of reflexivity, tired of partaking in the hustle and bustle of the human drama. We are the observers of deeds and the stewards of the planet, acting only when critical levels of insanity are reached and irreversible deconstructive motion is about to be engaged. At the time of the Tasmanian case, we had observed the midnight clock merely seconds ahead of all going dark, so close in fact, that the potential for a savior was lost among a plethora of failed attempts. From where we stood, there was no other chance at saving the world from a slow descent into irremediable catastrophe, than the reality in which Henri crossed that metaphorical line into his greater being. I rested assured then, that all of us at Vertex had also moved a notch up the ladder of awareness.

— o —

We have never considered ourselves anything but servants of the natural order. By it, I refer to the creative spirit that weaves energy into form, builds patterns that interface seamlessly with each other into vast, cohesive systems of existence. Of course, as odd as it may sound, there is order and purpose to destruction, through which, ultimately, balance is restored. In the case of the human experiment, a careless race will end its tenure at the work of its own hands, be it through brutal, viral pandemics or natural disasters. A careful one, on the other hand, will see to restoring the balance from planetary abuse. At the time of the case, we found ourselves facing a dilemma: was the race worthy of guidance or not?

We deemed it deserved another nudge in the direction of redemption, not out of pity, but in honor of the work already started by some exceptional individuals, some who would eventually join Vertex. Behind them, we saw a collective strong enough to tip the scales. And so, in a rare move by observers, we took direct action via the global judicial system, an instrument of incomparable powers when dealing with "corporations that couldn't fail." I must say we barely cut it, as beyond the case depicted in these pages, the few traces of hope left failed to reach vibrance. In simpler terms, it was make or break for Henri and Liz, and the teams behind them. And why them and not others? Well, let's just reason that it took the combined energy of these two unique souls to build a whole much greater than the sum of its parts, because of their love for each other. There was enough power in that union to attract the disparate elements of the case into coalescence. Whereas in the failed attempts, as explored within previously mentioned probable scenarios, that union was potent enough to engage the gears of progress, it regrettably lacked in definition—Henri hadn't come into his own potential early enough to commit to the love his relationship with Liz required. I, and everyone at Vertex, as well as those dwelling amid unimaginable layers of consciousness, will never say it enough—love is the essence of life. Period.

— o —

The lack of personal drama around Abraham's disappearance was one of the vital elements that made the case possible. Liz and Henri saw waste in letting emotions run the course of the logical path; instead, they relied on the power of the intuitive and invested their trust in it. It wasn't that they believed the elder partner was safe or dead, but that there were inherent reasons for things to have turned out the way they did. They simultaneously arrived at the clean slate of their assignment, addressing each element as it came into inner focus as an object that would eventually find its place, never dwelling on it past the point of recognition, as in saying *hello there* and moving on.

The reality of which I speak, as delineated in these pages, was the one-and-only in which the outcome of life on the planet wasn't fully at stake. It pitted itself against probabilities that pushed back at its yearning for activation. In all of those variations, the court case reached a point of acute significance, but never strong and far enough to break through the resistance. Each of those failed scenarios had moved from trace to full reality on the premise that the leases could be defeated. Unfortunately, too many miscues prevented forward motion in the optimal direction, such as Henri foregoing the trip to the mine on the premise Harold Freeman was corrupt, and missing on the opportunity to discover Jeremiah Jones's flash drive—or worse—taking it for granted that Liz's father had died in the slide and never finding out about the body swap.

It must be said that those failed scenarios shared the common thread of accumulated knowledge from error, of which potential for another chance at it shot from the rootstock, so to speak. That was when Henri, on a plane of parallel activity, boarded a flight to Tasmania for the fifth time and arrived at that trip with Liz on Gordon River Road along Lake Pedder, having by then furrowed a groove deep into the derma of the case.

We at Vertex crossed our fingers, for there were still many unsettled items anxious to derail our progress, and, obviously, quite a few unknowns surrounding the ubiquity of a certain Jeremiah Jones—notwithstanding the role played by Xing Liu, the mysterious Chinese executive on the board of *Branched Resources*.

Speaking of mystery, where was Abraham Elliot Garner and how did his note find its way to Lips Waters Café, awaiting the arrival of Liz and Henri? Well, it could be said that probabilities were pretty much alive around sequential reality and that with each forward step, side ones were also made, which, in *toroidal fashion*, recycled data back into the root past. Simply said, I was in no position of knowing at the time, and neither am I in this present—also the future of the case—because the pages following these very thoughts are still blank, although they won't be for long, if one gets the drift of my analogy.

This is what understanding Vertex is all about, to not envision changes to coalesce into the staticity of the established. Everything is always in motion across many interactive realities, as we, the observers and occasional participants in the affairs of the world, travel those lanes to engage in the fixing of what appears likely to break down at fundamental levels; mostly, we provide the tools, but we have been known, in dire cases, to do the job ourselves—after all, we are also human.

Now back to Liz and Henri.

———— o ————

22 – A DANCE OF SHADOWS (Liz)

Just as Henri returned to Launceston, Leopold Eisenberg, James King's attorney, came to the office to meet with me and Jack. The murder trial was a week away, and what was to come of it would decide the course of the case against *Branched Resources*.

Eisenberg was intent on finding the psychological angle on the criminal's motives, especially regarding coercion and blackmail. The point was to indict Gerald Harrison on charges of accessory before the fact in the murder of Yang Wu, and expose the face of his shady connection with the company—certainly, "environmental consultant" was hardly the nature of his work at the mine. Eisenberg had also opted to represent Stan Markalay, the arsonist at Paul Desmond's house, since both cases as a whole carried substantial weight against our villain. It was a not-so-rare instance of both defendant and plaintiff aligning in the pursuit of common cause without compromising positions. King and Markalay would be charged for their crimes, albeit with attenuating circumstances, a win for Eisenberg; and of course, the same charges would be the beginning of a deeper investigation into *Branched*'s hiring of Harrison.

— o —

Lelo Eisenberg was a large man who moved his body in series of grunts, as if every articulation worked under duress. He was quite old, and certainly beyond retirement age, which, in the field, could actually mean anything depending how fast you made your money and invested it. In the case of our man, there had to be other reasons beyond money to keep him on the job. On first impression, I sensed that the court was his raison d'être; without it, life was devoid of significance and purpose. Perhaps it tied to his choice of serving the underdog, the crestfallen, the beleaguered black sheep of the system, but as I came to know more about him, I arrived at a place of admiration for that gentle behemoth of a human. Even the smell of must and old liquor enrobing his girth and stature had an element of age-tested wisdom about it. But nothing could match his keen intelligence and acute flair for what weakened the prosecution in a court of law. We, at the office, understood clearly that the inertia of a large body in motion was unstoppable when it came to judicial matters, and it was perfect for what we were after—the goal wasn't to stop Eisenberg; we were going to let him plow right through us. In the meantime much light would have been shed on a multiplicity of villains; that was of course if we could put our hands on pieces of Jonathon Weisman and his ex-crew now holed up in Albany.

— o —

On John Lehman's recommendation, we sent one of our Front Shield officers to Albany to track Weisman's engineers. It was no coincidence that the city was the locale of Southdown Prospect headquarters, whose site of exploitation was a mere hundred kilometers northeast of town. As proven with Stanley, a community sitting directly across the smelter of Port Letta, the bad apples never fell too far from the tree; and whether *Branched* was directly involved in the crimes or not, it still had a lot of explaining to do. As far as we knew, Jonathon Weisman had remained stationed at Savage, making the communication between him and his crew difficult, but, on the other hand, it could be said that some distancing was part of opacifying the waters of culpability. What annoyingly persisted was the lack of direct connection between Harrison and Weisman. While the former had his crew on top of the wall the night of Wu's murder, the latter and his men were at the bottom, sorting through the rubble to extract an unrecognizable corpse. Technically, Weisman was untouchable; yet without his chief insistence on blowing up the wall that very night, there wouldn't have been a case to speak of.

The way to look at it was with two different kinds of lenses. On one side we had Harrison, King, and the crew that operated atop the dam in jail, while, on the other, Weisman and his engineers roamed free. That distinction alone was testament that each was governed by different rules, functioning independently from one another. I just couldn't think of a way to bring them on the same platform, even when it was intuitively evident a link existed. While I suspected Weisman to have been the man behind keeping Wu's earnings alive, I couldn't understand the logic, unless it was a prop placed with the specific purpose of either guiding or misleading. I guessed it was a bit of both. I also came to recognize much significance in the swapping of the two bodies; while Harrison and his gang dealt with Yang Wu's demise, another team had to be in charge of making my father disappear; and that was when, with shocking abruptness, Jonathon Weisman's face came into full focus—he was one of the many that visited the ranch back in the days of my youth!

I had to double-check. John Lehman must have known him, although that left me confounded as to why he didn't make mention of it. I first hesitated, and then fully recoiled from the thought; it was too odd—I had to see for myself first. I didn't even wish to share my discovery with Henri—it was my thing, something private between my father and me.

— o —

The house was as he left it before taking off on that hike with Harold. The caretaker in charge of the landscape and general maintenance resided in the east wing. Despite the property being in my name, I chose to not live on it or sell it. Now that my father was likely alive, it made sense to pay for the upkeep. I realized that I should have come there more often; it was after all a lovely place on a large wooded lot that begged for lovers like Henri and me to indulge in its offerings, namely, a glorious Olympic-size covered pool, and many secluded grounds crying for nudity.

My father's office looked as if he conducted his main business from it, although the term "main" was debatable in his case. There were the typical, heavy oak shelves containing the innumerable hardbound volumes of state, federal, and international law, as well as an inestimable collection of rare hand-printed books, some of them kept behind the glass of temperature and humidity-controlled display cabinets. There was also the obligatory bookcase door that led to the archive room where all things Ranch Acacia were kept and itemized: the photos, videos, minutes of the meetings, accounts of various experiments, séances, businesses, affairs—

everything to know about that side of Vertex without ever mentioning the name.

I was after photos, eight-millimeter reels, video tapes, proofs that my mind wasn't playing tricks on me. If Jonathon Weisman's face truly belonged to my memories, it would then certainly emerge from among my father's relics from times that didn't only mean the past, but also a quality of life that existed inside the one inhabited by the larger population. That world was a space within the greater makeup of the universe, an impenetrable sanctum, unperceivable to the common eye.

And there it was, amid a group of laughing faces, a young gentleman with the matching features of the man whose dossier had been the preoccupation of the office for weeks on end—one of the major suspects in the evils surrounding *Branched Resources*. It was a long time ago, when mother was still alive and vibrant. I could see her radiant face among those friends sharing the preciousness of extraordinary meetings, timely convergences of spirits full of hopes and glory.

Based on the dates, I was six by then; too young to attach meaning to experience, but definitely old enough to remember my surroundings. I couldn't say the man struck me as being exceptional, but there was a certain *je ne sais quoi* about him that spoke of a uniqueness of character; someone a child could neither love nor detest, but definitely the kind that could hold a child's play just long enough for a lasting memory to take root. Beyond the face, there wasn't much I remembered of Jonathon Weisman, aside from once seeing him in the company of my father, walking the path that followed the creek all the way to the end of the property, nearly half a mile from the main house. But that was more than needed for me to grasp that my parents were close to him then, although I don't recall the two of us crossing paths after that summer. Mind you, I began losing interest in adults the moment I became preoccupied with the self, so there was that, plus mother became ill and the groups stopped meeting after she died.

The fact was that my father and Weisman were old acquaintances—the kind of news that drastically changed the angle at which to approach the case. Also, John Lehman's lack of disclosure about the engineer's presence at Vertex gatherings was most perplexing. I felt that Henri and I were being kept out of vital information; but for what reason besides keeping a relationship between my father and Weisman concealed from the case? If so, did it imply the two were involved in something that could potentially jeopardize our chances against *Branched*—a set up?

— o —

Henri was just as befuddled as I was by the news, but rather than raise suspicion about John, he simply said that the omission was likely to benefit the case. Best was to not mention the discovery until the first trials were over with, when Harrison, King, and the rest of the upper wall crew were put behind bars. In other words, looking for clues of a Weisman involvement in the murder of Yang Wu was a waste of resources; something would just fall into place by itself. In the meantime, fattening up the file on the operation out of Albany couldn't hurt, for if the head engineer was untouchable, it didn't mean that his crew was irreproachable. Interestingly, two individuals were now exempt from scrutiny: Xing Liu, and Jonathon

Weisman. Obviously, a return to the archive room was de rigueur if I was meant to find a relationship between my father and the Chinese businessman.

— o —

That time around, I turned my father's office into my own. I needed a few days to immerse myself more deeply into the chronology of the gatherings at Ranch Acacia, starting with the first meeting—all the way back to just before my birth—right when mom and dad, still fresh out of Oxford and HEAD, opened for business under A. Garner & H. Garner, at our present location on Macquarie Street.

Without my father's love for details, there wouldn't have been a meticulous file system, completely digitalized and saved on various external hard drives ready to accept my laptop. Needless to say, the passwords for each year and event were part of a mnemonic code system only we, Garners, could interpret.

John Lehman was the ubiquitous entity of the group, and no wonder, since he and my parents went to university together, as it was said that he was a toss away from stealing my mother's heart. Personally, I don't think it was meant to be, but colorful stories must be told.

There weren't any sign of Xing Liu at that first Christmastime gathering, but he showed up in the cold of the following July for what appeared to have been a private meeting between my parents, Lehman, Weisman, and others I didn't recognize. The year was 1978. I was a month old then.

It was evident mom and dad were close to the two men in the utmost position of evading culpability

198

regarding the case. Although, things were still unclear about Weisman, it remained that those were meetings likely tied to the birth of that chapter of Vertex, internally known as the Tasmanian Team, or TT.

It wasn't until the middle of the following year that things became really interesting, right when Harold Freeman and three others, two men and a woman, joined that group. They always met at the half-way point between summer gatherings, generally around June or July, to discuss Vertex related affairs, most of which I was familiar with in loose terms. But I was now interested in the minutes, the intricate details that culminated in Henri, Jack, and I being taken for a spin.

Let's make it clear; I was far from amused. No doubt the brunt of the excuse would come landing in the form of a condescending, sugar-coated bit of rationale about how it had to be. I was getting weary of being taken the long way round for the sake of some pseudo-training—it was now time to spill the beans about how I felt and how I was no longer going to play the game!

I wished my dad had been around, so that I could have told him myself, daughter to father, woman to man, privately, like all family affairs should be dealt with and resolved, that I was no longer a child roaming among adults; that the voices praising the importance of matters of humanity and beyond, weren't part of the background noise a young soul innocently basked in. I hated him for holing up in a scheme that, frankly, made zero sense. Where was he anyway, and why subject his close ones to the pain of departure, the agony of loss? Were we, Jack and I, supposed to have been aware of a subplot orchestrated from behind the blind side of the case, or had the elders simply gone mad? The time was ripe for making some calls, first to Henri, and then John Lehman who deserved to get a piece of my mind!

As usual, Henri was of a rare stoicism regarding the boulversements that took place within my mental space. He asked me to reason with my emotions, which, he said, were totally deserving of expression. Even though I despised him for saying that, I knew deep down he was right, and that I was possibly overreacting, but I wasn't done yet with the anger. After I abruptly hung up on him, I endeavored to dial Lehman's number when the caretaker, Janice, knocked at the office door.

"Sorry, Liz, but there's a man wishing to speak with you about something important, he says."

Who knew I was there, and how important could unwanted solicitation be?!

I was about to unleash my fury on the impostor standing outside, when I came face to face with Jeremiah Jones.

I almost lied to myself that it was no surprise, but his presence actually startled me. I let him in.

"Sorry for the impromptu visit, Elizabeth, but I believe the time has come for some clarification. Although I don't show up in any of the pictures of the gatherings, I can assure you I was there, starting with the first one. Actually, I was also at Oxford as well as the French sister university when your parents and John Lehman prepared for their Master of Laws degrees. But unlike most attendants at those convergences, I always preferred to remain in the safe zone of invisibility—call it caution if you wish."

"Please, don't waste my time with hogwash, Shadow Man; I'm in no mood for small talk. People are dying because of this charade. Was Yang Wu, one of our own, the sacrificial lamb in a power game involving the trickery of old men? My own father, John Lehman, and Harold to boot? What about some decency!"

"None of these men are what you're thinking, Liz—all remains as it stands. Jonathon and Xing are untouchable because they simply have nothing to do with your father's disappearance. You and Henri have made much progress, but you must now open your eyes to the obvious before you become blind to it. And please do not call John Lehman about this until you know for certain that you must. Keep on looking into those gatherings; that is all I am permitted to say. Goodbye, Liz!"

That was quick—he had stood inside the door, not wishing to come into the office, and was now gone. For sure, the man wasn't from here, I meant the planet or this sphere of reality in general—maybe from a probable one closely rubbing against ours—who knew? After all, he just popped up for the first time at Swansea in the form of a self-addressed envelop, and had by then appeared a grand total of three times, leaving more enigmas in his wake than answers. Since my time at Vertex, no-one had ever mentioned such an entity capable of appearing from across the thin veil separating sympathetic paths. There had never been mention of a Jeremiah Jones, J.J., or *Shadow Man* in the course of my entire exposure to the groups as child or adult—I couldn't even tell whether he was Vertex or not. But now, I was—we were—facing a new, yet unchanged horizon splashed with the gun grey tones of uncertainty. It was a matter of cloud direction and where the storm would land, whether we were in its trajectory or merely to be brushed by its might. As the future of humanity hung on the fine balance of time and placement, it was clear by Jones's words that we had to shift position in order to orientate our focus elsewhere, which meant abandoning our pursuit of Weisman and Liu. I momentarily wondered if that included letting go of our investigation into Albany; but no, something in the back of my mind told me that there were gains to be made from it.

I called Henri again, apologizing for my rudeness and lack of patience. This time, I had his undiluted attention.

"Is Jones warning us that if we don't start looking into what's missing out of Acacia, we're about to come to a dead end? Did you get that or is it just me?"

"Correct, I've got to go through the entire records of those gatherings, films, photos, letters, minutes of the business meetings, etc... I'll be in there for days, but it could be worse."

"If you need me there to help, let me know. We're kind of tidying things up here with the Ambassadors, plus Upton, Harold, and Aleksei will remain in Devonport and Launceston just in case we hear of Dorset's whereabouts or something new pops up at the shed. So, if you can't manage, I'll be available."

"I don't need you to do my work, but I wouldn't mind a shoulder rub while I'm doing it."

"Put Janice on it till I get there; didn't she say she was a masseuse?!"

"Fair enough, I'll let you know what I come up with. I'm not going to rush it—too much at stake!"

I could have used Henri's presence, but to be frank, it would have been unfair to him. My mood was on the dark side of the spectrum, with too much information gnawing at my emotional sanity. I went down to the wine cellar, grabbed a bottle of Snake & Herring chardonnay, and decided to make it a night shuffling through the past.

— o —

While I was sorting through the files, a call came from Albany. Jason Saëns, the Front Shield officer sent to look after our engineers, confirmed that the three resided in various parts of the broader city, regularly getting together downtown at the Earl of Spencer for drinks. It was also confirmed that on the last two occasions, they were met by no other than William Dorset, our man mysteriously absent from his residence in Somerset and presumed to be on his way to an ominous fate—something for Upton Clay and Henri to ponder on.

OK, so we had something like this: the man holding the grudge of having been unfairly knocked off the pecking order—a perceived victim of foul play at the hand of Jonathon Weisman—had just found his ass in the crosshair of suspicion. It was a rather mind-stretching reversal, but sincerely, one that didn't surprise me at all. I was suddenly confronted by the notion that instead of Weisman having made the call of blowing the dam wall, Dorset and his cronies, in cahoots with the men on top, could just as well have put pressure on the head engineer to get the job done.

If that idea held water, what was Weisman's true role at the mine then? The unorthodoxy of his hiring suggested a decision made at the highest level—nothing too far-fetched in imagining Xing Liu behind it. After all, I had proof the two knew each other from the meetings at the ranch. Perhaps it was a matter of calling Harold Freeman and asking him to explain why he held the fact of his acquaintance with Weisman away from us. For the third time in a row, I dialed Henri's phone, more prone this time to being open to suggestion—no doubt helped by the wine—and also weary of my own bad mood.

Henri wasn't surprised either, which took me aback since he seemed so sure of himself that Dorset had been a victim of circumstances. But he was quick to explain that after going over the material I provided him with during the last two calls, he had changed his mind.

— o —

If the engineers weren't working for Weisman, and Harrison wasn't either, who then was the mastermind? According to *Shadow Man*, it wasn't Xing Liu, the most likely suspect, and my father was out of the loop—at least, I hoped. That didn't leave too many candidates to do us the honor of coming forward. The three worst offenders, O'Reilly, Harrison, and King were either dead or in jail. Speaking of Harrison, he was the man better placed to know the truth. I had always assumed that, one day, Xing Liu would reveal the face of a true villain, but now, without him in the picture, a large question mark threatened to topple the little accomplishment the team had laboriously put together. The notion was assuredly worthy of sarcasm.

If I hadn't known any better, I would have thought our bad guy was Jeremiah Jones, but intuition being intuition, that route was nothing more than a descent into a rabbit hole. We had to trust someone after all, especially if that person made the effort to connect at critical junctions. That left the doc, Paul Desmond, presently living at my house—brilliant!

— o —

While going through some of the films taken at the gatherings, I pondered on the reason why Xing Liu offered to have his name put on Henri's list of questionable relations (or did he say enemies?) following Jeremiah Jones's suggestion of choosing his friends carefully. Henri was supposed to know what that meant. My mind being on the restless side, I called him again, for I needed to be reminded.

"Liz, that was an allegory for the way one perceives his friends and/or enemies from the standpoint of assumptive beliefs; didn't we go over it once?"

"We did, but I sort of lost the feel of it, like I'm presently losing the thread of this crazy case... Should I call Harold about Weisman?"

"Someone's going to have to do it; so yes, give him a ring, or we can do a conference call if you like."

"Nah, I'll do it! I think it has become personal at this point."

"Let me know what comes of it—I'm also closely invested in knowing who my friends are. Not that I think Harold has been playing us—I've already been through that one and proved myself wrong."

"I know; it almost cost us our last chance at moving forward with the case. I'll keep that in mind when we speak. Bye, love, I think that's enough for tonight—big hugs!"

— o —

I rang a dour-sounding Harold, who had just gotten the news that Dorset was spotted with his crewmates in Albany—he felt frustrated. For a second I thought I had called at the worst possible time, but there was never going to be a right time to address what was bothering me deep-down.

"So, Harold, any good reason why you omitted to mention your past connection with Jonathon Weisman?"

"You found out, hey?! Damn, that's going to be hard to explain, but give me a moment here. OK, when I reached the bottom of the dam on the night of the collapse, Jonathon Weisman and I came face to face. I hadn't seen him in a long time, although I was aware he and your father had maintained contact over the years. The little we exchanged, considering the circumstances, might as well have been spoken while in a state of dreamlike numbness. I don't even recall being surprised to find him there in the least probable of places. His exact words were, 'For the love of God, I beg you to keep this between us!' And that's what I did, not that I wasn't tormented for keeping it a secret."

"And the same applies to Xing Liu, I suppose?"

"Did I have to? Wasn't it clear from John's words that he was to be left alone? As long as he wasn't suspected of foul play, knowing him was irrelevant."

"What can I say Harold, the way I found out felt like a total letdown, a betrayal if you get the drift. How can you expect me to trust you from now on?"

"How has my silence about it been detrimental to the case; you tell me, Liz! Weisman was untouchable from the start—you knew it, Henri knew it, we all did. It's not like you wasted your time going after him and then found out later that I could have saved you the trouble. Yes, your father, Xing, Jonathon, and I were well acquainted with each other; in fact, we discussed the many ways to bring big businesses on their knees in the event of a catastrophic outcome regarding their practices. You may say that our discussions became the platform for what we are presently mounting against Branched, *but I swear there is no plot deserving of a conspiracy theory here."*

"Fair enough, it's not like I should know all of your secrets, Harold, but what about Jones; what's your connection with him?"

"Abraham and John spoke of him, but I never met him—he's a myth. You and Henri may have received his visit, but from where I stand, he may be nothing more than a construct. I dare you to prove his existence."

"Nice one, smooth escape, but you know better than to make a fool out of me. We at the office have come to accept constructs as integral expression of intuitive knowledge. Why are you doing that, Harold?"

"We all have our angles—I respect yours—but I'm too rational to rely on intangible information. For the time being my focus is on Albany, and I wonder why Aleksei and I aren't already there."

"If the firm didn't require you to go there, it's because we have our reasons. You may be surprised by what you don't know about me."

"Well, that makes us even then. Keep me posted on what you expect of us up there. As far as I know, we're wrapping things up. You'll have my report by morning's end. Goodnight!"

It was relatively possible that I had blown it; but nonetheless, I felt much better. Harold had somewhat tested me since the beginning of us working together, and I must say that in spite of the mist surrounding the other versions of reality, I sensed it was the case there as well.

— o —

What happened between Harold and I was the result of something long in the making. I had always felt he saw me as dad's little girl—definitely not someone belonging to the head office of a law firm. He was never one to have much esteem for women, but when I took over as part of my father's wish, his antipathy turned somewhat misogynistic. Perhaps it stemmed from his deep friendship with dad, the kind of bond found on the battlefield, the tough love of men towards their kin, what they couldn't call love because they were too scared of the word. Whereas my father could live comfortably with a bit of pink-hued affections, Harold was all gun metal grey. Closeness was best expressed through endurance and exhaustion—joy had no place in it—life was work.

I'm not saying he was rude to me; he, of course, wouldn't have dared because of dad, but condescension needed not be rude to reach target. Humor and innuendos were legitimate channels to carry dislike to destination—the more confusion the better—and it kept on piling up as part of the routine of crossing paths.

Did that make Harold a traitor? Hardly so, but hurt could turn the world ugly and friends and family into caricaturesque figures out of the reach of awareness. That was what Harold had become to me, a fundamentally good man, wrought by the hammer of male conditioning.

But I had work to do—eventually he and I would figure out how to iron out our differences.

— o —

So, what hid amid the gatherings at Ranch Acacia that I hadn't seen with my own eyes? I didn't particularly believe that the summer affairs, the frolicking, the laughter amid the pouring of wine and fine scotches concealed mysteries worthy of lifting our case from the bottom up. It had to be within the loam of those winter meetings that the first roots of malfeasance found their vitality. But unlike our fair weather parties, those encounters were rarely filmed or photographed; what happened behind closed doors was at best documented in writing in the form of minutes. What I was looking for were those metaphorical roots that tapped into environmental concerns, but it was difficult to find acts of misdoing around firming the legalese necessary to defend the land. The misconduct had to be in the exploitation of those ideals with the aim, instead, to protect an industry at war with the wilderness. In other words, there was at least one insider that didn't belong.

I mentioned that with the arrival of Harold, there were two men and a woman that also joined. I had one of the rare photos but no names, and I didn't recollect having met them at the summer gatherings. The minutes of that meeting were also missing, which automatically raised a few red flags in my overactive mind. I needed to put names on these faces, and those capable of helping were either gone or inaccessible, leaving John Lehman as my only hope. Since I had already stirred up the pot with my conversation with Harold, my earlier intention to wait for further developments was now moot—I had no choice but to call Quebec City.

"Hi, Liz, what is it?"

"Going through dad's files and wondering if you could enlighten me on three individuals in one picture that appears to be from the meeting first attended by Harold—two men and a woman? I never saw them at the summer gatherings."

"My, so long ago, give me a second... Right, one of the men and the woman were the Swensons, George and Monique, attorneys from Adelaide, the second man's name was Karl Gilbert, a surgeon from Sidney."

"Thanks! By the way, you could have told me about Weisman."

"I agree; you needed to know. Now you do!"

"Why the secrecy?"

"You create your own reality, Liz, the secret was always yours. Please, stay focused on your Vertex training, now isn't the time to come unraveled."

"I will always be daddy's girl to you John, won't I? Same with Harold, right?"

"Come on, Liz, you sound inebriated. Get yourself some sleep and we'll talk again tomorrow—goodnight!"

That wasn't exactly what I had expected, but there was indeed something sobering about his words. I could take a hint and own it, but before going to bed, I had to put some order to my thoughts. Swenson and Gilbert were surnames I was familiar with, especially when two of the former were the attorneys for the latter. That was too odd for words—so, a few notes and I'd be on it in the morning!

— o —

It wasn't the smartest of move to drink an entire bottle of chardonnay on an empty stomach, but I prevailed, save for the pounding headache—nothing coffee and a solid breakfast couldn't correct. When I returned to my computer in dad's office, it was with the intention of unmasking the connection between those three individuals and the players in my present reality. It turned out that the Swensons were no other than the parents of Justin Swenson, defense attorney for Gerald Harrison—and wait for that one—Emma Swenson, his wife and firm partner, was of all things the daughter of Karl Gilbert, indisputably making her Alec Gilbert, or, Gerald Harrison's sister. All that within minutes of checking the Vertex global database!

Now, I didn't expect Harold Freeman to have been aware of the compromising connections, but that pivotal meeting had way too many cooks in its kitchen. In recap, the man who accompanied my father on that fateful hike to Savage River had pretty much known all the key actors in the case, at the exception of Jones, whose existence he waved off as a mere abstraction.

To use John Lehman's rhetoric, if the secret was mine all along, how could I have been aware, at the tender age of one, that the people meeting at my parent's new office on Macquarie Street that day, would eventually be connected by blood to a future lawsuit played in half a dozen probabilities, one of which finding me with my present, wicked hangover pondering on the very question? The one thing that struck me though was that those were the children of the olden crowd we were speaking of; Alec Gilbert, Emma and Justin Swenson, and of course myself were all youngsters of around the same age then, and the likeliness of us having played together was remarkably plausible. The difference—I had become Vertex, they had not.

— o —

Henri absorbed the information with an odd mix of surprise and indifference. I believed the surprise side was to show support towards my work; overall, though, he was moving with the flow. To him, my findings were only the continuation of what we'd been doing all along—separating the layers to the best of our abilities and cauterizing those that, mistakenly, were lifted from the wrong onion, so to speak. He simply didn't want to arrive at Vertex having engineered a complicated game of hide-and-seek just for the two of us. Although, when I thought about the way Henri had been advanced onto the case, I wondered how much of it wasn't just that: a series of initiation steps as part of a right of passage—and that applied to us both! Naturally, I found my mind running on empty when I tried making sense of it, and frankly, I was glad Henri could retain his balance within what could be best described as puzzling.

But John Lehman was right; I had been exposed to methods and training for too long to not ascribe to them. To see Henri run with the program, contrasted sharply

212

with my newly acquired resistance towards it. Well, it was my dad at the centre of it after all, and I could see how much his disappearance had affected me emotionally, even if for the longest time I held the front of my character without flinching. I had been overdue for a good look at myself—I guessed foraging into dad's secret files was the mirror whose reflection no longer displayed the youth of those ages, but the face of a woman characterized by recent hardship. I had worked myself raw as a means to escape my sorrow. Pushing against what was rightfully mine distorted my perception of reality, as the result of which I began to hate my father when, instead, I should have been with him in heart and soul. I recognized then that the process had been utterly counterproductive, as it prevented me to hear his voice weave through the elements of the case.

Did I think my father was alive in the end? Well, for one thing, it wasn't this body that went down the dam, but it had been more than a year since he vanished, thus the likeliness of his return was fading with every day passed, every snag in the case, every time we went after the wrong guy... Yet, part of me, back in the recesses of the subconscious, felt he was the man behind it all, and that, one day, he would walk into the room as if nothing happened, proposing a toast for the *fait accompli*!

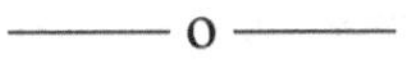

23 – UNRAVELING (Henri)

Liz's last series of calls worried me. It wasn't in her genes to get drunk. I was afraid reality had finally hit home and I was in no place to challenge that process. I understood too well what the case had demanded of her, and I couldn't conceive interfering with the release necessary to assuaging the pain. Nonetheless, it raised a logistical issue as to her abilities to keep going with the task, but I doubted she would be willing to step out—pride wasn't a quality she had waged on parting with.

Harold confessed that concealing the information about his past connections was his choice. Professional guidelines dictated the conditions under which vital data was to be made available, namely, the right time and place, which he claimed hadn't yet materialized. So, yes, he knew of the Swensons and that Emma was Gerald Harrison's sister, but it was fundamentally true that it didn't change the larger picture; if anything, I understood how that knowledge could have been a distraction. Harold's place was to work a specific agenda based on how the case progressed—not to volunteer input on the erroneous notion that it could have helped. As he put it, there were already too many revolving doors preventing coalescence. While I deemed his choice to remain silent acceptable, I didn't wholly agree with the logic. But that was Harold!

The fact *Branched Resources* did some wheeling and dealing with the state and the feds behind closed doors didn't necessarily evoke wrongdoing. Yes, it was unethical on many levels, but that facet of corruption was a big part of mixing business with politics; and while it skirted illegality with outright affront, only its pathology was reproachable—hence, nothing to build a case on. So, until we could prove that the company had engagements a few notches below the layers of approved criminality, we had to keep on searching and focus our attention on the four engineers holed up in southwest Australia.

Sure, it was true that Liz, in a bad mix of pain and alcohol, had threatened to unman Harold, but we all knew, she the better, that Jason Saëns wasn't cut for the dirty work. And so, on John Lehman's insistence, Freeman and Yegorov flew a private charter plane directly from Launceston to Albany.

— o —

Upton and I were left with the job of extracting all pertinent info out of the *Ambassadors of the Wild*, a task whose challenges and frustration were consistent with the fickleness of disenfranchised youth. It was evident the group was aimless, and even if their sentiments for the protection of the wilderness were earnestly felt, the methodology of going about it was absent. Their meetings were unfocused, often drifting off-center through disagreements and distractions. Actually, their most critical militant work was done under pressure from Harrison, as it transpired James King didn't know the first thing about sabotaging logging or mining equipment, and that Stan Markalay couldn't burn a house, even if he tried. I was hoping Eisenberg would give the kids a break by showing some brilliance in court.

With Weisman temporarily out of the picture, pressure was on finding a connection between Harrison and the Albany crew, as well as unveiling the significance

215

of the Swensons representing our most reprehensible villain besides a family tie. There wasn't a doubt in my mind that orchestration played an important part in fostering that arrangement. The whole thing had a feel of rehearsed preparedness pointing to Harrison having chosen the particulars of his arrest. The thought was discomforting in that a stealthy unknown was felt edging my blind side, distinct in its omnipresence by existing in the shadow of an outsize obvious. Did Harrison's team anticipate the case to be thrown out of court on the basis of infallible alibis? We had recordings, witnesses in King and Markalay, proofs of coercion and blackmail from testimonies by O'Reilly and Desmond, yet their visible assurance was at best unsettling. I sensed something geared at destroying our work was about to happen, why I picked up the phone to reach Lehman in Quebec City.

— o —

"Hi, John, don't tell me you weren't expecting me! Now that we all know about the connections between the Swensons and the respondent, can I ask you how you feel about seeing Harrison walk?"

"Not a good prospect, Henri, but a distinct possibility based on what we don't have: a motive for his actions."

"Exactly my point; they know we don't have a face for the mastermind, that our testimonies are shaky—thanks to O'Reilly's demise—and that our witnesses are admitted criminals. Plus Eisenberg could tip the scales and make us look like fools."

"At least, you have a solid head on your shoulders, Henri, and that counts for something. But

don't underestimate Jack Lewis; he's a monster the minute he gets his chance—he's been known to own the courtroom when under adversity. Remember, you're not alone in this and there are still a few days left."

"Thanks, John, I needed to hear that!"

That was all I asked for now, some measure of reassurance, even if nothing new was learned.

— o —

At that point, the case played on two legal fronts, one with Ehuang Wu—the applicant—against James King, Tony Sanchez, and Gabriel Turner—the respondents; and the other with the state as the plaintiff against Harrison and Markalay, the defendants. Of course, with court terminology varying to some degree between countries, let it simply be said that, for our purpose, plaintiff and applicant, as well as respondent and defendant, were interchangeably used. The Uri Dudko murder was defined as state against James King. Naturally, the case was plagued with innumerable convolutions, but the office had it under control with Jack Lewis and Front Shield at the helm. Of course, my turn would soon come to face *Branched Resources*'s lawyers—a test of the limits of my skills—and though, I looked forward to it, I enjoyed the relative safety of my present role as field investigator.

— o —

Harold and Aleksei were quick to latch on the tracks in Albany. After a brief exchange with Jason Saëns, they split roles in observing the men's actions. It was immediately obvious that none of them were working jobs, rather, they moved around town and its suburbs, meeting with a number of individuals, which oddly played like a game of musical chairs, very much as if they expected to be under scrutiny. It was unclear as to whether they did it as calculated disruption or as a means to protect the sanctity of their meetings. That incessant crisscrossing of activity totaled their numbers at much higher than just the four engineers. It was demonstrable that we were in the presence of an organized group whose identity was yet to be recognized by our tools. Whereas environmentalists played on the theme of visibility, these individuals favored operating incognito. We, at the office, immediately homed on the conceivability of a right-wing cell bent on wreaking havoc amid nature conservation laws—and for the first time in weeks, I heard in my mind's ear the sound of clutch plates locking and of gears truly meshing. There was a sense of forward movement that jolted the case out of its lethargy, shedding with it the deadweight of false assumptions. The obvious: *Branched Resources* was and would always remain a villain, juggling profit and politics in the name of jobs and demand; in fact, nothing unlike any other big businesses invested in the exploitation of planetary resources. What it wasn't though, was a reprehensible criminal organization; thence lay the nuance set forth by Xing Liu through his metaphor of friends simultaneously making the list of enemies.

I had arrived at the conclusion that, at some point in the Ranch Acacia era of meetings, the Swensons and Karl Gilbert had fundamentally veered off Vertex's vision, and that Alec Gilbert's change of name was conceived on far more than a whim. It reeked of a plan to muddy up the identity waters during the infiltration of the mining company's infrastructure. I was looking at an elaborate set-up geared to destroy any chance at mounting a case of environmental concern against *Branched Resources*. Its wickedness reached the core of the observer within me, as I witnessed from afar the fate of the world unravel onward to an unfathomable reset to default settings, that time, however, at the exclusion of our present version of humanity.

— o —

Technically, my work in Launceston was done. The *Ambassadors of the Wild* had given us all they had, which distilled into them having been used by much bigger and meaner fish. Upton Clay remained in Somerset to check on Dorset's house, while Harold and Aleksei went on sniffing tracks in Albany. It was time to return to my desk in Hobart and help Liz out of her funk. The office needed her strong and focused ahead of the uncontestable string of villainy about to unspool, for I suspected the future rooted in unusual places.

A report from Quebec City put the Albany cell on the short list of potential underground organizations aimed at sabotaging environmental work and progress. While Abraham and the rest of Vertex had sought to prove corruption in the behind-closed-door negotiations between state and mining industry, a group of slick players had crossed the line into indecency by forcing the hand of a pseudo-protectionist gang of misfits into committing criminal acts. All the Swensons had to do now was to prove Harrison's innocence and move the entire blame onto James King and the rest of the kids.

It fell on Liz and me to find the compromising affiliation between the lawyers, Harrison, and the Albany cell. We were well aware that the Swensons, by partaking in the narrative at Xing Liu's estate, had stepped into their first mistake. We had to momentarily refocus on Stanley to reassess the roles of the participants. At the time, none of the engineers were on the list of suspects, so we didn't expect any of them there, which, based on the latest, didn't mean they weren't.

— o —

Whereas Freeman couldn't be seen by any of the bad guys in Albany, Yegorov was free to roam with nary the risk of being recognized. That was how he managed to get close enough to the group at the Earl of Spencer to catch a few names and profanities rising above the noise, notably, Garner, Emma, Ger, the Chinese cunt, and Desmond—enough to congeal the notion that the topic was about the people we knew. For the occasion, Aleksei had let his hair down to assume the looks of a local hand straight from finishing his shift at the port, while joined by a female happy-go-lucky regular willing to share some short-on-supply fun. It also helped that the Russian was extremely handsome. It worked, and according to the report, the group never suspected they had been eavesdropped on. It wasn't much mind you, but enough to point to a plan in the making. Emma was of course the attorney; the "cunt," Xing Liu; Ger, Harrison; and Desmond, our doctor still staying at Liz's place under the watch of Harold's henchmen, while, for the time being, my fiancée resided at her father's place. Naturally, the mention of Garner and Desmond was the enigmatic item,

220

since we didn't know whether the reference was for Abraham or Liz, and in the case of the doctor, whether he was friend of foe. We had carefully presumed that he was friend, but with reserve—that was why he was under surveillance as much as protection. After all, trying to put his house on fire while it could have been easily known he was out, had long ceased to qualify as an attempt on his life, at least from the office's standpoint. As we stood, Paul Desmond had moved up the ladder of suspicion.

What it boiled down to was that the engineers were aware of some of the critical players in the case, which automatically disenfranchised them from innocence. But we had to move a step closer in order to gather evidence of wrongdoing; something that wasn't as straight forward as it sounded. What Aleksei pulled off at the Earl of Spencer was a one-time shot, which, against the odds, yielded enough to prove we were in the right place. Without hard evidence though, we still had nothing of strong-enough substance to dismantle the Swenson's projected strategy. We did have the recording from Xing Liu's home and his approval to use it in court, in which the lawyers were caught discussing matters with their clients that dangerously skirted the razor's edge of impropriety, notably so in the fact that said meeting happened ahead of Gerald Harrison's arrest, but we needed quite a bit more for the coup de grace, and that came when Harold caught, on his trusted Leica, George and Monique Swenson, accompanied by an unidentified woman, being let inside the suburban house rented by Donald Weber and Mervin Saunders. The shots didn't lie and the ring of suspicion had closed on the group.

Technically, we had enough to reduce Harrison's defense to ashes, but time was no longer on our side. The evidence would have to be introduced during court proceedings at the risk of being ruled as irrelevant to the case. No, the Swensons would be better served with the introduction of the recording by Eisenberg in the King case, an item they couldn't object to, since they had relinquished representing the killer. The one glaring issue was that the Chinese man, one of the powerful directors of *Branched Resources*, was at the center of the most incriminating data, for if it worked against the company—a good thing—it diminished Harrison's implication of malfeasance—a bad one. We had arrived once again at a play of contradictions.

— o —

Since there were a number of juxtaposed court appearances related to Yang Wu's murder and the missing of Abraham Garner, I am in the obligation to distill things into simple components:

- Lelo Eisenberg represented James King and Stan Markalay.
- Jack Lewis represented Ehuang Wu and the Garner Estate.
- The Swensons represented Harrison.

I deem it irrelevant to enumerate all the details spent on schedules, on defining applicants, respondents, or dealing with the secondary case involving Tony Sanchez and Gabriel Turner, the two crewmen that assisted James King in throwing Wu down the tailings dam, and who Eisenberg declined to represent. Our prime joes were Harrison and King, two cases that were to establish the means by which to go after the wilderness leases. At that point, it didn't matter whether the mining company was guilty or not; the main purpose was to expose the corruption that lay within its day-to-day operation and how it fermented into foul play.

— o —

As data kept on percolating from Albany, I was struck by an item that nearly eluded me—Harriet Donovan, the accountant at Southdown Prospect, with whom I had interacted on a number of occasions regarding Yang Wu's wages, and whose photo ID of a younger self was now part of the files at the office, strangely matched the facial features of a ubiquitous Ranch Acacia attendant. I immediately called Liz to have her look into a possible cover-up by the woman, who, recently and so conveniently, had retired from her desk. Her response was swift.

"Darling, you have an eye for details—Harriet Donovan was indeed one of the guests—it's right here in the file! I'm sad to say that even though I recognize the face, I failed to make the connection. Not all of the Ranch Acacia meetings made it to the forefront of my memory. Oh dear, the woman lied to you about the pay stubs and the clocking at the mine—she must have known Wu was no longer alive from the time my father vanished!"

I was beginning to feel bad for Jack, but I remembered John Lehman's comment about his resilience through adversity. As in all things proportionally opposite, Lewis was likely going to be OK.

223

Nonetheless, little time was left to get Harriet Donovan to the bench. It was up to Harold to convince the local authorities to have her comply, but Vertex was on it, and before anyone had a chance to realize what had happened, she was put into police custody. At last, we had what we needed to get the ball rolling in the Garner versus Harrison case.

— o —

But before I finished packing my belongings, just ahead of rejoining Liz at her father's house, an unexpected visitor knocked at my hotel room door.

Xing Liu, dressed in a perfectly tailored suit, shone a confident smile as I let him in.

"I hope it's not an inconvenient time, Henri, but I thought I would stop by before flying back to Canberra."

"Please come in, but I thought you left after the Stanley gathering."

"Well, that was what I told Gerald, but in fact, I only flew to Melbourne for a few days before coming back to the island to conduct business in Hobart and briefly swing by the Savage River operation to meet with Jonathon Weisman."

"That's right; it has come to light that the two of you have known each other for quite some time. Liz found that out when she went through her father's files about the Ranch Acacia meetings."

"As she was destined to, Henri; I'm glad her intuitions took her to the logical place."

"Would you fancy a drink before I drill you with a few nagging questions, Xing?"

"Just water, I don't plan on lingering though; I have a driver waiting for me outside."

"Well, you may answer just that one: are you not concerned about the content of the recording taken at your house; after all, it does incriminate you as the worst possible villain?"

"Not really, because I doubt Eisenberg will need to produce it as evidence."

"He'll have to in order to demonstrate James King didn't kill Yang Wu of his own volition."

"Not if he discovers ahead of his court date that the Swenson's are planning on proving Wu is alive and well."

"Am I hearing you right, Xing; are you saying it wasn't Wu's body that was intended to pass as Abraham's? That is utterly absurd!"

"The river has no choice but to follow the bed it has carved. It was a pleasure seeing you again, Henri— my regard to Liz and Jack!"

He didn't touch the water. He was out the door before I could even say goodbye. I immediately called Eisenberg.

———— o ————

24 – STATE AGAINST KING

Lelo Eisenberg expressed no surprise at the news of the Swensons preparing to bat out of the park, but I intuited that deep within his massive intellect, the seed of one-upmanship had germinated. Although, technically, Jack Lewis was going to end up on the wrong side of the fence, it wasn't in our interest to put up a fight beyond the mere formality of it. After all, James King didn't know who Yang Wu was aside from what Harrison had told him, and if he killed another man instead, it was altogether a different court matter. At that point, I began to doubt the veracity of King's confession about the murder of Yuri Dudko, which more or less translated as an arrogant expression of assumptive untouchability. If so, how much had he been assured full exoneration by pleading guilty, and whose promise was it? James King wasn't very sharp overall, being prone to bragging and toughing it up under pressure; if anything, he was an easily-conned bully. In the end and in few words, Eisenberg summed it up the best:

"Well, Henri, by the look of it someone believes they can outsmart the fox. Thank you for the heads-up."

— o —

If John Lehman hadn't assured me that Xing Liu's words were as good as gold, I certainly wouldn't have bought his story past that of a skillful spin master. But considering there was the ongoing sentiment among us that something was bound to be amiss somewhere, there was no reason to be shy about moving in the direction of yet another unexpected turn. After all, it had been that way all along, a ragged trail of contradictions consistent with every element striving to write its own story. So, if Wu wasn't dead, whose body, then, was flown to North West Regional hospital?

Of course, it sufficed to bring O'Reilly back in the equation to imagine a corpse scheduled for cremation to have been substituted. I called Liz, first apologizing for my delayed departure, but most importantly, to ask her to look at Savage River's logs for a possible inbound flight from North West regional on the day of the accident.

To no-one's surprise, flight records for that day failed to materialize, but Liz made quick work of locating the owner of the helicopter that flew the body out of the mine, Alan Grieves, of Ground Sky Ground Ltd, who confirmed the chopper had taken off from North West Regional in the late afternoon of that fateful day.

— o —

Since Gerald Harrison had taken the reigns by the time the call was made from the tailings dam and with Samuel O' Reilly at the receiving end ready with a corpse matching Abraham's stature, the game was on. Following that logic, James King and his accomplices placed the deceased at the top of the slide, while Wu followed Abe's fate. As much as the scenario lacked in veracity, it fell into place by firming up character placement within the general settings. O'Reilly's role was better defined, Harrison's breadth of activity more substantial, and King's actions more fitting in their pathology. The larger choreography gained in substance as well, with the engineers in charge of extracting the severely damaged body hurrying its removal from the premises—the whole of it playing like clockwork. After the dust settled, all that remained was the enigmatic disappearance of Abraham Garner and Yang Wu.

Either the men had been abducted, leaving the door wide open for the participation of unknown parties, or they were complicit in the making of a farce. Whichever the case, as seen from that mental viewpoint, the prospects for a timely resolution were slim. Since no-one recently volunteered to walk into the limelight of the case, I concluded there were no concealed agents of mischief and no kidnapping. At once, all pivoted on my ability to process the entirety of our work into its coherent conclusion. I solely focused on Vertex's purpose to bring me into its affairs and trusting my abilities to achieve closure. In simple fashion, I was a free pawn on a game board of probabilities, with each of my thoughts, choices, and moves an agent of restriction or expansion. There no longer was the option of lingering—friend or foe, it was in bridging the two halves of the courtroom that the arbitration would reach its point of power.

— o —

Jack Lewis and Lelo Eisenberg kept to their side of the case, neither of them making use of their newly acquired knowledge. James King pleaded guilty and was sentenced to the minimum of thirty years in prison for double murder. If he flinched at all, Jack couldn't tell. The convict took it like one receiving a medal after battle, his mind still on the field. Whether his lawyer had assured

228

him or not that the case would eventually be reversed amounted to mere inconsequentiality. He had been hardened by a life bereft of hope and where nothing good ever came out of expectations—prison and death were the only foreseeable destinations for his kind.

— o —

Liz and I had nicely settled in her father's house, but it had been difficult to convince her that the kidnapping scenario had lost its legs and that we were now looking at a coupage of time-related clips belonging to disparate realities. Somehow, in spite of my deep trust in her, I couldn't totally ignore my sense of unease around the disconnect between father and daughter. Lurking in the shadow was a mounting suspicion she knew more than she was at liberty to share. The thought called for laying the cards on the table. So, in between the first two hearings, and amid the quiet of an intimate evening by the fireplace, I broke the ice.

"Liz, I need to know what you're keeping away from me regarding you and your dad; if you don't mind the timing."

"It was all arranged that the timing would be right when you'd ask. Where do you want to start?"

"Alright, but first, were you aware Wu was alive before Xing Liu pointed me in that direction?"

"No, and for the record, I never hid anything from you in regard to our work on the case. On the other hand, if you want to learn something, ask me about my doubts and suspicions, and you might unearth some relatable truth about how you and I fit in."

"OK then, we spoke on many occasions about the possibility Vertex and your father could have engineered a way to strike a debilitating blow to Branched's *plans to take over the wilderness, but how was it possible you were kept in the dark about it?"*

"Dad and I shared many things, including various scenarios about how to defeat the leases, but ultimately, when it actually came to walking the talk, he reverted to the outdated notion that certain tasks were better handled by him alone. I can't speak from the standpoint of probabilities, where relationships are likely different from those here. I don't know where you and I stand in them at this very moment and how much trust exists between us—nothing I care to focus on, even if I knew how. If you, on the other hand, wish to investigate, ask Jeremiah, I'm sure he has the means to demonstrate the futility of visiting our areas of failure. But as of here, I don't know for certain whether dad had this all planned out or not. I can only guess he's behind it, something that's been on my mind from the get-go. It doesn't mean that I never felt unfairly slighted or hurt by his methods—case in point, my recent fall from grace after going over his memos."

"Alright then, I'll only ask once: is this all about me and my initiation into Vertex?"

"Oh, Henri, I thought this was all clear to you; I guess I was wrong. You are presently Vertex's one hope at righting all of those adjacent wrongs. John had known that about you for the longest time, but it wasn't until our relationship firmed up after your first visit to Hobart that the opportunity presented itself for us to commit to your deeper involvement. Yes, we're going through various versions of us together, but only in this one have all the anchors reached seafloor, if you get the analogy."

"I'm deeply sorry for doubting you; please forgive me for the digression. What you're saying loud and clear is that you've always been suspicious of your father's actions, but you didn't want to play that card?"

"Yes, and neither did John, for if you think hard enough about it, there was nowhere to go. Only in the perceived reality that dad had been either killed or kidnapped could a potent scenario ferment into a case, and our life together reach its present level. So, let me ask you a tricky one—first thought: where and how do you see yourself in any of those variables?"

"Let me guess... representing Harold for the wrongful death of Abraham Garner and tanking it?"

"That was an easy answer, don't you think?"

"Yeah, it rolled right off the tip of my tongue."

"So, you realize it was never John's intention to put Sackman in your shoes; it's just that, here, we exist in a multilayered, best case scenario."

"Then, would you say Harold is in it with your father and Yang Wu?"

"Harold, no, but at this point, I can't see how Yang wouldn't be working with dad."

"Here's a confession: we're failing in so many scenarios because we've no reason to believe your father wasn't set up and sent to his death. Here, on the other hand, and owing to a mix of circumstances, Wu was found the victim. I don't think the Swensons counted on him to replace your father, and I can't fathom how they could presently be aware of a third body. Following this train of thoughts, we arrive at the dilemma of being the only ones moving the dead around. That's of course ridiculous, but we've been known to err before. So now, if your father is truly in charge, he's then responsible for placing the

corpse atop the dam, which puts James King and his crewmen in an odd spot. It also makes O'Reilly an accomplice of your dad. Meanwhile, the Swensons discovered Yang Wu was alive, and how exactly?!"

"I can only guess they were drawn to it—I think it's a trap. They aren't aware of what Vertex presently knows about them. It's clear though that dad was hoping we would figure a few things out before it was too late."

"Courtesy our 'friend' Xing Liu, but he's Branched Resources; *what do you make of that?"*

"I can only speculate that the mining company isn't interested in the leases, but only pretending to be. It sounds absurd, but looking at the larger picture, Branched *isn't the only player in the big game."*

"In other words, you're saying that there won't be a case against them?"

"You've got a way with rhetorical questions, but yes, at this point I'm convinced the company has been aware of something going on across its departments, and with the help of Vertex, is working on extracting the malignance from their staff."

"So, according to you, Branched Resources *sees no future in the exploitation of the wilderness and instead is aiming at preventing anyone from accessing it. It sounds like an enormous compromise, but we have known heroism to have redeeming value. So now, what stops me from thinking the Ranch Acacia meetings involved many of* Branched*'s insiders?"*

"Bingo, you're saving me from preparing you for it; mom and dad's files revealed it all! It was also how, I believe, the Gilberts, Sullivans, and Swensons found ways to infiltrate the company with the intent to undermine global environmental work."

"OK, love, I hope you don't think I have no trust in you, but you must admit I had reasons to express my concerns, no?"

"Yes and no, I'm sure you know more than you're willing to credit yourself with. Never doubt your intuitions, and that stands for me as well! There's still much to uncover, but that'll have to happen as we go; for now, we can't turn back—it's time to join dad's camp and play our part like he intends us to do!"

"Well, Liz, nice to see you've pulled out of your funk with renewed vitality—how inspiring!"

"Thanks, dear man, any lingering suspicions?"

"Nope, I'm forever grateful for what I gained out of this conversation. I'm now ready to wrap up the Harrison case, are you?"

"You bet I am!"

——— o ———

25 – MALIGNANCE

Liz here.

Even though the case against Harrison was geared at casting the net of culpability over *Branched Resources*, it was obvious, based on new evidence, that the company would be fully exonerated from wrongdoing, while the blame would instead be spread among the corrupt at multiple private, state, and federal levels.

What Harold and Aleksei had unearthed in Albany was a cell powered by the wealth of those intent on draining the planet of all resources—the anti-Vertex, so to speak. Although, the organization favored the cover of anonymity, its code name was *Man over Matter*, a reference to humanity's rule over nature—with *Man* as in *male Caucasian*, naturally. Of course, one assumed that the display of women of twisted allegiances such as Harriet Donovan was on par with portraying the notion of equality between sexes, false as it may have been; but overall, the pathology of sexism and racism, through extreme right-wing rhetorics, suffused all over their image. There was enough evil there to add an entire era of darkness to known history, and likely, in the form of a grand finale.

—o—

Much thinking, meetings of minds, speculations, and last minute amendments set the tone to the days preceding the first hearing. Henri and I had our hands full trying to make sense of who knew what in regard to the accident at the mine, and we came up with the unbelievable notion that James King, his crew, and Samuel O'Reilly could, instead, all have been agents working for my father and posing as abettors to Harrison's grand plan. The way I saw it, no other plausible path to the third body theory came to light. The net was cast over *Man over Matter* from the start, with dad having, in some form or another, advertised his visit at the mine. So, while he was expected at the top of the dam wall ahead of its collapse, Harrison never suspected my father had been the de facto coordinator of his own demise all along. In that line, and contrarily to what Harold was led to believe, Wu was to meet dad above the dam instead of behind the equipment building, with the engineer's subsequent disappearance becoming an item of perplexity for Harrison and Harriet Donovan; although, nothing compared to the later pronouncement that the engineer was the dead man instead of dad. The checks sent to Ehuang Wu for the one year period preceding that discovery were testament to the uncertainty of that transitional period—Yang Wu wasn't supposed to have vanished. And so, in the light of the mystery, and with their plans teetering on the edge of uncertainty, *Man over Matter*'s only recourse was to silence those in possession of too much information. Problem was, James King wasn't working for them, and of course neither was Xing Liu, whom they trusted to be an easily manipulated insider, as long as he believed he was in charge—hence the, *ahem*, endearing term, *"Chinese cunt,"* overheard by Aleksei at the Earl of Spencer.

Then how were the Swensons going to use their supposed knowledge of Wu's alive-and-well status to turn the case around? Well, in a perfect world, proving that the engineer wasn't killed in the accident was sufficient to lift

Harrison, an environmental consultant, above all suspicions of masterminding ill-intent against the protection of the Tasmanian wilderness, turning all eyes instead to *Branched Resources* for negligence in keeping their dam walls secured—a wicked diversion as the mother of all irony!

But it wasn't a perfect world. Any blame thrown at the mining company was at the risk of backfiring. If the elements weren't good enough for us to mount a case against *Branched Resources*, they were just as insufficient for *Man over Matter*; notwithstanding that said negligence had been skillfully exploited by the rogue cell itself to the end of murdering my father. By the look of it, the Swensons were about to close a can of worms by opening a new one. Proving Wu was alive was one thing, but could they also attest to my father's well-being? The office certainly doubted it. In the best case scenario they could free Harrison from the grip of justice, hoping nothing would trip them on the way out. It wasn't difficult to see the work of a master puppeteer aiming at inculpating the Swensons in one of the most back-handed ways known to my profession: to turn the defense into their own prosecutor and collapse the argument. At our end, we ran the risk of having the judge throw the case out of court— something we couldn't afford.

— o —

Naturally, we weren't going to allow Justin and Emma Swenson to come forward with their evidence of Wu's well-being—whatever that was! The plan was to beat them to it with the introduction of our last minute witness, or rather, suspect, Harriett Donovan, the one

236

individual most likely to shamelessly lie in the courtroom, a trait Jack Lewis had all the intentions to ruthlessly exploit. In spite of Eisenberg's promise to allow James King and Stan Markalay to testify against Harrison, we needed something definitely more sensational.

— o —

The mention of the *back corridors of power* as used by Lehman and my father wasn't just a myth; men and women of influence were known to tread their marble floors and leave fingerprints on the gilded handles of their oaken doors. It was of course a potent metaphor for the ways to bypass the morass of inefficiency, or another form of saying one had friends in high places. In the case of Vertex, those corridors were of its own making, areas where thinkers of all provenances and professions figuratively conglomerated to assist each other when the call was made. As it turned out, Judge Raphael Montgomery, the man behind the bench in the Harrison case, was one of them, and for that reason had long suspected Wu and my father would eventually resurface. I agree it was corrupt for the act of favoring one side of the courtroom over the other, but that wasn't entirely true as long as the trial was conducted in a fair manner, which Montgomery insisted it would be. But I must bow to the fact the case had become its own gestalt, to which the courtroom was a merely a prop. To further the analogy, the entire world was the stage on which the fixity of the rule of law was allowed to soften its steely stance to serve sanity and the perpetuation of physical existence.

In a situation where position and perspective mattered most, it was always best to acknowledge the odds against which you stood. In the case of Vertex, all balanced on bypassing the game while maintaining a sense of normalcy to the overall picture.

— o —

I can't tell you enough how much of a relief it was to have Henri by my side again. Honestly, I had been far from expecting circumstances to ever separate us once he got to Tasmania. It made me value the time spent together in Swansea, Launceston, and Lake Pedder all the more. It didn't matter how big or small the distance, the emotional vacuum spoke loudly of how much of my heart had been kept in that man's own. Whereas I relished the solitude of the self following my breakup with James, I now couldn't fathom moving back to that place of private beatitude with Henri in my life. My freedom was no longer at stake, and neither was the prospect of a no-man cluttering my inner space an option. To me, freedom was an investment in trust, and trust was aplenty in my relationship with Henri. All I can say is that it was nice to be back together on the job as a physical team.

Meanwhile, Paul Desmond was still staying at my house—Russians on watch across the street et al. But as time went on, it became apparent that the doc was in no real danger, especially with most of the bad guys in Albany. Nonetheless, as an important witness, we couldn't slack on his protection. Intuitively though, I wasn't totally sure I had the complete story about his relationship with Harrison; and for that, I regretted O'Reilly was dead, incinerated with the information about their time together as medical students. Based on the latest information, and provided it wasn't just another false lead, Desmond's role teetered between the good and the bad. Something smelled rank in his recollection of Harrison's arrival at the mine, as in an item of reversed complicity. For now, he looked genuinely defeated, but was he? Once again, my intuitions advised to proceed with caution.

— o —

All data collected from interviews with each member of the *Ambassadors of the Wild* had been sifted and chronologically catalogued. The interesting thing was that the group's history only went back to the time of my dad's disappearance, as in emerging for the sole purpose of being instrumental to the case, which put James King at a totally new level, while making the kids at the shed much better actors than imagined. There was a surrealistic quality emanating from the whole thing, a looseness of execution leaning on the spontaneity of an improvised avant-garde production that barely veiled the elements of precise choreography within it. In sum, it was unlikely that King's main purpose at the mine was simply reducible to sabotaging equipment and being a tool for *Man over Matter*; undoubtedly, his role eclipsed all we had assumed about him, and for that, we could only count our blessings for not having totally messed things up from the onset. Looking back at the case's chronology, I guess it was meant to be that way—extracting by addition, succeeding through error.

I had to give credit to King for having played his role to its useful end, without ever raising suspicion about his true identity while keeping a straight face as a con man. Although it was evident Harrison and the Swensons eventually gave up on him as soon as the news of Wu's death registered as not just a prank by our team and the media. But even then, his arrest fit like a piece of the puzzle by providing him with the protection he needed. No, there wasn't an item that wasn't meant to belong, aside from O'Reilly's death.

— o —

The malignance that had penetrated the Ranch Acacia winter meetings was carried over from the summer gatherings. The Swensons and Gilberts, among others still to be uncovered, had come to hear of those events through the relentlessness of their convictions and work—though it was still unclear what those convictions amounted to. Vertex database classified the group as the resurfacing of a sect dating from Newtonian days, whose dominant article of faith lay in the marriage of science and religion, the pedestal on which man, having antecedently been made in the image of God—and now in possession of the tools of creation—was free to rule and exploit his domain as he wished—a gift from father to son. Predictably, women weren't factored in.

I very much doubted that my father and John Lehman weren't cognizant of the presence of nuncios at those guarded winter meetings, which I hoped were traps for reasons only they and their old friends saw fit to justify. Perhaps it was premature on my part to flirt with conclusions; regardless, elements wanted to coalesce into a clear picture and this one was as clear as they came. I was integral to it, a shadow in the background of a moving set, shaped frame by frame, flicker by flicker by the hand of time. I was in that picture then, as it was in me now, a reversal dictated by the forces of memory. My mind whirled in a cycle of winters and summers, those of the lower half of the world, where Christmas parades marched under the heat of sun-drenched afternoons. Forget the files, the photos, the streaked eight millimetre reels; I was in it amid the secrets, the infidelities, the plots, the stories by the evening fires, the laughter and sometimes the tears. I ran, danced, dashed out of hidden corners into the open of attention, soaking every moment as if it were my last, never realizing that one day it would be all gone into the recesses of the mind, neglected—forgotten.

How bold of my father to bank on my recollection of the past, how reckless! But yet, I savored the trust invested in me, and undoubtedly, in Henri as well, my loving partner, without whom I would never have found the strength and courage to forge ahead with that oddity of a case. For the first time since the accident at the mine, I felt the loss. Dad had been gone for far too long; I now very much yearned for his return.

— o —

Such recollection demanded that I travel paths never trodden, into the subliminal elements of memory; not what I saw and touched, but what was recorded in the deeper layers of awareness—to remember not just the forgotten, but also the omnipresence within it—what was witnessed that didn't conjure the senses into forming recognizable markers. For that, I needed to leave my present body and assume those of the past as an invisible observer of my own experience. In other words, I had to make time disappear and peek into each room, each event, moment; become the proverbial fly on the wall of my own psyche: the me within the me, yet free of the constraints of direct accountability.

Henri knew about my inner work; he assisted me while contributing with his own soul-searching. He had his plate full with sorting out the meaning of probable events, and how they could all work together to add to the pot—not exactly your standard spelunking of the self!

My main objective was Jeremiah Jones and how he existed in the background of the Acacia days. I couldn't recall seeing him there, yet it didn't mean he never attended, especially the winter meetings for which I had little interest, even though my parents insisted that I be by their side.

It was on one of my many "spectral" outings that the most peculiar thing happened: I was a young self, lying flat on my belly, working the pieces of a puzzle, while, in the room around me, my father and a group of men and women where conducting what appeared to be adult matters—when suddenly—from the corner of my eye, I caught a shape quickly shifting against the dark of the wainscot. The child failed to register the apparition, but I was far from wishing to remain the passive observer. I energetically pulled out to follow in the steps of the interloper, who, as it turned out, was no other than the appropriately-nicknamed, *Shadow Man*. We immediately found ourselves outside the house, impervious to the icy rain drumming against the veranda roof.

"Here we meet again, Elizabeth, this time under the most curious of circumstances. I must confess that you startled me. But, at last, you have, in a giant step, crossed the threshold of possibilities into the most significant and rewarding phase of your work."

"I'm surprised you didn't expect me."

"Let it be said that I have been waiting for this encounter to happen on so many failed occasions that I became distracted by your younger self's puzzle, at the risk of revealing my presence to her. Luckily, her focus was amid the pieces."

"You make it sound like she wasn't meant to see you?"

"She wouldn't have understood; notwithstanding that seeing me could have altered your recollection of events and jeopardized this very encounter."

"I presume you're speaking from the standpoint of my physical reality?"

"As well as its probabilities."

"So, what's in it for us, Jeremiah?"

"For one, there are no other 'times' factored in for us to meet—without the information provided by your presence, I would be left with no indication that the case against Man over Matter *was happening."*

"What?! But you met with Henri and me, while leading us on the trail to Swansea and Wynyard!"

"But no further than the time I swung by your office. Without you here, there is nowhere for me to go and help you with advancing the case; the Swensons, until now, have had a distinct advantage—something you, Henri, and Jack will discover soon enough."

"Considering that what you're saying isn't any more perplexing than my very presence here, I have no choice but to trust your words. But how in the world could the Swensons have had advantage, considering the evidence we hold against Harrison? Proving Yang Wu is alive and well isn't going to do it."

"Once again, it is for you to find out."

"Same place as you, but you already knew that."
"What?"
"If not, it'll come back to you."

Same exit indeed. I was back in body looking at the coffered ceiling, imagining a younger self eyeing me from above—what a trip!

If I was to make sense of that encounter, I had to better regroup my thoughts into a coherent heap. At least, that was the reasoning. I called Henri, who was presently in his office on Macquarie Street, helping Jack prepare for his court appearance. Only two days left before the big date and so little time to figure out what advantage the Swensons had over us! I asked my darling man to meet me for lunch at the wharf; I could no longer bear the sight and smell of a law office—at least not till we were over the hump.

— o —

A laughing Henri: *"Jeremiah Jones blending with the walls of the old office—nothing odd there!"*

"Nothing odd either about me meeting my younger self, I suppose?"

"Liz, you are your younger self on so many levels—I can barely contain the pleasure it gives me."

"If you keep on saying the right thing, Sir, I may melt back into the past and take you with me."

"I don't believe I could resist the opportunity to follow you there, even if you didn't ask."

"Is that so, dear man?"

"Growing up with you would have been a blast; too much of an age difference though."

"Little do you know that I always had a taste for older boys; but what are the odds of you having been there and the two of us not remembering?"

"Pretty low, since to my knowledge, I had never been to Tasmania until we met."

"Not even for a short visit?"

"Well, if it ever happened, I have no recollection of it. It's possible my parents took me here on their many travels, but I would have to have been pretty young to not remember."

"Certain memories prefer seclusion until they are gently required to step into the light."

"At any rate, you wouldn't have been born yet—we can put this one to rest."

"Tell me, Henri, are we just wasting our time talking about nonsense, or are we trying to breach the gap between this present reality and a time at which one of its roots took hold? In my opinion, putting it to rest may not be the most suitable of decisions. I'm not suggesting that you invent a memory; rather, what I'm alluding to is that some of the deeper layers of awareness are often concealed within the experience of childhood. Obviously, I'm not asking us to be children again, but to revisit that quality. I understand it's a stretch, but can we not, for a second, imagine the two of us being there by simply breaking down some of our preconceptions around what's possible and what's not—or is that too crazy?"

"You were there, Liz; I wasn't. That's why it's more difficult to imagine me being there, since my sole memory of those times is through what you and Abraham shared with me. But I'll do my best."

"Good, if you can imagine probable events, this is a lot simpler since you already believe it never happened; just be creative!"

Asking Henri to be creative must have been the understated request of the day—he was right there with me on a day my parents and Jonathon Weisman were taking a walk along the creek. We weren't children but our very selves, blending with the scenery like *Shadow Man* in my father's office during the previous encounter. The quality was that of dreams—atmospheric, timeless. Henri spoke in thoughts rather than words, but it made perfect sense, for we strived to not be intruders into a past that couldn't be disturbed, even in the flutter of a single leaf. Short of a better word, we were spirits whose bodies had no place in the landscape of revisits, or, in Henri's case, of a first-time, *special* visit.

As we zoomed in closer to the trio, the dynamics of the conversation gained in clarity. Henri looked at me, conveying his warning to keep at a distance, as to not alert anyone's inner senses—no distraction, even of the utmost minuteness, allowed.

Abraham Garner: *"Xing knows of the plan, but he cautions that it might require time and patience before implementation."*

Jonathon Weisman: *"I'll be ready when you are. In the meantime, I'll keep an eye on our suspects. I noticed Karl isn't letting go of his boy, Alec. Don't you think he should be playing with the other children?"*

Helen Garner: *"I'm sure Liz could loosen up that child, but I've heard Karl is holding to Alec as a means to compensate for his failing marriage."*

Jonathon: *"You mean to that strange woman, Harriet Donovan, her real name if I recall?"*

Helen: *"Yes, they act like they don't know each other, but if you care for my opinion; it's nothing but a put-on."*

Jonathon: *"If so, is she opening herself to sympathies, aiming to attract a lonely heart?"*

Abraham: *"Please, make a note of it as part of your watch; it might have some relevance."*

Change of scenery—it was evening, food and drinks awaited the hungry on a long serving table a short distance away from the crackling campfire. Harriet Sullivan and a man still to be identified partook in an animated conversation sprinkled with giggles and short bursts of laughter. If there was any truth to Jonathon's playful remark, now was the time for revelations. It only took one gesture, a man's arm around a woman's shoulder—an act bereft of resistance—to seal the deal. Harriet had lured the moth to the glow of her charms, an individual whom I recognized as one of the doctors and surgeons that attended yearly.

It came as no surprise that Jeremiah Jones would join in at that precise moment.

"It may be of significance to you both that his son, Paul, is presently under the care of Karl Gilbert—it seems the two boys are hitting it off—his name is Alan Desmond, father of the man enjoying the convenience of your Hobart residence, Liz."

Me: *"What happened to his wife?"*

Jeremiah: *"She died in a private plane crash while on business. Alan never remarried."*

Henri: *"Let me guess, on a flight to or from Albany?"*

"Perth, but close enough. Her husband's involvement with Man over Matter *is only starting as we speak. Alan and Harriet interacted for the first time a couple of days ago."*

Me: *"And Karl is of course OK with the flirting, if not downright complicit in drawing Alan to the web, am I correct?"*

"It's as good a recruiting method as it gets for this particular environment. But I'm done here; I'm sure you can finish this on your own. Until then!"

Nothing unpredictable there, *Shadow Man* was gone in a flash.

— o —

In an instant, we were back within our personal present, relieved that the experiment yielded a sense of completion rather than of bewilderment—Vertex training worked in curious ways.

"Alright Liz, we have a change of plans, but what do we do about Desmond?"

"Best is to not ring the alarm yet; there isn't a doubt he has been in touch with the Swensons, and, as one of our witnesses, it's likely those attorneys count on him to jeopardize us in court."

"I guess Jack won't be able to call him to the bench anymore."

"Unless Jack wants him there in order to beat him at his own game."

"Of course, that requires an entirely new approach, but nothing outside Jack's bag of tricks. I trust he's used to last minute reversals."

— o —

After a long meeting with Jack Lewis, Henri and I chose to revisit Ranch Acacia to pick up the trail following that pivotal union between Harriet Donovan and Alan Desmond. We seamlessly arrived at one of the winter get-togethers in my father's office, one with Alan and a young Paul flanked by the usual suspects. The topic was on land preservation and the means by which to work the legal system into dismantling state and federal leasing regulations. Xing Liu proposed that infiltration was to be considered, to which a consensus followed.

It was at that precise moment that our thoughts converged onto the realization that the *Branched Resources* insider was setting up his game board and surgically positioning his pawns. He had lured the Swensons, Gilbert/Donovans, and Desmonds into his room of mirrors, being now recognized as the man to defeat my father's grand vision. The level of deception was as cruel as it was brilliant, and it was obvious from our unusual perspective that *Man over Matter* had been all along the target of a game of wits in which the prey was kept believing it was the hunter.

—— o ——

PART SEVEN

26 – GHOSTS OF RANCH ACACIA

Henri here.

Liz and I returned to the ghosts of Ranch Acacia nearly a dozen times in the days preceding the trial, each trip adding another peg to Jack Lewis's board. The man seemed vitalized by the relentless shuffling of the case elements, and instead of showing the stigmas of a discombobulated mind, he laughed at what would have added to a mammoth clusterfuck to any other clear-thinking lawyer. His stance was a lesson to me as the one scheduled to switch places. Obviously, I was far from ready to tackle the task, notwithstanding that Liz needed me by her side to search for clues into her past.

For me to travel to those places and vividly be present was beyond logic, but it felt natural in the sheer sense that I was following Liz on an energy path born of her memory of those times, our closeness providing the backstage pass, so to speak.

As we witnessed a young Elizabeth age and *un-age* across random settings, we were able to focus on the lives of two boys, Alec Gilbert and Paul Desmond. Unlike other children impervious to adult reality, these young minds were prematurely subjected to the rectitude of their parent's missionary work, with the understanding they would one day be instrumental to the execution of *Man over Matter*'s master plan. Worth pointing again was that said plan was on a close parallel with the one Abraham, Jonathon, Xing, Jack Lewis's father, Robert, and others were laying out to draw the group in.

Even though the winter meetings ended in the wake of Helen's passing, the Christmastime congresses resumed only after a one year hiatus. It was clear that the missing presence and voice of Liz's mother had the effect of emboldening Harriet Donovan to move into the role of the Alpha female, a detail that too clearly suggested Abraham and the woman had enjoyed a moment or two of physical intimacy. In a flash, we were transported to a night scene in which the two entered the guest cabin beyond the open area of the campgrounds and fire pits.

Liz's words joined my thoughts.

"Oh, I remember those nights, but I didn't know who she was—now I get it!"

Flash to another quick change of scene with our boys Alec and Paul sitting side by side, occasionally glancing at each other with a complicit smile and a glitter of elation in their eyes. While children their age would have likely felt out of place in such settings, they, without a doubt, understood their position as one of special status; ergo, as belonging to an elite group whose work and responsibilities soared amid the atmospheric heights bequeathed by *God* to the chosen few. Sadly, they weren't aware of the long con laid before them by Abraham Garner, Xing Liu, and to an increasing degree of suspicion, John Lehman, who, if he wasn't always present, was mentioned ever so subtly as "our friend." What the boys knew, on the other hand, was that they had infiltrated the work of environmentalists for the purpose of, one day, striking a deadly blow to their progress. In their minds, I very much doubted purpose was anything more than getting a thrill at watching the world burn, especially when said minds lived under the ills of parental manipulation, expectation, and deceit.

When it came down to it, *Man over Matter* was akin to a sect modeled after Nazi ideology, where religion was both inherent to its shadow and deviled in the open of its principles. For the sake of comparison, it possessed in tunnel vision what Vertex owned in latitude.

— o —

Jeremiah Jones joined us on one last meeting at the ranch. Harriet Donovan sat in between Abraham and Alec Gilbert; next to him were Paul and his father, Alan Desmond; then, going around, sat Karl Gilbert, the Swensons—who for the first time had brought in their son Justin—with John Lehman, Jonathon Weisman, Xing Liu, and Harold Freeman tying the circle. Not once did Karl make eye contact with his wife, which only deepened their connection at the strategic end. It's worth pointing that Emma Swenson, née Gilbert, never attended any of those meetings. Young Liz was also absent.

Harriet Donovan: *"Now that we all agree on the need for infiltration; how do you propose we begin penetrating* Branched Resources, *Xing?"*

Xing Liu: *"With your background, you could apply for a position in accounting, say; and I'd make sure you get the job. That is, if you're into being on the inside. You essentially would be a spy with access to restricted information—just an example."*

Harriet: *"Actually, that sounds like the perfect first step in preparing the terrain for others to come in, such as our boys here."*

Abraham: *"It doesn't have to be you, dear, but you'd make a good scout, since the job requires unshakable integrity."*

Harriet: *"Xing, you can sign me up for it as long as I don't have to go through the shenanigans of standard applications."*

Xing: *"I can take care of the decorum; all will look legitimate."*

John Lehman: *"With Harriet in, we'll be in place to map the entire organization from the inside out and locate our strikable zones."*

— o —

It would take years until the boys made it to the staff of *Branched Resources*, with Paul as the in-house doctor, and later, Alec, under the pseudonym of Gerald Harrison, as environmental consultant. But Harriet Donovan was the first to infiltrate the mining company, not as a proponent of wilderness protection, but as a counter-agent at the service of destroying it, a role she was never aware had been specifically engineered for her. She was too close to being the main con artist to be cognizant of the true puppeteer, Abraham Elliott Garner, the man whose wit and charm she had fallen prey to while acting the role of the deceitful seducer in her husband's eyes. Karl Gilbert eventually caught up with the humiliating truth. According to Vertex files, the two parted amid unspeakable resentments and animosities, the whole of it culminating in Karl's death by poisoning. It was ruled suicide, but Liz very much doubted it had been the case.

As the love affair between Abraham and Harriet served the dual purpose of snaring the two into opposite schemes, it also had the power to affect allegiances and weaken the original purpose of that very alliance, at least for Harriet, who had imperceptibly softened her stance vis-à-vis her role in *Man over Matter*. But Abraham needed her to remain the force behind the group's vision, and after Karl's death, while they took one of their many walks along the creek, he announced that the relationship was over.

She appeared to not have heard, for she kept with the pace before proposing they turn back because of the cold. It was their last walk together, and before long, she was employed by *Branched Resources* as head of accounting. From that point on, her relationship with Abraham remained strictly focused on business, albeit with a pronounced emphasis on making sure he and John Lehman would be utterly defeated in the end. All was in its proper place as Vertex saw it.

—— o ——

27 – HARRIET DONOVAN

Liz here.

As Henri and I neared the completion of our latest outing into a past forever dwelling among the settings of Ranch Acacia, Jeremiah Jones walked in unannounced with the wish to share the evolution of the *greater case* from a moment he characterized as pivotal.

"Harriet Donovan did her job well, unearthing, over the next decade, a wealth of internal information for Vertex to sift through and organize into mappable data; although, as anticipated, the material was primordially aimed at taking the group on a false trail, but that was precisely the point. I must stress that Man over Matter *never knew of the existence of Vertex as a powerful global entity, instead downplaying its importance on the limits of its satellite law office in the middle of nowhere. For all intents and purposes, Abraham, John, Harold, Jack's father, Robert Lewis, and many others were deemed arrogant fools, easily manipulated and just as easily discarded when the time would come; and by discarded, I imply that the end would justify the means. When, later, it was intentionally divulged by Yang Wu that Abraham and Harold would be visiting the mine to pick up confidential files, which by now I trust you've gathered never existed, Harriet arranged for your father to be assassinated. Of course, it wasn't entirely her choice, since she acted a role specifically tailored to her character, but only on the premise of a very fine line, for we must assume that if she*

didn't show her hurt from her breakup with Abraham, it made her all the more dangerous and determinate. After all, if it was easy to get rid of Karl, Abraham's demise would be child play.

Xing Liu was always the in-between, which deserved him the title of The Traitor, amid those less flattering, as spewed from the mouths of the white supremacists making for the majority of Man over Matter—but never in his face, due to the man's unshakable psychological command.

But before you ask, it is time to explain who Harriet Donovan really is, which I'm confident will lead to understanding the nature of my presence, as well as uncovering Xing Liu's true identity and mission. Although for that, you must follow me to a place best suited for such disclosure."

The place in question was my father's home office back in our regular time. In fact, it was where Henri and I had conducted the experiment from; rendering the notion of following *Shadow Man* there contradictory, at least until we observed the two of us stepping into the room, which must have been somewhat before we sat on the couch to enter the meditative state. In other words, we were still in that state, looking in onto a close past point. Rather than falling to perplexity, the three of us looked at each other with airs of distinct amusement, if only for Jeremiah's idea of a joke being laced with comic ridicule.

Oddly, rather than going for the experiment, the me of the scene poured wine into two glasses and handed one to Henri with the words, "I guess we'll never know!" It was a toast to an end, to the death of a beached vision—the syntactical components of a resigned failure.

Henri, too, sensed doom in those words, as our short-lived amusement was quickly replaced by dread, if, of course, amusement and dread had been part of the spectrum of emotions felt by observers, well-knowing that observers could only contemplate emotions as something felt by the observed. But call it splitting hair, for we knew too well what we were looking at—the Henri and Liz in the scene never revisited the past. Instead, they found themselves a day away from the first court date without a suitable foundation to support months of investigational work. Without the face of a mastermind, Harriet Donovan was nothing more than a suspect loosely incriminated through a series of procedural mishaps by Garner, Lewis & Desgardes and the Albany authorities. In fact, she had outfoxed Abraham, John, and the rest of Vertex by simply staying the course in the face of the changes thrown her way. All she focused on till the end was revenge for the deep insult inflicted onto her person by her breakup with Abraham—the affairs of *Man over Matter* came a distant second.

Henri read me, as Jeremiah read us both. We had entered a probability a mere degree removed from the meditative state that brought us to witness one of our failures. Jones quickly broke the spell, indicating it was time to resume with the rest of the story.

"Some of us don't belong to your present. That applies to me, to some extent Xing Liu, and definitely Harriet Donovan. In fact, and unbeknownst to him, Gerald Harrison isn't Harriet's son. Both he and his father, Karl, were nothing but mere items of convenience in a complex agenda, one she tried to coerce Abraham into as well, but from a different angle and for disparate

reasons. Harriet Donovan's sustained presence in your time represents a level of sophistication rarely seen from my perspective. Will is nothing but a mischaracterization of her powers—she is driven by forces that exist far beyond the reach of those capable of traveling the corridors of time. But I must first refine the narrative about what that means. We all travel in time through the ubiquity of 'incarnational realities,' albeit with a level of fragmentation useless in the sense of true dimensional traveling. It takes particular advances in consciousness to become aware of the various processes behind the makeup of the physical world, but for those with access to skills earned through relentless journeys into their personal unknowns, many doors have opened to expose the principles of time, space, and probabilities, something you are both aware of since you are here. The same skills apply to Xing, but I, unlike he and Harriet, cannot exist in the physical of your rightful present. My various interactions with you over the last few months have only been made possible by taking advantage of small windows offered by some of the convolutions in your work and the confusion they harbored—your minds became amenable-enough to accept my presence. Do I need to explain why such convolutions were necessary to arriving at where we are and why I was instrumental in choosing their placements? I'm sure you get the picture.

Metaphorically speaking, Abraham and Harriet are made of the same stone, each a half separated for the benefit of the common freewill, each containing an aspect of the other. While the Harriet identity doesn't originate from your world—her form strictly being an image reflecting the power of her skills—it doesn't mean that, at some point, she couldn't be not only physical, but also very much unlike what she symbolizes as a part of Man over Matter. *The aspect of Abraham present in her half of the stone was physically manifested in Helen's existence.*

Do you have any questions before I continue?"

Me: *"Am I supposed to remain unaffected by your definition of my mother?"*

Jeremiah: *"I am expecting some kind of response upon your return from this visit, if that is indeed what you mean."*

Henri: *"As long as 'metaphorically speaking' holds true, I'm so far comfortable with your depiction of the deeper layers of the case. I trust it will serve us well in due time."*

"It will indeed. Now, was Helen aware of her connection with Harriet? The answer is yes, but from the intuitive standpoint only, and mostly in the form of controlled antipathy. As to Abraham, the revelation came to him upon Helen's passing, well into his sexual relationship with Harriet, which was the main reason why he wanted out of the affair and position the woman in the open of retributions. It's possible that he retrospectively perceived Harriet's presence as having been the cause of Helen's failing health and death. Naturally, our main culprit was well tuned into who Helen was, observant that your mother catered to the part that lived in Abraham's metaphorical half of that stone, in a—needless to say— complex arrangement. In other words, it was a union of opposites that ran counter to the extramarital affair. In a curious twist of priorities, the fate of the planet momentarily balanced on the will of two entities seeking avengement for perceived wrongs.

But Harriet didn't kill Helen—the sanctity of the self doesn't permit for that kind of psychic violation. Seeing herself in another body wed to the object of her desire wasn't necessarily cause for disempowerment; if anything, it was the manifestation of Abraham's inner yearning for unification. Helen's failing health was the item of permissibility—nothing else—and the reason for Harriet to court Abraham had nothing to do with Man over Matter.

All of this doesn't mean the issue of world sustainability is a sideshow to personal vendetta, but ignoring the history behind Harriet and Abraham will unlikely fail at getting to the bottom of the case, and that is why it all plays on multiple probabilities, whose concept was introduced to you through a mixture of intuition and direct experience.

As I said, Harriet is not of this world in the pure sense, although she obviously exists in it. Unlike your father, Liz, she wasn't born in your chronological time— Helen was. Abraham's equivalent to what Harriet is was an Oxford University professor at the time of the disputes in the early twelve hundreds. By equivalent, I mean at the evolutionary level, for the two didn't interact in that time. To further muddy the waters, the professor, Edward Sexton, has zero knowledge of Abraham in spite of the fact Vertex is his brainchild—I'm choosing the present tense purposely here. Any questions?

The information didn't appear any stranger than the way the case had evolved from the onset. Henri and I were now aware of the number of probabilities involved in arriving at that conjuncture. It made a lot of sense at the level of the observer standing across the fine line of intimacy. Yes, we were outside, yet the closeness and focus were unparalleled. The entire picture was coalescing as awareness gained in stature, as memories originating from restricted areas converged amid the outer layers of my father's office, where a couple belonging to another reality toasted to the imminent failure of the case. All was unfolding as a stage act whose script could be altered on a whim at any moment. And yet, there was a sense of inexorable firmness to these intertwined sequences, bonded as much in their disparity as they were in their resemblance. Henri and I existed in all versions, but only in that one were we looking from the outside in—something I find somewhat difficult to translate.

Henri: *"It looks like Xing Liu is the wild card."*
Jeremiah: *"You could say that, but he likens himself to being the creator of balance."*
Me: *"The man whose allegiance is to the whole?"*
Jeremiah: *"Exactly."*
Henri: *"Like yourself?"*
Jeremiah: *"My wish for balance extends beyond the mechanics of the case, but without Xing on the inside, my work would be far more complicated. It's bad enough that, unlike Harriet, I cannot exist in your present other than as an image under specific mental conditions."*
Me: *"I'm ready to move on, if you don't mind."*

Before *Shadow Man* got to continue, we found ourselves in yet another room, looking in on a group loosely seated around a low table. Harriet Donovan handed a tarot card to the man next to her, seemingly amused by something he had just whispered in her ear. The year was eighteen ninety-nine, more precisely the twenty-third of September, the day of the equinox in London, England. The man was Harriet's lover, a law professor by the name of August Alexander. The apartment stood above the wet cobblestone work of Great Cumberland Place, overlooking Marble Arch.

Harriet: *"August is hoping for visitors today; anyone else intuiting on its possibility?"*

A middle-aged woman: *"By Jove, please, not the Farnsworths again, so coarse and unimaginative!"*

August: *"I am thinking perhaps something novel."*

Harriet: *"I concur, the day calls for the unusual."*

I didn't know for sure, but I had a sense we had been spotted by the hosting couple. In chorus to my thoughts, Jeremiah seconded my suspicion.

"August picked up your scent, Liz, he is an in-between personality related to both Edward Sexton and your father, not by physical lineage, but the three rise from the same consciousness. He's also Vertex."

The information rang of common knowledge; the reawakening followed its steady course. At the core of my being, August Alexander was one of the familiar faces.

It occurred to me that Jeremiah Jones, in showing us around, was also flirting with altering the course of all connected events, especially if our presence was divulged in the midst of what appeared to be a séance in the making. My understanding of events and probabilities was basic, but the notion of any disturbance to the thin veil defining past from future was bound to affect how time positioned history. There wasn't a doubt that, should we be seen, our waking present wouldn't be the same as how we left it.

Jeremiah: *"The changes can only happen upon your return, since they are dependent on you being here, and being here is dependent on you being there. Consciousness doesn't allow for self-erasure—it's a contradiction that transcends the concept of what is possible and not. If you wish to alter the course of these people's lives, here is the perfect place to start honing your skills. But know it will not destroy the existing course, just create a new one from the standpoint of your proper reality."*

Henri and I looked at each other with the common question, "How will changing the past bring closure to the case?" So far we had simply peeked into past events; now the offer—for indeed it was a suggested opportunity—to alter their course brought us to the brink of testing uncharted territory. As lawyers, the first thing that came to mind was the unspoken legality of such an act, legal or illegal in the sense of ethics rather than law, which immediately sounded hypocritical in the context of the profession, for ethics and laws had long become estranged relatives. In the end, it wasn't a matter of good or evil in the biblical sense. If the only way to move the case to a successful conclusion was to announce our presence at a gathering in nineteenth century London, what rule could possibly be broken?

Jeremiah shone a smile, which might as well have been an agreed go-ahead. Within seconds we appeared as spectral figures encircled by ashen faces; well, save for

Harriet and August who had instead gained colors to their cheeks. Silence fell to its lowest decibel as motions froze to stillness. When a voice suddenly cracked the air, it was reality shaking itself loose from a momentary malfunction.

Harriet: *"Well, well, guests from the future, Elizabeth and her husband-to-be Henri, what an unexpected surprise; you actually did it!"*

August: *"Harriet hinted at the possibility a while back, and it has since become the subject of much research at my end concerning personal matters of the highest importance."*

Oddly, Jeremiah was nowhere near, while the rest of the group had remained stilled, revealing that our two hosts were also impervious to the bounds of time.

Harriet: *"It isn't as much you barging on us as it is us coming to you. You see, we don't wish of you to disturb the way things are in the minds of our guests—they will soon forget the whole thing as yet another failed attempt at meeting the unknown. They are far from prepared to face the nature of your presence in their space anyway. Because of the method by which I have chosen to lead what you may call a unique life experience, my memory straddles the many branches of time; hence why I remember you from Ranch Acacia and, of course, from the case you both are presently—in your time that is—mounting against me and* Man over Matter. *I am not at all concerned at the personal level with the outcome of your work—I will never be in a position to lose, whatever the appearance. But I hope that before your return to your bodies, it will be with a deeper comprehension of my involvement as well as how August is about to shape things to come down the line for Abraham and you two. If you have made it thus far, I trust you will be able to make good use of the information."*

Again, the observer in me remained unaffected by the stunning revelation. Harriet Donovan was indeed a very unique consciousness, but so were we to find ourselves in that room; although, she did a better job at maintaining a semblance of physicality, for it was exactly that—a focused appearance. Henri and I immediately awakened to the reality of her arrest back in Albany. It made no difference to her—she could be gone in a blink, leaving the fate of the case hanging over the edge of some unfathomable precipice. Best was to let her tell her story.

"Although I never met Edward Sexton, I was made aware, through connections at Oxford, of his essay on the concept of creating a watchdog society for the purpose of alleviating conflicts and the tendencies for the male ego to find release in the art of savaging land and flesh. It pleased me that such a man was capable of seeing beyond the limitations of his race, and courageous enough to propose that the wise could soothe the beast within the imbecilic aristocracy and masses. At that point, my goal was to contact the consciousness, in all of its facets, behind such a warrior, and for that I had to remain intact, undiluted by the process of incarnation; although, as you can imagine, it didn't prevent others from rising out of the core of my being. Of the facets in question, I have met the many men and women, with whom, over the ages, I was able to create useful

relationships, and in the case of August, a strong working partnership. When it came to Abraham Garner, things got somewhat complicated, since, as you know, he married Helen, a sister-self, so to speak.

I am well aware I have been made the villainess of your case, in part for my association with Man over Matter, *and for my perceived short-lived affair with your dad, Elizabeth. In reality, what you have arrived at until this meeting is one of several possible scenarios, but not the one you need in order to reach closure. For one, I have always known about Vertex—something that eclipsed the scope of your findings, as it has been my duty all along to keep the group alive and growing by introducing Sexton's work to all those receptive to it. August is the force behind globalizing Vertex and making it what it is in your world. But back to Abraham!*

Contrarily to what you know, he and I met at Oxford when he studied there with John Lehman. It was through me that the two became receptive to Vertex, and through my recommendation that they joined. Abraham and I were lovers before Helen showed up on the scene, but I chose to move on when it became obvious she had replaced me in his heart. She was me to a great extent after all, but, unlike me, she had her legitimate place in your reality. It was only natural that upon hearing of her failing health I yearned to reconnect with the man I loved.

Based on this short history, you may naturally assume that I come from the past; but no, I'm from your future, albeit from a probability that failed at regaining its balance, due to your case coming to an impasse. And the reason it came to that was because you fixated on the markers instead of wondering where they led. But now with you here, I trust that finally someone got it right and that my job is nearly done. If you wonder how I plan on changing the reality I come from, wonder no more; it simply cannot be done. I'm not here to change the past but to create a new one from which will spring the one probability missing in my legitimate time, a sane and sustainable world.

Henri: *"What is Jeremiah Jones to you; do you even know him?"*

Harriet: *"Good question, actually, one of most importance. He isn't someone I personally know or wish to know, since he only exists for those who believe he does. That being said, Henri, he is to you what I am to Helen, a part of your psyche that belongs to another dimension of reality. I know he's here, but inside you as opposed to a third visitor in the room."*

Me: *"So, you're saying he's Henri?"*

Harriet: *"They're related, which isn't the same, dear."*

Henri: *"If I'm correct, what he has told us is subject to interpretation, wouldn't you say?"*

Harriet: *"It is your interpretation, but you seem to have stayed fairly close to what was said—you are here after all."*

Me: *"I did see him and speak to him though."*

Harriet: *"Through windows created by mental lapses, I gather. Your closeness with Henri must have made it possible. But then again, you have abilities of your own that are awaiting your approval. And remember, your mother is a sister soul, which makes of you and I relatives, as distant as we may be. But if you're wondering, Helen is your biological mother; I was gone from your father's life at the time."*

Me: *"What's the scoop with* Man over Matter *and your involvement in seeking my father's demise?"*

Harriet: *"All interpretations based on looking for a bad guy as opposed to seeing the larger picture, which as you have now realized involves more than one development."*

Henri: *"And this hopefully being our best-case scenario?"*

Harriet: *"Only if you can convince yourselves upon your return that this meeting wasn't just another dream, since it obviously doesn't belong to memory like your previous forays into the past."*

Henri: *"None of it was ever part of my past."*

Harriet: *"The level of sharing between you two begs to differ."*

Henri: *"What do you know about Xing Liu and his agenda?"*

Harriet: *"His agenda is parallel to mine in that it appears to work out of both camps simultaneously. Mainly, he's an actor right out of the Vertex school of infiltration, a close ally of John Lehman, Jonathon Weisman, and Abraham's. The four of them, upon entering Vertex, were initiated by the first group of teachers trained by my partner August Alexander, here."*

Me: *"What is your relationship with my father in my time?"*

Harriet: *"Let me put it this way, the night before my arrest, he and I were having dinner at my place to both celebrate your achievements and say goodbye to a long partnership—you'll understand soon enough."*

Me: *"How did I not know you two had been together all that time?"*

Harriet: *"You were not meant to, dear, at least not*

until this moment. I was in your life from a safe distance for both our sakes. Whenever Abraham wasn't within your line of sight, he was with me, and I'm glad you never sought to investigate. I guess we were good at it."

Henri: *"Are Gerald Harrison and his lawyers, Emma and Justin Swenson, untouchable too?"*

Harriet: *"Unfortunately for them, someone must end up being the bad guy. Where would the balance be without some of those? Alec was rotten to the core and so was his friend Paul. Their fathers Karl and Alan were the same, bad seeds from the inside out, just to say that schooling and status have nothing to do with decency. Man over Matter was their work; I chose to take the reigns as a means to protect myself from scrutiny, especially after Karl's death for which I was partially blamed. Actually, he was poisoned by Alec, who already knew a thing or two about medicinals."*

Me: *"So your love for my father is genuine?"*

Harriet: *"Like it is for all whose roots tap in that magnificent consciousness that brought us Vertex, starting with Edward Sexton."*

Me: *"You're almost saying that my parents are incarnates of you and Edward's."*

Harriet: *"And I'm almost saying that you're like a daughter to both of us."*

Me: *"But you two never met?"*

Harriet: *"Not in the flesh, dear."*

And with that, we left nineteenth century London to open our eyes on my father's office, back in our legitimate time. The phone was ringing; Henri answered. I looked around, making sure I was back in my skin and not still roaming the lanes of memory. Although everything was in its proper space, I couldn't disengage from the feeling that I wasn't back to the place I had left. I remembered *Shadow Man*'s words, *"The changes can only happen upon your return."* It could only have meant that the eminent nature of the case had shifted to accommodate for the new awareness born of our latest extracorporeal exploration. Harriet's dinner with dad the day before her arrest was most resonant—a celebration and a farewell.

Henri hung up the phone.

"Jack called to let us know that Harriet Donovan has been released. Her lawyer picked her up an hour ago—her case has been closed!"

Well, that was one major change. For one second, I wondered who her attorney was, but I knew better.

———— o ————

28 – DIVERGENT PASTS

Henri here.

I poured wine in two glasses, a picture reminiscent of how we saw ourselves from the perspective of a couple of observers looking in on an alternate reality. But instead of us celebrating an abandonment of hope, Liz and I forged ahead with sorting out what Harriet and Abraham had been concocting all along.

It wasn't a simple matter of connecting the dots since they were all over the place, but of making sense without the tools of logic. At the center of the case we had a love affair within which another was cocooned. We had Vertex and *Man over Matter*, bad guys in Harrison and Desmond, good ones in Liu and Weisman. There was Freeman and the Russians, the *Ambassadors of the Wild*, and lest we forget, Jeremiah Jones, aka *Shadow Man*, now my inner self, positioning incomprehensible markers along our path. And of course there was Liz, who made the case central to our relationship. The true missing link was my role, the reasons why I landed in Tasmania in the first place in an array of scenarios involving unavoidable missteps, each leading to an impasse; except for one—this one—walking the fine line defining failure from success. What was I blanking out of my past that kept me from seeing the obvious? Then I remembered, and so did Liz.

My parents, Jean-Pierre and Cecile, owned a small farm in Pointe-Saint-Michel where we spent a week each fall in the company of friends. The excuse was the colors and the golden glow of the lower sun on the St-Lawrence

River. Just like Liz, I was home-schooled and my folks were lawyers. Among the friends in questions were John Lehman, and to no surprise, Abraham and Helen Garner from down under, accompanied by their young daughter, Elizabeth, a precocious mind behind probing eyes that made my heart flutter. The memory came as a revelation of what my projection, Jeremiah, had said, *"The changes can only happen upon your return."*

We didn't change the past—we changed the future, which came with its own version of it—while all the time, we never left the present—a concept out of my reach when I began my new life in Tasmania.

— o —

Indeed, my parents took me to Ranch Acacia on their yearly visits to the Garners, while Liz and I came to enjoy each other's company on increasingly intimate terms, not sexually obviously, but through probing the many mysteries of life as seen from the standpoint of fertile minds.

Following Helen's passing, neither of us made it across the equator, relying instead on the occasional postcard for news, until we practically forgot about each other. While the Gilberts, Swensons, and Desmonds never made it to Pointe-Saint-Michel, Harriet was once seen there when Helen was still alive, and later, accompanying Abraham on subsequent visits. We interacted on one occasion, a conversation that ended on a mysterious note. I was eighteen and preparing for my first year at Toronto's Faculty of Law, both eager and apprehensive in regard to living on my own, both sure and unsure about my choice of studying law in the first place, but Harriet's words put a twist to the whole thing. She looked me in the eyes, unsettling my nerves—there was something pulling me in that stare that spoke of unusual depths.

"Forget Toronto; you must go to Oxford just like Abraham, Helen, John, and myself. Of course, you make your own choices, so it's OK wherever you go; but the true path is England. You may want to think about it."

She didn't allow for clarification; she was gone and never seen again until she resurfaced in the case.

— o —

When our Quebec group came to Hobart on that shared assignment and Liz and I reconnected, both just as stunned by how much we had erased the memory of our earlier friendship, Harriet wasn't in Abraham's life and no mention of her was ever made. I never thought to ask and even if I did, people changed, relationships came and went; I just wasn't in the business of nosing around the affairs of others.

But now wasn't a time to juxtapose memories. Even though we were blessed with the ability to travel some of the lesser-used passages of the psyche, it was no reason for entanglement. The setup had changed, but the case was on, with or without Harriet. When we told Jack about what had happened, he countered with the classic conversation ender, *"Doesn't it occur all the time, except most people don't tune into those things?"* Of course, it came with a certain level of soul-searching and general awareness of the self, which was Vertex's modus operandi, something I practically took for granted. After all, it was the whole purpose of the gatherings, both at Ranch Acacia and Pointe-Saint-Michel, although not all that attended latched onto their purpose. The rule of thumb was that those who traveled to only one of the two locales were generally non-cognizant of what the group was about, which made it simple in isolating infiltrators such as the Swensons and Desmonds. Figuratively speaking, these individuals swam against the current and were perceived, in subtle ways, as elements of either resistance or disruption. Although that level of group cluelessness was just as common to both places, the Canadian get-togethers lacked the element of foreboding posed by *Man over Matter*. For what they were worth, these celebrants provided the sort of necessary brouhaha consistent with the drama of gossip, skylarking, and the impetuousness of remarks under inebriation.

— o —

I ended up applying for a scholarship at Oxford. Harriet's forceful suggestion had piqued my curiosity, notwithstanding that the idea of studying abroad had erased my doubts about my choice of going for international law. In a curious way, it all made sense, even if Liz and I missed each other by a few years because of our age difference. Being from Quebec, I was a natural to finish at HEAD in Paris, as did John, Helen, Abraham, Liz, and of course, Harriet; although it was unclear on what virtue the latter attended Oxford and *les Hautes Etudes Appliquées du Droit*. But knowing August Alexander had studied and taught there as well, it was obvious that Ms. Donovan, through her barely guised insistence, had something in store for me.

Nothing out of the ordinary came up in my years at Oxford; I made friends, shared a flat with a young fellow from Glasgow, but mostly, I plowed through the courses with unbound vitality. It wasn't until I joined the Garners that I began to evaluate the importance of my studies, even if I had already heard it from John Lehman that my Oxford and HEAD educations were the determining factor in me being hired by the Quebecoise Law firm.

"It's been here a tradition in choosing partners, Henri. All we ask of you is a performance as good as your excellent grades, and in ten years your name will join those of a prestigious few."

As it turned out, my name joined those of another firm in a faraway land. The fact was I had been groomed to replace Abraham Garner, the senior partner at Garner, Garner, & Lewis in Hobart, whose disappearance eventually brought me to his private office, where his daughter Elizabeth and I were presently commenting on the legs and finish of his favorite chardonnay.

— o —

I strived to find significance in the importance of studying at Oxford instead of Toronto, or McGill, say, but as John pointed out upon hiring me, it was tradition and not mystique that drove the choice. It was a distinction of commonality, a branding that assured order was ever preserved. To give credit where it belonged, Oxford was where Vertex had been conceived centuries ago, and perhaps that fact alone had sentimental value in some eyes, if only in those of Harriet Donovan's.

In the end, it came down to selection. Harriet had chosen me on abilities I wasn't fully aware of at the time, simple ones such as being open to suggestion even if it meant reconsidering an existing stance. That turned out to be the ground zero of adaptation, not by necessity, but by choice, something to mature into rather than be taught. It was why youngsters like Paul Desmond and Alec Gilbert, whose aims were driven by self-gratification, were ushered onward to studying anything but law at Oxford. In their case, though, medicine wasn't exactly a calling, but selection spread wide at the hand of Ms. Donovan, especially if it served a specific purpose.

— o —

The basic issue in holding multiple sets of memories was to recognize them from each other. Liz and I held two primary pasts at the conscious level, but only because we had arrived at beholding the skills at our disposal. As we peeled the layers of awareness and identified the nature of choice, probabilities, and the volatility of our notion of time/space, we could see how the exploration of the inner reality was paramount to explaining the mechanics of the physical. Life was in continuous movement at unspoken, ever-intertwined dimensional levels that made *surface reality* look as if it were held captive. And in a way, it was—not by hostile, outside forces, but by self-imposed limits.

The ability to detect change and recognize it as part of the evolutionary process enabled us to reconcile memories of the early stages of the case with the data harvested along our exploratory sessions. The core remained solid as the players moved around, switching roles, dying and un-dying, committing to an act only to exit from it and walk into another, et cetera. Without the skills of event-recognition all would have been experienced as a seamless set of merging timelines, each accompanied by their relevant pasts, albeit not without a mild sense of confusion. But to the many, confusion was merely the nature of existence.

In the end, though, it was the essence of perception that dictated the path ahead, and the more we narrowed its scope in defining our work, the more we specialized in an area that, even as it seemingly represented the whole, only touched upon one of its interpretations. Inevitably, the recipe for success lay in a balanced mix of straight focus and peripheral alertness.

— o —

Looking at the case from a distance, with its players rearranging themselves, or sharply veering from one direction to the next, the thing was that for every change, a probability was allowed to thrive, within which a unique version of the future developed to its useful conclusion.

Until our recent visit to eighteen ninety-nine London, no variant of reality arrived at the level of usefulness that foretold a successful closure. The restriction pertained to an upset balance between humanity and its environment, to choices driven by the outdated notion that Earth's resources were inexhaustible, and a combination of blindness to mounting evidence of its falsity and rejection of the facts. The one and only component that could counter the weight came in the full realization of Edward Sexton's vision. It took someone from the future to journey along its virgin path, all the way to the source, to figuratively relight that candle and carry it to all latent markers and beacons until, finally, it came to rest on the mantle of Abraham's home office, amid which the ghosts of Ranch Acacia dwelled.

— o —

Many items in the two sets of memory did not align, but they didn't have to. Players like Harriet, who had left the spectrum of culpability, were still very much instrumental to shining light on the real culprits. Angles and perceptions had changed, but the elements remained the same. The whole of the case, when broken into sequential fragments, highlighted courses leading to unique outcomes, some dependent on reactive projection, others on objective observation. In terms of linearity, two successive fragments might have only been separated by the minutest of details, explaining why the search for *waters*, for example, started and ended without us noticing the disconnects at both ends—when it stopped making sense, we just moved on. From the standpoint of Vertex, we strived to link each of the fragments that showed a promise of arriving at a place of balance, and by the look of it, we cognized we were there.

From our most recent perspective, Liz and I had been two beacons emitting at resonant frequencies, she from Ranch Acacia, and I from Pointe-Saint-Michel, whereas in the first set of memories the Canadian gatherings weren't factored in the case. To drive in the point, in other versions of reality, various degrees of change left the Acacia meetings bereft of tangible reasons for the case to take hold, or to even exist in the first place.

279

So, yes, many sharp turns left unseen at first, but as we went, the fog began to dissipate on the playing field. As we rethought the various processes, it became obvious that too much rationalizing was the cause of many instances of bottlenecking; thus, we slackened the mental process until intuitive information seeped through the cracks in logic. There wasn't a doubt that, in spite of our advancements, more was still to come, especially in dealing with Abraham's disappearance.

——— o ———

29 – HOMECOMING (Liz)

Locating my father's whereabouts and the reasons for his absence had preoccupied me from the minute I fully absorbed he wasn't dead, for as he went from victim to instigator, I was caught in an emotional storm that yanked me out of sorrow to loft me into the space of rage by betrayal. I couldn't bear I had been kept out of his plans, me, his one and only daughter, the child, adolescent, and adult that had stayed by his side throughout those phases, all the way to heading a law firm together. And yet, I then realized that there had been another life beyond the settings of our relationship, something of major importance I had failed to acknowledge in order to keep on purveying to the pain of having lost my mother. I had barred all notions of another woman in his heart, thus rejecting Harriet to the point of deviling her and making her disappear. No, my father didn't shoo his lover away after blaming her for the loss of Helen—I did it by conceiving an entire *constructural* sequence around my own misguided pain that eventually would coalesce into a legitimate past. It was only in revisiting that past that I saw the results of my creation from the outside in; that Harriet Donovan wasn't who I had made her to be, not someone outside my pain, but an integral part of it. She had loved my parents to the point of leaving when their relationship started taking hold. She was there through the later years of Helen's life, not to prey on an emotional condition, but in support. The fact was that my mother wanted her there, by her and her husband's side. She wanted Harriet to make love to dad, knowing she had lost both strength and desire to be physical with him, all in spite of their insistence that they didn't have to. No, she didn't want it any other way! I heard it loud and clear when, while eavesdropping, she said, *"You made this relationship possible by opting to a graceful exit; now allow me to return the favor. I mean it!"*

— o —

Yes, Henri and I had grown to see beyond our choices as makers of reality—we had ventured to the observatory high grounds of our own life process, two figurative flies on the wall of whatever room we chose to visit, or, on a grander scale, two souls flying high above the vastness of worldly experience. Not bad for a couple of attorneys often associated with bottom dwellers!

I knew my father was alive somewhere, but I no longer wished to be part of his choices, at least, not as an arbitrator of right and wrong. I loved him for being the eccentric he would always be, and finding that very trait in me pleased me greatly.

His and Harriet's plan to defeat *Man over Matter* was rooted in something that ran deeper than some ad hoc committee of testosterones on the war path. The group itself was only one of myriad facets with a grudge against the natural world. Actually, the greater villain nested within the human psyche, a resilient power that blindly sought the destruction of its source of existence. I was in no position to explain why an infant dependent on the teat for survival would strive to poison the mother, but that was what it felt like at the gut level, an illogical bit of ill-fitted reasoning that had no bearing on decency and relevance, and yet it was there, fanning out its feathers.

The irony behind immense resources put at the disposal of such insanity didn't escape those with the might to counterbalance it; equal means had to be utilized, not in an open battle whose victory yielded no winner, but through subtleness and efficiency via complex channels endeared by Vertex as *the back corridors of power*. The point was to provide a contextual environment for opposite views to come under the limelight, and such an environment was the case. I then realized that my father wasn't meant to return in the proper sense—the sustained mystery of his disappearance was crucial in bracing our side against the Swenson's argument of no wrongdoing if Yang Wu was proven to be alive and well.

— o —

In fact, Wu's fictive murder was part of the playbook. It was deemed a closed chapter until another corpse came knocking at the door. So convinced were we at first, that we based our case argument on it well into the final stretch. But things had shifted, while it remained to be seen whether the Swensons had heeded the winds of change or not. My take was that it was unconceivable that our groundwork could have fundamentally been recast—Henri agreed. In his words, all useful convolutions had been exhausted; there was no longer a need for them—we had arrived.

This was when it became interesting. I sensed that rather than having merged with the new reality, the case teetered on the fulcrum edge of two probabilities, with the Swensons in the *old* one, and us afoot in the new. Contrarily to the notion that a blur in perception would occur in such an instance, the weaved realities appeared as one, in which actors played from related scripts, close enough, though, to evade anything short of rare acumen. And perhaps, reading from the new script was what being ahead of the game simply meant.

Jack assured us he was in control of the situation and that whatever happened had to follow its course unimpeded. We sipped our wine, confident of having covered all angles. As we returned to the living room and looked through the glass, a thin layer of snow had spread over the grass outside. Then my phone rang—Harold Freeman was on the other end with the information that Samuel O'Reilly was willing to testify. Apparently, the dead had the uncanny habit of *un-dying*. Henri was wrong; not all useful convolutions had been exhausted.

—— o ——

30 – CIRCULAR HORIZON (Liz)

Whether O'Reilly perished in that car crash or not was now a matter of perspective. If my notion that the Swensons were working of the old script was right, then the surgeon's reappearance was likely to create a stir in the courtroom.

In light of the new situation, we had no intention of allowing the defense to bring Yang Wu's name to anyone's ears, and even though the suit was centered on his murder at the hand of James King, on Gerald Harrison's order, Jack was ready to go full reversal by bringing O'Reilly to the bench as his first witness.

— o —

The objection was waved off by Judge Raphael Montgomery in the manner of a man taking no objection before settling into a pace. He had already been informed by Jack that O'Reilly would be called to the bench and saw no harm in the introduction of a last-minute witness.

I would have paid to watch the Swensons' faces as they recognized the man who was thought dead from burning in his wrecked vehicle, as Jack swiftly moved with his first inquiry.

"Where were you the day your car was found burning by the side of Bass Highway, near Port Letta?"
Justin Swenson: *"Objection!"*
Judge Montgomery: *"Objection overruled, the witness may answer the question."*

O'Reilly: *"James King and I were watching it burn from a distance."*

All objections were subsequently overturned.

Jack Lewis: *"Can you identify the driver?"*

O'Reilly: *"Derek Gunn, a deceased homeless and familyless man scheduled for cremation."*

Lewis: *"The coroner identified you as the driver, how was that possible."*

O'Reilly: *"A substitution of dental records—not unheard of in my field."*

Lewis: *"In other words, you and James King placed the dead body in the driver's seat of the crashed vehicle and lit it on fire, right?"*

O'Reilly: *"Correct."*

Lewis: *"Can you explain why?"*

O'Reilly: *"Because I was supposed to be the one to die in the accident."*

Lewis: *"Please clarify."*

O'Reilly: *"Gerald Harrison ordered James King to have me removed, not knowing that Jimmy and I were associates."*

Lewis: *"May you please define 'associates'?"*

O'Reilly: *"We were part of an investigational team hired by the company."*

Lewis: *"Who hired you?"*

O'Reilly: *"Head engineer Jonathon Weisman."*

Lewis: *"I understand you are a surgeon, not an investigator; how did that come about?"*

O'Reilly: *"My capacity as surgeon at North West Regional was what the team needed of me."*

Lewis: *"Please elaborate."*

O'Reilly: *"North West Regional is under contract with the mine to address medical emergencies. I was, until recently, the surgeon in charge of admitting the injured flown from Savage River."*

Lewis: *"Were Abraham Garner and Yang Wu some of the injured you admitted from the mine?"*

O'Reilly: *"No."*

Lewis: *"Your report of the body flown from the facility on the night of the tailings dam accident identifies the victim as Abraham Garner, please clarify."*

O'Reilly: *"The body was identified by his friend, Harold Freeman, and Elizabeth Garner, his daughter, the day after the admission."*

Lewis: *"But you knew the body was neither Garner's nor Wu's; am I correct?"*

O'Reilly: *"Yes, you are. The body was borrowed from the morgue, helicoptered frozen to the mine, and dumped down the wall as it collapsed, and then flown back to North West Regional as the victim."*

Lewis: *"Who was the real victim meant to be?"*

O'Reilly: *"Abraham Garner."*

Lewis: *"And why wasn't he?"*

O'Reilly: *"Because he already knew he was supposed to be."*

Lewis: *"Who told him?"*

O'Reilly: *"Nobody—he was ahead of those who wanted him dead."*

Lewis: *"Who were those?"*

O'Reilly: *"Gerald Harrison, doctor Paul Desmond, William Dorset, and most of the men involved in blowing the wall."*

Lewis: *"Why did they want him dead?"*

O'Reilly: *"Because of his role in the leases."*

Lewis: *"Would you say those people exist under a collective name?"*

O'Reilly: *"Yes,* Man over Matter.*"*

Lewis: *"Aside from the suspect and without naming anyone, do you recognize any individuals in this courtroom as belonging to that organization?"*

O'Reilly: *"Yes, I do."*

Lewis: *"That will be all, your honour."*

Rather than switching to cross-examining the witness, the Swenson team opted for a recess. They were more than aware than the judge had kept the ball in Jack's half of the court; unfortunately for them, O'Reilly's mysterious reappearance had shaken the foundation of their argument, and now that the jury was informed Wu didn't die in the mine accident, objecting to the surgeon's open testimony was their only recourse. In other words, their case had sagged under the weight of Jack's calculated maneuver. But since nobody died at the dam, they momentarily lived under the assurance that their client was innocent of the crime. Nevertheless, intent was still punishable by law, and Uri Dudko, as far as everybody knew, was still dead, unless, of course, he wasn't, since James King's criminal status was undoing itself, piece by piece.

— o —

It remained that my father's disappearance and the charges of kidnapping were still looming large; although, since we now were certain that dad had orchestrated the whole thing with Harriet, Jack deemed it inconsequential, at least for the time being, to pursue those charges.

At that juncture, I wondered where Judge Raphael Montgomery's cutoff point was. I suspected he counted on the Swensons to prove Wu was safe before dismissing the case and letting Harrison walk. But the defense had to first tackle O'Reilly in order to dispel the impending accusations set forth by his words. The court was back in session.

Emma Swenson: *"According to your statement, Mr. Yang Wu was never admitted to North West Regional Hospital on the night of the mine accident; can you confirm?"*
O'Reilly: *"Yes, it is correct."*
E. Swenson: *"Did you personally know Mr. Wu?"*
O'Reilly: *"No, I didn't."*
E. Swenson: *"But you knew of him, right?"*
O'Reilly: *"Yes."*
E. Swenson: *"And how did you know of him?"*
O'Reilly: *"That shall remain confidential."*
E. Swenson: *"I'm asking about the circumstances of that knowledge; can you please answer!"*
Jack Lewis: *"Objection, Your Honour!"*
Montgomery: *"Objection overruled. The witness may answer the question."*
O'Reilly: *"His name was mentioned at my briefing with Jonathon Weisman."*
E. Swenson: *"Can you recall the exact words used by Mr. Weisman?"*
O'Reilly: *"Yes, equipment engineer Yang Wu was to make contact with Abraham Garner at some yet to be disclosed date, that's all."*
E. Swenson: *"And what were the reasons for that meeting, Mr. O'Reilly?"*

O'Reilly: *"I am not at liberty to tell this court."*

E. Swenson: *"Yes, you are!"*

Jack Lewis: *"Objection, Your Honour!"*

Montgomery: *"Objection sustained—please, may the defense get to the point."*

E. Swenson: *"Based on your statement, it is obvious Mr. Wu is alive and well. You are of course aware that you voluntarily destroyed the plaintiff's argument against my client, Mr. O'Reilly?"*

O'Reilly: *"I'm in no position to disclose information about Mr. Yang Wu's present state of health, since we never have met and I wouldn't know where he lives. On the other hand, I am alive and well, yet you thought I was dead. As far as I know he could also have met his fate; after all, not all corpses go through North West Regional Hospital."*

Following a quick deliberation, Emma and Justin Swenson switched places.

Justin Swenson: *"Since the report of your accident actually made the news, it is simply natural that we didn't expect to see you with us today. But our team is glad to find you in good health, Samuel. The point here is to establish that our client has been wrongly accused of ordering the murder of first, Abraham Garner, and then of Yang Wu when the authorities convinced the state that the body had been originally misidentified. I believe that by you saying that neither of them was admitted that night into North West Regional is reasonable evidence that this case should be closed. So, unless you have something else to say that proves otherwise, I see no point in wasting the time of our judicial system."*

O'Reilly: *"I actually have something to say that may show the court that our judicial system isn't being taken for granted. The reason why I survived an attempt on my life was because I was a step ahead of your client. The fact was I worked for him, not because he had blackmailed me into it, but rather out of satisfying the requirements of my assignment. You see, Gerald, or Alec as he was previously known during our days at the University of Sydney, got a bit of help getting hired by* Branched Resources *as an environmental consultant since the company was in no need of such an individual—our team, with the push of one of the firm's executives, made it happen. We were well aware that his drive to get inside the mine stemmed from motives that were far from benefiting the environment. My role was essentially to make myself available as someone easily corruptible."*

J. Swenson: *"Whatever you say, Samuel, none of your diatribe is admissible to this court—you're still wasting our time!"*

Montgomery: *"Since the defense asked the witness, on behalf of the respondent, to prove that we may have reason to continue with the case, I don't see why he should be interrupted while fulfilling that request. The court has all the time in the world to hear to the end of his statement and I shall be the one to decide when enough is enough. Please, continue Mr. O'Reilly."*

O'Reilly: *"Since Gerald threatened to harm my family if I didn't do as he asked, I had the perfect excuse to act the part of the willing victim, which also made me an eventual candidate for elimination. James King was Gerald's hired killer, a loud-mouthed environmental fanatic from a fringe group out of Launceston, whose aim was to sabotage mine equipment, or so he bragged. The thing is the* Ambassadors of the Wild *were the brainchild of a group of art students partnering with the University of Tasmania's Newnham campus, who collaborated with our team to provide a background of legitimacy for James's depravity of morals. James was not only ordered to push Abraham Garner down the wall, but to also kill Yang Wu, the man he and Harold Freeman had planned on meeting clandestinely north of the dam. It had also been arranged for Freeman to be spared for reasons I am not qualified to explain. Technically, I was told to prepare for the arrival of two bodies, but, of course, I knew ahead of time that it would never happen. Instead, Gerald forced me, under threat, to accept a single body, which unbeknownst to him, I had sent ahead for James to collect, put in a hiking outfit, and place on top of the wall scheduled for collapse. When, a year later, James was asked to eliminate Freeman and his partner Aleksei Yegorov, I knew I was next in line and that James would soon be left to rot or be killed in a prison cell. But none of it was meant to be as it seemed, since the mastermind was under the strings of a greater puppeteer without whom I wouldn't be telling this story here today."*

Montgomery: *"Thank you, Mr. O'Reilly; we shall reconvene tomorrow at 9 o'clock. I expect all parties to attend and be on time. I will arrange for James King and his lawyer to be present as well. This session is adjourned."*

— o —

It was unlikely the Swensons had foreseen their argument to be swept under the rug in favor of the opening statement of a last minute witness, but I had no

292

doubt they saw where they had missed on a couple of opportunities to slam the door shut on the case and claim a victory for their client. Certainly, arrogance, and also some desperation had contributed to it, but one thing for sure, O'Reilly had comported himself as a true pro, in the process of which his old persona had melted like ice under the sun. I was beginning to really appreciate this new reality of ours.

— o —

Henri was convinced the judge was only in it for the sake of not leaving any stone unturned. As he put it, the case was already blown out of the water. Harrison was being tried for the murder of Yang Wu, and if the engineer was alive, the accused walked free—end of it. That was Henri being rational in a non-rational environment. But things took a turn when Jack announced that Montgomery had ordered Paul Desmond to appear for questioning at the Department of Police. Apparently, O'Reilly's composure and directness had left such impression as to warrant further enquiry into the peripheral matters of the case. In other words, there was enough substantiated evidence of wrongdoing to justify a procedural rearrangement of the terms defining the trial. At that point, it no longer sufficed that Wu was said to be alive; he had to appear and dispel all notions that his life was ever in danger while working at the mine. Short of bringing the engineer to the bench and have him testify in Harrison's favor, the Swensons were at an impasse. Whether Jack had it planned all along or that he counted on an element of fortune to turn things around was left unmentioned, but he certainly took advantage of an

293

opportunity when he saw one, making it part of the flow rather than an item of disruption meant to shock the opposite camp. That was why, I surmised, he asked only questions that begged for others to be asked.

— o —

When the recording of the meeting at Xing Liu's residence was replayed at the office, pending the decision to use it in court, the Chinese businessman was unsurprisingly absent from the interaction. Instead, the order to kill Harold and Aleksei came directly from Harrison, while the Swensons' role as *Branched Resources* lawyers was switched to representing the core of what would eventually surface as *Man over Matter*.

Henri and I, as well as the rest of Vertex understood a thing or two about the multiplicity of scenarios when it came to traveling across probabilities, but this one change was particularly striking. The question teeter-tottered between whether the mining company was originally guilty or that we had inculpated it from our own mental model, consequently developing a sequence that later would come to an impasse. The answer, of course, lay in the rhetorical nature of the second half of that very question, hence the importance of not getting too attached to such models, for they came with powerful blinders. The Swensons must have then spoken on behalf of the company, and not as their representatives. As to Xing Liu, he wasn't there; his niece, Tanya, was—she was the person taking the shower during Harold and Aleksei's visit of the premises. She also was James King's girlfriend, the reason why the back door had been left open for our two investigators to let

294

themselves in. In fact, the Chinese man wasn't even in Tasmania at the time—a sharp departure from what that phase of the case had yielded. It kind of left me curious about what happened to him in that version of reality, but I sensed he was simply untouchable irrespective of the situation. To the discriminating mind, things were not necessarily as they seemed.

It was all too clear that *Man over Matter* had believed they could use Liu as a means of penetration into *Branched Resources*, while Liu himself had all along acted by the Vertex playbook of facilitating each of their position within the company in anticipation of their every move. In that regard, it suited Xing particularly well to act both the puppet and the master puppeteer. Needless to say, the latest version of the recording reflected the shift between those two sides; as the result of which the Swensons no longer assumed the reserve of their previous selves when they once advised to tone down the dead body count; this time, no such consideration was made, as they seamed openly responsive to Harrison's suggestion of working on an alibi for King. It was consented upon that the recording would be introduced when James King was called to the bench.

— o —

My general feeling upon reviewing the many forks in the case, each with its own development, was that of observing the circular horizon from a high place. I was at the intersection of myriad angles opening onto vastnesses of possibilities. Yet, the case within each was finite, with those possibilities eventually sharing a common end; save for that one tight wedge that, because of forces external to the picture, had opened, radiant, from center to as far as the eye could see. It was the path chosen, where tomorrow and the days of the trial to come lined up inexorably intent on forging ahead.

— o —

Frankly, it was a relief to get Paul Desmond out of my house. The man didn't resist or even seem to be surprised by the presence of the police at the door with a warrant for his arrest. Harold, in spite of having been informed, had oddly left security on watch. I received a concerned call from Dimitri Osminin asking me what was going on, which, of course, left me to wonder about the reasons for the omission. Without explaining, I resolved to prompt the Russian surveillant to pull his men out and call Freeman for details.

Henri, who had been sitting beside me, raised a *what-the-fuck* eyebrow and stood up abruptly as if jolted from mental standby. Far from expecting such an extreme reaction out of my darling fiancé, I simply uttered, *"Henri, he must have just forgotten!"* to which he responded forcefully with, *"Harold doesn't forget!"* He had a point; absentmindedness wasn't a Freeman trait.

— o —

31 – SAVAGE TRUTH

John Lehman here.

When I met Abraham and Harriet at Oxford, they lived together as a couple. There was an alien quality to their bond that I found particularly attractive; it was ancient, as if borne of the very stone the university was built on. We quickly became close friends, spending our time looking ahead to the future, imagining ways of making the world a better place. One at a time, Harriet and Abe introduced me to their connections, and before I knew it, I had stepped into my first Vertex gathering. One wasn't invited—one either belonged or not. Those who didn't, relished those get-togethers as the customary parties catering to intellectual chit-chat and a sense of answering to an elite chosen by the graces of good fortune; but for those who heard the call, it was in the tradition of crossing a distinct threshold into a new kind of awareness, amusingly referred to as the back corridors of power. I was immediately overtaken by a sense of belonging, ready to join the larger discussions at the core of world sustainability. Eventually, I came to realize it had been Harriet's mission to draw me into Vertex, at which time I also understood who she both was and wasn't. It made all the more sense when, later, Helen came on the scene and Harriet stepped out of the picture. She had seen what we, at the time, were a long way from comprehending: our multifaceted reality in all its past and future manifestations. It took me a while to grasp the concept before it settled into core awareness.

By the time she joined the Ranch Acacia gatherings, Harriet was ready to expose the hard reality of what we were up against with *Man over Matter*. She had recently entered into a relationship with Karl Gilbert, widowed father of Gerald Harrison and Emma Swenson, and had made tight connections with Alan Desmond, also a single dad, and many within the anti-conservationist group. Her plan was to facilitate the agenda of *Man over Matter* by positioning each of its agents within what essentially consisted of an anticipated model overseen by Vertex. For that, we had to know all of the players without an iota of suspicion on their parts, one of them, a close associate of Abraham Garner's, Harold Freeman, the man slated to send his friend on a plunge to his death down the west wall of the Savage River tailings dam.

Unfortunately for Harold, the secret of his betrayal had reached its expiry date. Far from caring to inform the Russians of the arrest of Paul Desmond, he was on a flight to Melbourne, en route to Canberra.

— o —

If Freeman's getaway spelled trouble for Harrison and the Swensons, it certainly amounted to a monumental headache for Henri and Liz, who had depended on his relentless work to free the case from the shackles of insolvability. Henri's reaction upon hearing the news of the omission was far from exaggerated considering the implications if the investigator were to indeed be a peon of the other side, or worse, the organization's top dog. But as far as the larger picture was concerned, he could have spared himself the trouble, for if it hadn't been for his and Liz's investigational skills, the outcome of the case would have been far different; in fact, it was bound to end just like all the others, with a court failure and a crippling loss to humanity. If anything, Henri deserved to congratulate himself for having had the nose to sniff inconsistencies around Freeman's actions early in the case, even if no clues coalesced into forming a track. In fact, he has my deepest respect for never having trusted the man in the first place.

— o —

Aside from me, only Harriet and Abraham knew what Harold was up to, and most spectacularly, none at *Man over Matter* had any idea he was the brain of the operation. They answered to a higher authority, never guessing that voice belonged to one of the men they wished to make disappear. It was all along a game of deceit, a complicated one that threatened to come apart with every move. It was Freeman against Abraham, *Man over Matter* against Vertex, but the fox was forever Harriet—always a step ahead, adjusting, suggesting, shifting scenarios, or rewriting the script. She did it from the past, the present, and the future whence she truly came, or, from adjacent timelines, close and far. In doing so, the case veered off-track on many occasions, memories joined or replaced others, while villains swapped coats with the good guys. She fooled Freeman into believing she was the driving force under his orders, while he stood merely where she needed him to be. Orchestrating the mine accident was particularly tricky; for it required a decade-long assessment of case topology, the skills to hand-pick all of the suitable actors, notwithstanding getting the timing right, while banking on Liz and Henri's parallel paths to get the ball rolling in a direction that was far from linear.

By the time of the trial, it was still to be determined whether Harriet's work would pay off or not. All hinged on Judge Montgomery's assessment of the verdict's long-term outcome, and how much he was willing to go with the tedium of endless convolutions, as opposed to staying within strict procedural guidelines. It also balanced on Henri and Liz's ability to see to the last details of their assignment.

32 – URI'S REVENGE (Henri)

I immediately called Upton Clay. It felt like something had awakened within me. An old suspicion had festered below my skin and was now oozing through a visible wound. It was there all along, yet I had repressed the thought as a forbidden one. Of course, I knew from the very beginning, but where could have I had gone from there? I was too new at it, plus I lacked the proofs and the angle from which to seek them; and perhaps, just perhaps, I wasn't meant to pursue that route. But all was clear now; the case path that had so far been lined with incomprehensible markers, moving banners, and mind-twisting illogicalities, was free of all artifacts, pending what was still to poke its head through the veil of Harriet and Abraham's magnum opus.

Clay: *"No, Henri, I haven't seen Harold since we closed shop; I assumed he was back in Hobart."*

Me: *"Didn't he say he needed to tie a few things up in Albany?"*

"He did, but he went alone; Aleksei is presently in Launceston looking for clues into Yuri Dudko's death."

"Why would Harold send him there in the first place?"

"He didn't; the Russians are on it. Apparently, they're not buying the official story; Aleksei confessed he didn't believe King when he questioned him."

"Well, as it turns out, he was probably right. King isn't who we thought he was. You heard about Jack bringing O'Reilly in as a witness, didn't you?"

"Yep, Saëns is keeping me updated; I would have paid to watch the reaction of the defense."

"What do you make of it?"

"Looks like Harrison's attorneys should be worried for their own sake."

"So, if King didn't kill Dudko, who did?"

"Elemental—someone who couldn't afford to be uncovered and who knew exactly how close the Russian was to the truth."

"Like, say, someone Dudko reported to?"

"For example."

"Uri was after a document that never existed; what kind of truth are we looking at then?"

"The answer is in the question; he found out the document was as bogus as his assignment."

"The one thing is, nobody at the time believed the document was inexistent; how could he have known?"

"Since it's assumed he got to James King, what if the two got to know each other just long enough for Dudko to get suspicious of the list he was working off?"

"I'm starting to get the picture, Upton. Thanks mate; let me know as soon as you hear from Harold!"

— o —

Yes, Uri Dudko had been on the true path while we were lost on an imaginary one, chasing the meaning of *waters*. From the distance, it looked completely absurd. Somehow, I must have known since Jeremiah Jones kept on trying to rectify our course—*Shadow Man*, or J.J., my inner guide, working relentlessly to instill sense into me. Who could have killed Uri Dudko besides James King? Who else but Harold Freeman or a hired gun, of course!

When I shared my thoughts with Liz, she first looked at me, incredulous, but quickly aligned with my suspicions.

"Oh, Henri, this is so sick! But isn't Harriet in Albany with, possibly, dad?!"

"That's a critical question, considering Harold is now aware he has been played all along. It couldn't be too early to put Aleksei back on the payroll; I'm sure he would appreciate a fresh scent to his track."

"But aren't he and Harold close?"

"Sure, but it's also time to see whose side the Russians are working for; I've got a hunch it's not Freeman's."

— o —

Aleksei Yegorov was quick to accept the offer. He was joined by Dimitri Osminin and two others from the Russian investigational collective, which I learned, for the first time, operated under the acronym, T.I.E., for *Tasmanian Inner Eye*. Without getting into details, the detective let me in on his doubts about the circumstances of his friend Uri's death. In his words, *"If King didn't do it, then Harold lied to me."* I took it as a hint Freeman was no longer a friend of the group.

As the foursome staged their plan of action, I retraced every step of my trip to Savage River. I began to see how the hike through the wilderness was nothing but an excuse for Harold to test my character for tenacity and endurance, and also to evaluate my level of gullibility. He must have known that I clearly had reservations about the idea in the first place and that my doubts extended well past our safe return to the vehicle, when I opted to go separate ways back to Hobart. But what struck me most was the plausibility of him, Freeman, or one of his allies having, in the first place, planted the thumb drive in the rear of the maintenance building where Yang Wu had his office. In all likeliness, the contents of that drive were intended to send me and the Russians on a wild goose chase, along which the elements of culpability would evenly shed their ballast, burden our investigation with costly delays, and eventually render the case too weak to stand a chance in court.

But somehow, Uri Dudko had homed on the one item on the list that sent him straight to James King, just as Liz and I almost did when, instead, we took the road to *Lips Waters Café* and then Swansea. As we wrongly intuited King was code for *King's Bridge*, he, Dudko, found the real James and met his fate; except that wasn't the way it happened. At the time, Freeman believed King was a member of the *Ambassadors of the Wild* on a mission to sabotage mine property, who subsequently got hired by Harrison to do the dirty work, when in fact the evidence pointed to him working for Harriet and Abraham on the same team as Samuel O'Reilly's. What seemed likely was that Freeman was done with King and counted on the encounter to end in bloodshed, with Dudko holding the smoking gun. Instead the two must have found kinship in the light of the deception lying at the base of their encounter.

Now, had Liz and I followed that route to James, how could it not have benefited Harold? After all, getting rid of us had its advantages, especially if it came before Dudko found King. With us murdered and the assassin downed by the Russian, Freeman and *Man over Matter* could plow ahead with the leases, while simultaneously, and in double entendre, deploy the veil of castigation over the mining company's greed, the whole ending in a court show of the absurd with Freeman suing *Branched Resources* for negligence in the death of his best friend, Abraham Garner.

— o —

Liz was quick to highlight that perhaps Freeman had always been where Harriet and her father wanted him to be, a step behind from accomplishing his goal of demolishing Vertex's raison d'être. Her point was well-taken, considering Harold's influence and relationship with the group. My question was, at which point did Vertex actually become aware of the subterfuge, and what was the trigger?

Liz: *"I'm more inclined to think Vertex drew Harold into its circle, which of course would benefit him immensely."*

"So, in your view, your father, John Lehman, Xing Liu, Robert Lewis, and of course, Harriet always knew Harold was the head of Man over Matter *Australia?"*

"It's my understanding we wouldn't be here to talk about it if it had been otherwise."

"And you are arriving at this, how, exactly?"

"Deep inside, I feel it was the reason for the gatherings: to draw Man over Matter *into the circle. Originally, mom and dad advertised the meetings in trade magazines as a merging of minds on behalf of global awareness, in order to attract thinkers of all provenances and forge the first Tasmanian chapter of Vertex. Of*

305

course, it could never be divulged that such a chapter existed, especially to potential infiltrators. I don't believe Harold ever was aware of the name Vertex and of the group's global wingspan, but he undoubtedly recognized the power behind the gatherings and how much influence and leverage my parents and their firm had in the state, which was of utmost concern to Man over Matter. *"*

"You're aware you're saying this as if you had always known it, right?"

"At this point, I'm taking anything new as part of forgotten knowledge, which seems to be enhancing memory."

"You weren't even born."

"Neither were we when we visited Harriet in London."

Liz obviously had a point—there was much to gain in probing her thoughts. We had to know the stakes—going after Freeman was a deal that could only go one way. On the other hand, a lack of precipitous action would endanger Abraham and Harriet. It was now clear why Abe had chosen to play dead: first, of course, to convince Harold he had succeeded, and then second, to secure his hiding place. Let's face it, Freeman essentially sent the Russians on a hunt of his friend's digs, without ever disclosing the true nature of his goals to them. But Uri Dudko figured it out, and that was why his body was found floating in the South Esk River.

— o —

It was assumed Freeman was in Albany looking for Abraham, although, as in all assumptions, there was a strong propensity for error in that judgment. It was strictly based on the fact Harriet had been apprehended there. But now, with the truth of her dinkum assignment exposed, Albany was probably the worse town to hang out for the two of them; and at that point, no place in Australia was truly safe. And then the wildest thought occurred to me.

"Liz, did Harold ever visit Pointe-Saint-Michel?"

"I was just about to ask you that very question. I think not. As a matter of fact, I don't remember dad ever speaking of our travels with Harold."

"I don't recall seeing him there either. We're on the same page, aren't we?"

"Yeah, I think that's where dad has been mostly staying since you moved here, and now Harriet has joined him. It makes so much sense on so many levels—like in you and him merely having swapped places. How brilliant is that?!"

"It also means he's been in my parents and John's company since that time; now that's crazy!"

"Yes, but can you think of a better scenario for them to oversee our moves?"

"And move us around like pawns?"

"Come on, Henri, you know better."

"Only humoring the self, but you're right. So now, what about Freeman?"

"Are we sure he's after dad, as opposed to fleeing before the authorities get hold of the truth?"

"He doesn't look like the type to be worried about the cops—he's been around them for too long to not know their weaknesses. No, if he's going to get busted, he'll want to finish the job first."

"That leaves Xing's place, in Canberra!"

"Because that's how he's going to figure out where my dad is, by getting the information out of Liu."

"That means our man's in danger..."

"And that's why Aleksei and Dimitri need to get there pronto. I'm calling now!"

— o —

The Russians were on their way. Xing Liu's phone wasn't answering and no-one, not even John Lehman had any idea where the Chinese man was. I had the odd feeling that we might have been too late and that Harold already had what he needed. As always, John was quick to assure me things weren't as bad as they looked.

Lehman: *"Delighted you and Liz figured it out about Abraham; I was wondering when you would start making the connection. I take it you and I are OK about it, but please be frank if you're not."*

"You've always been a lovable asshole, John—so dependable that way—how can I ever get mad about your manners. I'm sure you have Abe and Harriet under solid protection by now."

"Your folks and I have taken care of business, kiddo. And don't worry about Xing; he's got more than one hare in his hat."

— o —

33 – CANBERRA (Liz)

The trial was no longer my main focus; my mind was locked on the pressing matters of Harold Freeman's whereabouts. That said, court and escape ran parallel to each other, the most desirable outcome being dependent on proper meshing of the two.

Canberra isn't like any other city in Australia. For one thing it was drawn from scratch, like Brasília, except that it fared much better. It actually is one of the nicest spots to live in the country, probably why Xing favored it over Hobart. As the capital, it is more of an administrative center than say, a progressive one like Sydney. It's also a lot smaller and quieter, which for some reason, and from my perspective, made it the oddest of places for the case to choose its dramatic end.

— o —

Xing Liu's primary residence was located in the suburb of Forrest in South Canberra, on a well-concealed lot off Arthur Circuit. Simply put, Forrest is one of the most affluent parts of the city, which put Liu's wealth somewhere within the comfortable average of the richest, if that means anything. He lived there with his wife, Pamela, or Pam as I knew her, and a buff female keeper, Oscea, in charge of grounds and basic security.

Freeman vaguely remembered the address through his association with Liu, but since he had never been there, it took him forever to get it right. Somehow, he had counted on his investigational instincts to find the house, one similar to the many ambassadorial residences spotting the area, but the maddening circles and loops to get to it frustrated his compass to the point of threatening to send him into a fit—something to be said about the mind that drew the blueprint of the city.

— o —

Xing—in anticipation of the visit, with Pam safely away on a week-long shopping trip to Sydney—was getting prepared for the confrontation. Naturally, Oscea was ready too, and anyone familiar with the woman would have known that "prepared" has special meaning to her. In the meantime, the Russians had landed at CBR, where a Mercedes SUV rental awaited them.

— o —

Back in Hobart, James King, after having stated his name and made an affirmation, was asked to sit in the witness box. The court, save for the customary coughs and shuffles, was silent when Jack Lewis came forward.

"Mr. King, you were accused, tried, and sentenced for the murder or Mr. Wu as the result of an indictment written against your person; yet it appears, based on a recent witness testimony, that the complainant is alive. Can you confirm that you are innocent of the crime?"

Emma Swenson: *"Objection, your Honour, the witness is not on trial!"*

Judge Montgomery: *"Objection overruled—the witness may answer the question."*

310

James King: *"I was instructed to kill Yang Wu, but I didn't follow through."*

Jack Lewis: *"And why did you change your mind?"*

King: *"I didn't change my mind; Yang and I worked on the same team."*

Lewis: *"Who ordered you to kill Mr. Wu?"*

E. Swanson: *"Objection, the defendant is leading!"*

Judge: *"Overruled, may the witness answer."*

King: *"Gerald Harrison."*

According to the transcript, the orderly required silence in the courtroom.

Lewis: *"Mr. King, do you recognize Gerald Harrison as the accused?"*

The defense's objection was again overruled.

King: *"Yes, I do."*

Lewis: *"Did the accused instruct you to murder Samuel O'Reilly as well?"*

All objections were from that point on overruled.

King: *"Yes, he did."*

Lewis: *"Did he also request that you kill Abraham Garner?"*

King: *"Yes, but only if Harold Freeman couldn't do the job himself."*

Lewis: *"According to the indictment, he, the accused, ordered you to murder Harold Freeman and his partner Aleksei Yegorov as well; is that correct?"*

King: *"Yes, it is."*

Lewis: *"Then, how could Mr. Freeman have been a target of Mr. Harrison's? Based on your allegation, shouldn't they have been working together?"*

King: *"Gerald Harrison didn't know Harold Freeman was the one issuing orders from the top down; no-one in his group did. He was under the assumption he and Abraham Garner were long-time friends working against* Man over Matter*'s agenda."*

Lewis: *"So, according to your testimony, it all distills down to the group actions of a criminal organization that answers to the name of* Man over Matter*; would you say that assessment is correct?"*

King: *"Yes, it is."*

Lewis: *"That will be all, your Honour."*

— o —

Oscea was an ex-commando officer of the Johannesburg Civil Defense Program. She was trained in counterinsurgency, street-ready in the event of a terrorist attack, a role she took to an extreme until the threats subsided. Xing Liu heard of her through acquaintances in South Africa. Confident he had found the perfect bodyguard, he contacted her with the offer of a well-remunerated job in the Australian capital, under the guise of housekeeper. To his surprise, she accepted on the spot as if she had been anticipating the opportunity of a life change. Courtesy the efficiency of *the back corridors of power*, she was papered and on duty within the month that followed. Although Oscea wasn't a keeper in the proper sense, she didn't mind the cover and used it with the same passion a stage actor in the throes of their character would—something I loved in her when dad and I visited. When not in the role, she spent regimented hours in her private gym, keeping sharp and fit.

Freeman rang the bell.

Oscea answered the door.

"Who are you and how may I help you?"

"H. Freeman, I'm here to speak with Mr. Liu."

"Mr. Liu receives on appointment only."

"I was in the area; I thought I'd stop by for a surprise visit—Xing and I are old friends."

"Harold, right? Mr. Liu has spoken of you. He's presently out, but please come on in if you don't mind waiting."

"Thank you, and your name?"

"Oscea."

"Oscea who?"

"Oscea, as in Prince or Bono."

"Got it, my pleasure."

Actually, Xing was in, listening on the conversation between his bodyguard and the visitor. He was sitting at the desk of his subterranean office, facing monitors that showed Freeman leaving the vestibule and entering the living room.

"Mr. Freeman, do you care for a refreshment, or something harder perhaps?"

"Please, a Bundaberg root, or ginger if you have..."

"You must know it's Mr. Liu's favorite soft drink, especially the ginger beer!"

"Indeed, we go way back. But tell me, Oscea,

Xing never mentioned he kept a maid who looks like a body builder; you must be working the gym regularly."

"You would know Mr. Freeman, you look pretty fit yourself for your age, if you don't mind me saying."

"Let me guess, Johannesburg?"

"I see the accent gave me away once again. My turn: Durban?"

"Right on the money, babe! What do you call two expatriates from Mzansi, one colored, the other white, inside a Chinaman's house in Australia?"

By then, the hostess had homed on Freeman's mounting aggressiveness, which, as I well knew, often slanted towards misogynistic remarks, especially in the presence of a colored female. Oscea didn't have to improvise an answer—as if on cue, Xing Liu made his grand entrance.

"Ah, Harold, what a surprise! What brings you here, old chap?"

"As I'm sure you know, my work occasionally demands that I consult with the bureaucratic morass of government; in this case, a particularly puzzling instance of shifting allegiances."

"And how exactly would bureaucracy solve that for you, Harold?"

"It's a simple matter of knowing who and how to ask, generally through coercion."

"Of course. Tell me, Harold, when was the last time we saw each other?"

"Probably when you got the Gilbert kid hired. But I'm sorry I missed you when I stopped by your vacation home in Smithton—lot's of people there."

"Yes, I heard; you and Aleksei Yegorov. Did you meet my niece, Tanya?"

"She must have been the one in the shower, no, but it was nice of her to disable the alarm and leave the rear sliding door open."

"Anything to assist an investigation, Harold! But please explain how it served you to obtain an incriminating recording of your own people and make it available to the authorities?"

"Pretty much the same as how it served you when you turned the tables on Branched Resources.*"*

"As usual, missing on the nuance, Harold."

At that point, the game was up. The mention of the mine was Oscea's signal to prepare for action. She knew Freeman was armed; all she needed was a good read on his body language ahead of his critical move and strike before he could harm her. It was all too clear she was in the way of the visitor getting to Liu; timing was of the essence.

Just as Oscea's hailed projectile ferociously hit Freeman's hand, his shot widely missing target, the Russians rushed into the room and were on him before he had a chance at a second try.

Aleksei: *"I feel sorry for you, Harold. Taking Uri out like you did, because of a job you hired him to do, is some special kind of sick."*

Xing: *"As always, exactly where we need you, old friend; you never disappoint!"*

Oscea sealed Freeman's mouth shut with Gorilla tape, adding, *"As long as I'm around, I don't want to hear another word from you. Ah yea, the answer to your question: the white one, a lame ass from Durban; the colored one, a decorated sister from Johannesburg. And while I'm at it, I couldn't wait to show you, the second you stepped in, what my training could do to you. Too bad our brothers in arms here arrived too early. Until then!"*

The Russian foursome hauled Freeman away—I never heard from him again.

———— o ————

34 – COLLAPSE (Henri)

Justin Swenson's cross-examination of James King was a disaster. With each question, the lawyer buried himself deeper and deeper into the layers of culpability, as the witness kept on exposing his and Harrison's roles in the orchestration of Abraham Garner's murder.

During the weeks that followed, and as more witnesses were brought to the bench, many of *Man over Matter*'s members were apprehended, while a warrant for the arrest of Harold Freeman was issued globally. Multiple suits of state against individuals were mounted, as I saw some of my first court work since my arrival in Hobart, a time that seemed so far away already.

— o —

I tried to figure out how the Swensons had planned on proving Harrison's innocence by showing Yang Wu was alive. Even if they originally had the means, the case quickly ran away from them when O'Reilly took the bench. To their credit, they didn't have a window into their own past, for had they looked into the days of Ranch Acacia, and had they been observant enough, they would have seen the patterns of manipulation that turned them into servants of *Man over Matter*, as in each generation before them. But for that, they needed the kind of insight that was denied to them at birth. That said, they certainly weren't victims, as none of us ever were. Justin Swenson's bravado proved he was trained to be a victor, even when lacking the means, cast in the mold of entitlement and arrogance that lived at the core of *Man over Matter*'s inane principles. He came into the courtroom assuming that a proof of Wu's wellness was all it took to get his brother-in-law and best mate out of trouble. Justin and Emma Swenson not only lacked the savvy of their profession, but also the much needed perspective and peripheral vision vital to seeing the larger picture. Their thought process remained forever tethered to the group's central theme, and thus the couple missed on perceiving the nuances of complexity that persistently saw their markers repositioned by the countercurrents of dual gamesmanship.

As the case closed with a guilty verdict for Gerald Harrison, the state subpoenaed the Swensons' offices, leading in the arrest of the couple on murder complicity charges. Thanks to a solid defense, they were released on grounds of insufficient evidence, albeit with their best days as lawyers forever behind them.

— o —

Everything bespoke minute placement, including the arson attempt to Paul Desmond's residence. It didn't matter who did what; it was always as the result of a move under the hand that sought, amid a multiplicity of options, the most suited path for each time sequence. Stan Markalay wasn't required to put the doc's house on fire; it only needed to appear that way—under protection Desmond was less likely to flee—that simple. We deemed it essential that the Gilbert/O'Reilly/Desmond triangle be exposed as the pivot to the making and unraveling of *Man over Matter*'s plan to murder Abraham

318

Garner. It turned out that coaxing Samuel O'Reilly into the group's nefarious motives was a terrible idea, as the scriptwriter had already seen to the man's role as a reliable insider. The same applied to James King, the *Ambassadors of the Wild*, and of course, Xing Liu and Harriet Donovan. As to Freeman, he went for every pothole in the road, while Liz and I merely hired his services on the belief that he was capable of providing fodder to the case. Well, he did that—he had no choice— after all, he, too, was after Abraham's whereabouts, albeit with the goal of silencing him instead.

— o —

In perspective, it didn't matter what we did as long as we heeded the markers and moved the case accordingly. Did Abraham deposit the attaché case at *Lips Waters Café* weeks before we stopped by, or was Irene concealing some truth about its time of delivery? She likely was, in order to remove the element of proximity. The mastermind was ever so close, monitoring each of our moves—he or she couldn't afford to have us sense that nearness. Then came Jeremiah Jones, my alter ego from layers above and beyond; how was he connected to Abe and Harriet? Or did I simply project a self as a token of my suspicion of someone walking in every of our steps, or perversely, of Liz and I walking in theirs? No, it only appeared that way, because there always was a sympathetic distinction between the arranged and the improvised, as there was between the perceived and the projected. What mattered most was that we were in charge, however often we ended up feeling wrested by the latest twist. There was nothing to doubt in that process,

319

anymore than one should have doubted life for what it hadn't revealed yet. All balanced on trust when trust was the least candidate to attend the party. In fact, Liz and I didn't even think in those terms; we went along, never setting our hopes too high or too low, simply relying on the belief that unmediated forward action was preferable over debating to great lengths its merits and logic. We were fools without a compass, yet we never were lost in the true sense—the lesson always was in choosing the path of least resistance.

— o —

So much of the case appeared as ongoing inconsistencies, yet it only seemed so in due of us straddling a variety of scenarios that kept on leaving tails in their wakes. Case in point: the memories of my time at Ranch Acacia, absent at first and now fully embedded in my past. Under normal circumstances, I shouldn't have been able to discern one from the other. But I could, and so could Liz and most at Vertex. As to the rest of the players, I very much doubted that they perceived those shifts as anything beyond minor drifts, if at all.

How did it play at Justin Swenson and Alec Gilbert's ends when, in spite of me not visiting the ranch in one probability, I was now dwelling amid their memories as the case came to its conclusion? Likely, I was the guy they couldn't quite put their finger on. And so, when the time came for me to join Jack in the courtroom, it quickly became obvious that confusion acted its part in weakening the defense. I came from left field with arguments they were unprepared to counter, all extracted from our meetings at Ranch Acacia as well as other places. Yes indeed, things were fuzzy when lacking situational awareness, and how easy it had been for them to forget that I too was once part of *Man over Matter*; with the one added twist that they might have then known me as Jeremiah Jones...

— o —

It took me a while to come into my own and take advantage of my potential, but when I did, it was as if the world had unraveled like a ball of yarn under a cat's paw. As the wool remained unchanged, it zigzagged across the room assuming new shapes, to eventually be recaptured and knitted into objects of disparate complexity. Analogically, I was yarn, feline, and knitter, just like Liz, John, Abe, and Harriet were on their own terms. Helen was too, but she belonged to her own story, one that deserved to be told in full recognition of her ultimate sacrifice of effacement, a choice she made at the service of greater purpose.

If I deemed the process of my development to have been a cycle of falls, it was both in terms of the seasons and the missteps that took me back to them. Perhaps "cycle" was too dimensionally constraint to encompass the notion of limitless possibilities, but it stroked me as reasonably good in its poetic sonance.

Anyway, and to cut to the chase, arriving at that stage of transformation demanded utter flexibility on the part of the belief system, a quality I prided myself in being naturally gifted with. Going with the flow was in fact something I learned from Harriet Donovan when she suggested that I study at Oxford instead of Toronto—a marker I could easily have ignored had I been set in my

321

ways, but it came to my attention that within that moment a soft breeze had crossed the room, leaving a message that gently floated to my feet. From that time on, and in spite of some initial resistance, I heeded those messages as they steadily showed me the path to Tasmania, taking into account, of course, that only in my then-present version of reality did I stay true to that maxim.

— o —

My joining of *Man over Matter* was also Harriet's suggestion, which happened just before I attended my first summer meeting at the ranch. She also advised that I used a new identity. The name Jeremiah Jones came to me as a thought, but she might as well have spoken it. My stay within the group was meant to be short-lived, just long enough to get familiarized with its makeup and assess the long-term implications of its greater purpose. The reason for it was to basically avoid generating a lasting imprint of my presence that could have bled through the layers and intuitively alarm people like Harold Freeman. That said, it was of benefit that some channels were left open at my end, which explained my immediate suspicion of the man.

The complexity of it all begot the weakness of words, but I had become a natural at moving through the layers without the encumbrance of seeking answers to questions with no place to be. In other words, from where I stood, awareness never was the byproduct of thoughts, but rather of focused, silent observation.

Anyway, arriving with a sense of renewed awareness amid the fallout at the end of a long trial season, which of all things took us all the way into the next fall, was a great place to be. Liz and I soaked in the superb weather, ignoring the chill that blew from Bass Strait. We almost had all reasons to rejoice, save for the lingering sense of discomfort around Abraham's persisting silence. Last we heard from Pointe-Saint-Michel, he and Harriet had left for an undisclosed location, indicating that they either had unfinished business to address or that danger still loomed in unsuspected areas. John and Xing seemed to think that there was no cause for alarm, but some of the dust still needed settling before we took a chance at letting our guards down. It seemed like a wise choice at the time.

———— o ————

35 – MAN OVER MATTER (Harriet)

Man over Matter was as old as time. It sat latent for most of it, embryonic in form in the deepest recesses of the human soul, programmed to react at the first call. That call blew from an indescribable distance, when distance was measured in terms of what was probable and not; "not" being a notch past the farthest reachable point.

Any notion, as long as it could be conceived, and as ridiculous as to implicate the destruction of the space to imagine it, was given a chance at realizing its potential. The poison seed of control of the natural world and the savagery inflicted onto it, found nourishment in the bile of men who vied for immortality. They iconized their private gods into stone, robbing them of their vibrancy, and went on to take the world apart, leaving in their wake ashes and fear.

As humanity sought its balance through periods of renaissance, dark cells thrived in the background, feeding on the strength of what they strived to destroy, namely anything borne of the womb of creativity, or more precisely, the sacred feminine.

For us, women of the future, it was barely conceivable that such core separation hadn't already blown existence to smithereens; thus, we knew the wounds to the Mother Earth were beyond our hopes of mending; at least, as seen from the vantage of our explorations into probable realities. Therefore, if one didn't exist in which the world thrived beyond our time, someone had to go "out there" and create it—I was the one elected to travel amid multitudinous pasts to locate the vacant spot capable of birthing that new world. I found it in the darkest of ages, scattered through the near-forgotten writings of Edward Sexton, a place I called *Providence*, albeit one not of God's conception, but rather of the inner powers that lived within us all.

It was, without saying, unimaginable for most minds that such an individual as myself could travel through time; hence, it was paramount that I fit the best I could by remaining unassuming, something quite difficult when one had to also exult command. I found the balance upon realizing that the men of the past relished seeing themselves in a woman, which they translated as an acceptance of their powers, as opposed to the sort of submissiveness they unconsciously despised. To be like them was to gain their respect if not their trust.

Man over Matter was of course the work of men, a group that had mounted like an anthill on the forces of multiplicity. It was sickly natural in appearance and evolution, to the point at which its ominous presence raised the question of sanity to establishable order. If order meant balance, one-sided societies didn't; it was that simple, and yet, like some inky malignance, the movement went on tainting everything it touched. To add insult to injury, its members, in an élan of misplaced affection, went on to call the organization *MoM*.

— o —

What did Edward Sexton possess that other men didn't have? For one, he had sensibility beyond his time in the form of a deep understanding that without the wisdom of women in the balance the planet would suffer "the savage despoiling of its beauty"—his adjusted words.

Sexton was blessed with a sacred masculine unaffected by the battering forces of insanity. He wasn't the only one, but he possessed the eloquence and dexterity to put his views into spoken and written words. Even though his teaching voice fell to deaf ears and his writing was scattered to the wind, enough of his material was caught in the eddies of time to be found and regrouped into a whole under my auspice, and brought to the attention of men of vision and mettle. Although it would take centuries before those kinds of men became available.

— o —

In perspective, I managed to put my stamp on two philosophically-opposed groups, one of my making, the other of my undoing. Vertex and *Man over Matter* officially formed in the eighteen-hundreds during what may be referred to as the era of séances, although, fundamentally, neither was a produce of the occult. Nonetheless, with the nature of the psyche and its innumerable doors gaping into the unknown, it could thus have been said that both rooted in metaphysics, one— Vertex—aware of its source of being; the other, a reflexive entity intent on annihilating it.

To cut to the chase, the stuff of séances was the channel that purveyed to my needs of reaching into the kindred souls prone to join Vertex, as well as the darkness that courted their companies. The gatherings at my apartment in London teamed to those of Acacia and Pointe-Saint-Michel, represented three of the many portals used during my travels, albeit, with each existing in various probable forms, allowing for a multiplicity of options to be identified against the ideal *scenario isolate*, until a match manifested. That came when Henri and Elizabeth visited at Great Cumberland Place, at the exact point of reunification of Henri and his alter ego, Jeremiah Jones. The concept had materialized and a new past was born, with the two of them at its navel. Abraham, Helen, Jean-Pierre and Cecile Desgardes, and I had seen that quivering strand of potential come alive in the couple, but it had always been upon them first meeting as adults, for no scenario of an earlier encounter existed beyond the aforementioned isolate, which was nothing more than a projection of mine. Nonetheless, that spark was what we all needed to forge ahead with the case, in the hopes that its energy would morph into a stream capable of shape-shifting with the relentless tug of contradictions, forces that were essentially designed to confuse *Man over Matter*. The true miracle was Jeremiah Jones, who found his way through the layers to manifest before Henri and Elizabeth, a name suggested by me in the *new past*, but one that found its roots in the spirit of Edward Sexton. One may say that with the expansion of awareness, the reality of connection with all beings within their respective families of consciousness becomes inevitable.

———— o ————

36 – RIVER DERWENT (Henri)

It took nearly a year for all elements of the case to settle, the whole culminating in a shakeup of business and politics, while many individuals saw the course of their planned futures drastically altered. Freeman was believed to have fled to South Africa, but knowing the man, I was certain that he understood the value of a good rumor. My take was that he was probably where he fitted best: on the fringes of the Tasmanian wilderness, where some of his kin were hard at work planning their next move against the new generation of environmentalists. But, as I saw it, it was a ferment bound to sour up under the heat. So, what happened with the Russians? According to Aleksei, Freeman took the beating of his life, but since no-one had the heart to kill him, they left him where he lay, bleeding and unconscious, by the edge of Lake Burley Griffin.

— o —

When Abraham and Harriet finally came to the house, it wasn't to discuss the whys of the long absence, but to talk about wedding preparations. Naturally, we were overwhelmed with the joy of reunification, so ample room was made for the outpour of emotions; but us being Vertex, such emotions were strictly a measure of their rightful intensity, meaning that they were only allowed to last the course of their useful cycle. In other words, we didn't overdo it.

As to the wedding plans, Liz and I had our views set on something bereft of production and drama. We were overdue for a gathering, and though Ranch Acacia was long gone, Pointe-Saint-Michel begged for a human presence, at least in my parents' words. It was our wish that at the exception of a few peripheral guests, the assistance was to be composed of the members of the two firms, partners and Front Shield, as well as Xing Liu, Yang Wu, Jonathon Weisman, and on Abraham's insistence, Samuel O'Reilly and James King.

But in the end, regardless of where Liz and I stood apropos our symbolic union, it all came down to what Harriet deemed was the proper place and time. She was fine with Pointe-Saint-Michel and the guests, but she had something else in mind. In the trademark manner I had become familiar with, she took me under the shroud of confidence on a short walk to the edge of the woods, proposing that perhaps Liz and I deserved a ceremony fitting of the occasion, something out of the ordinary.

"You see, Henri, when the mind opens to the idea of limitless possibilities, it strives to garner dreams into cohesion. Mine was, and still is, to bring sympathetic elements, which had otherwise been too far apart, to recognize each other. Although your connection with Elizabeth was inevitable, it lacked the true closeness necessary to carry us here, thus why you and I met in the dream state, amid circumstances under which I suggested you infiltrate Man over Matter, *using the moniker Jeremiah Jones. From that point forth, Jones became an aspect personality that lived under the roof of your psyche, if you don't mind the inference. He was also the part that connected you to Edward Sexton, the entity behind Vertex's conception. In other words, without implying you are the man himself, you have a straight line*

to him and to me by extension. Of course, the same goes for Elizabeth, albeit in a somewhat more complex manner through Helen and Abraham. My point here, Henri, is to take you both where I come from, as a gift to you and myself, for a heart ceremony before a world that you helped save; then you can do as you wish as far as this reality goes. I don't possess the power or the will to coerce you into it, but I beg you to not decline."

"I wish Liz was with us to hear you; why just me?"

"Elizabeth needs you to be the one to relate my wish; such is the nature of the sacred order."

— o —

I had no idea that when Harriet, Liz, and I held hands before taking off for the future, we would end up on a craft in the middle of River Derwent, facing a not so different Hobart—but there and then ended all similarities. The air and water felt and looked cleaner. We could hear gentle splashes against the hull, free of the background drone of the habitual city soundscape. Bird flights broke and converged in wild murmurations from every part of the sky. The more we unlocked our senses, the more the minutest of differences exploded in insanely disproportionate revelations. It was as if our connection to the outside world had been rebooted from a state of corruption. Harriet smiled, aware of the bewitchment in our eyes.

"It is not at all as I left it, saying that as your past adjusted to the changes, so did mine. The way it looked before the abolishment of the wilderness leases would

have shocked you—no trees or birds; the river, a sickly brown with extreme levels of salinity; scorched hills and mountains across Meehan and Wellington Ranges; impossibly variant temperatures carried by temperamental winds; and that's just from a glimpse at the environment. As to living conditions, I shall spare you the agony. What you see here is a healed world."

Liz: *"On the surface, it doesn't seem that much different from our Hobart, but there's a lighter feeling all around."*

Harriet: *"That's what a lower population does, curbed at slightly over a billion world citizens, based on sustainability and equity. As to the lack of noise, we have harnessed energy sources still unthinkable in your time, but I assure you it won't be long before your first strides into true renewability."*

Me: *"I'm embarrassed to ask, but how far deep in the future are we?"*

Harriet: *"Don't be, because it is a pertinent question. In exactly one hour, from the median of our departure, Edward Sexton's release of his first paper on human awareness will equidistantly coincide with our private ceremony here. As to your query, giving or taking a few years—roughly eight centuries."*

Liz: *"Are you planning on performing the ceremony on this boat?"*

Harriet: *"Yes, but farther down, below New Zealand, at the exact point of Oxford's antipode."*

Me: *"And we will be there in an hour, I suppose."*

Harriet: *"Precisely, you are presently in a future where travels are deemed an art form—take it from me!"*

Me: *"I am missing on the significance of the time and space equidistance, can you explain?"*

Harriet: *"You beat me to it. I often speak of order, mostly natural order, but in this case it is mathematical order that is guest. Your wedding ceremony, which I will perform as a minister of my own world, thus making it official in some sense, is part of the convergence of forces that will seal this probability as its own irreversible reality. It represents the last phase of my work and foretells of my permanent return to this rightful world. Only a specific arrangement of lines and axes on the map of relative resonance will do to satisfy me."*

— o —

Naturally, without fully understanding how we got there, we settled amid eerily calm waters in the middle of nowhere, the three of us standing high up on a platform above the cabin. I at once realized that the boat was specifically designed for the performance of marriage rituals, judging by the arrangement of seats below us, and that it also was Harriet Donovan's home.

As the time neared, we held hands in a triangle, readying ourselves for the convergence. Little was said, save for the traditional vows and the customary references to love, purpose, and responsibility. There was no summoning of ancient powers, no storm forming amid the great skies, no rainbow or divine horns blaring from above Heaven's gates, just three humans standing at a rare crossing, two of them joined in the oldest contract known to man and womankind, the other, representative of the sacred order, officializing the rite—no witnesses needed.

It took much longer for the return trip to Hobart, on the account that future tradition demanded that the act of marriage be followed by a demonstration of love. For that, a special room was provided for intimate sex, or, if we wished, we could simply enjoy the open. We of course opted for the fresh air, while Harriet sunbathed in the nude a distance away. The experience was as close to conveying a sense of absolute release as Liz and I could ever have envisioned, and to this day it has remained the model by which all our lovemaking should be engaged.

— o —

If Hobart appeared only marginally changed for the distance of the waters, walking its streets threw all notions of resemblance out the window. For one, there were no personal vehicles, short of bicycles powered the old-fashioned way, which, for a second, conveyed pictures of Amsterdam, if the Dutch city had also foregone the combustion engine. Besides that, the comparatives were few, due to the spaces between riders, pedestrians, and the diminutive, twelve-seat boxes that served as public transportation, all painted in the style of kindergarten art. The reduced population was clearly apparent even though the town still spread over a reasonably wide area. Liz and I were surprised to find that One Eleven Macquarie Street still stood when all other buildings around it, save for Saint-Joseph church, had been replaced by much soberer structures. Harriet explained ahead of us asking.

"You stand before a historical building in honor of your work eight centuries ago. I hope it makes you feel proud."

Liz: *"You're not insinuating that we, as people, made history, are you?"*

333

Harriet: *"If you look closer at the commemorative plaque, it says 'Garner, Lewis, & Desgardes offices, eighth story,' does it not?"*

Me: *"And that just for a case?"*

Harriet: *"Not just any case when it implies the creation of an entire reality; plus, I couldn't help myself."*

— o —

That was Harriet, one of the finest human I had ever met. In some curious way, she went from a stranger working in the office of a dubious company to my oldest friend, a woman of extreme resources, talent, and compassion. In a way, our relationship spanned the spectrum of the human character, gradated in units of self-awareness, from a low reflexive to a high ascendant. But what stood for our connection in various probable scenarios, didn't necessarily apply to Harriet, for wherever she existed in time, she was forever the same, changed only in the perception of her person by the eye that sought to reach into the deeper colors of the soul. On some level, she had found me in Edward Sexton and returned me to where I belonged: amid the back corridors of power, a place that prospered at the crossing of endless possibilities.

——— o ———

37 – POINTE-SAINT-MICHEL (Liz)

The wedding went as planned with all the usual suspects taking their place on the grand stage of illusion. It was a delicious event all the same, for we knew, barring a few exceptions, why we chose to follow the present script.

For me, the true union was back on the boat, but a promise was a promise, and one couldn't just tell the guests that the ceremony had already happened in the distant future.

I had worried about my father and what would happen of him when Harriet returned to her world, but that fear was soon dispelled when I realized that he knew of the outcome all along. In spite of my admiration for him, I always managed to underestimate the reach of his boundless personality—he was, too, a traveler, an artist as Harriet would say. In the end, I had no doubts as to how much their union transcended the mere challenge of time.

— o —

I missed Helen, my dear mother and tutor to my young soul. She should have been there that day, her voice heard above the bustle, effortless, clear, and joyful, a joy that carried the secret of pain, like one held a jewel close to the heart. She was a complete being, too complete to fit amid the incompleteness of the world that surrounded her. In spite of her early departure, her involvement in the case was fundamental. Creating the firm was first and foremost her idea, and her willingness to take Harriet into her intimate circle was a deliberate act of cognitive purpose. In making room for a "bigger player," she demonstrated the firmness of her grip on what lay ahead. She made herself mortal, a sacrifice few were capable of conceiving at their clearest moment. She stood dignified till her last breath, always and forever the ascendant force of her own reality. To me, she was the angel that brought the sacred into the physical, spanning her wings over my young self, protecting, but never smothering.

In spite of her absence, I intuited Helen wouldn't miss her daughter's wedding, especially the one of the two that mattered most. Somehow, she had to be there, in her best dress, moving fluidly around the guests, brushing by like a gentle breeze. I knew she was, for my heart felt at peace—safe.

— o —

It was all the better that we eloped, at least in terms of guilty pleasures, because the ceremony as it stood was nothing more than an excuse for a long-overdue gathering of old souls. Of course, I wouldn't have wanted it any other way, but fact be told that tradition had been in special needs of a good dust up. Thankfully, this time around, there was no evidence of malfeasance inking its way onto the script, but I trusted that it wouldn't be long before Vertex had to utilize its clout to nip an act of global naughtiness in the bud. Needless to say that the human ego had a lot of sobering to do ahead of recognizing its true power, but by the look of it, it was on a promising course. That sense of reckoning was met by John Lehman's gaze; the man who always seemed to be ahead of anyone's thoughts. Odd that after all the wheeling and dealing associated with the case, he still remained a stranger to me. But as Henri once said, *"John's the friend you think you know until you realize the friendship is nothing other than the shield protecting the mystery of his person."* "Well put, Henri, you know your kin!"

How good it felt to humor the self and the love of your life in the ambiance of your own wedding! Henri and I had been looking to that moment for so long that the waiting practically became the stuff of the ordinary, to the point of us finding comfort in the numbness of ritual postponing. In the end, it paid off, as we likely wouldn't have found that depth of love amid the mundane of the predictable. Undeniably, there was love when we met, but only in the allotted amounts directly proportional to our levels of self-awareness. Our work made us whole, and by work I meant both the case and the personal growth that ensued in the wake of inner exploration. All things paralleled everything.

— o —

Being back in Pointe-Saint-Michel after all these years didn't bring the past into focus like I had expected. Rather, it was so connected to my present that a sense of belonging simultaneously to both dominated the intimacy of my thoughts. It was as if two parts of me walked side by side, adjusting each move for perfect synchrony. Metaphorically speaking, there was newness to the old the way there always had been history to the now, as in time going both ways, or going no ways at all. I felt the construct coming undone, its parts falling like scales off

337

an ancient edifice, the facade of reality showing the cracks in its making, the frescos turned to a dull powder at the base of its walls—my world was whirling, disconnected from meaning, drawn to the vortex of some unfathomable act of randomness. I seemed not to care, simply observing my thoughts coming unmade. And there I was, Henri beside me, the two of us gazing across the St-Lawrence's waters, looking into nowhere in particular, acknowledging existence through the stillness of momentarily silenced minds. We were young, facing the probabilities of our lives unraveling before us, cognizant of the choices made. But right then and there, we knew we were meant to spend a life together.

Harriet quietly joined us.

"If I may make a suggestion, please try your best to preserve the preciousness of this moment; it would pain me to not be invited to your wedding."

As easily as I had drifted, I was back in my time, Harriet looking me in the eyes with a glitter of amusement.

"Glad you heeded my words; I'm sure you now see their importance. I'll be leaving soon, so please, don't be shy and call on when you get the chance; there's a cabin on the boat with both your names on it, or if you prefer the open deck... Until then!"

———— o ————

END

ORDER OF APPEARANCE

- <u>Henri Desgardes</u> (Main character, investigative lawyer, Quebec City, Hobart)
- <u>John Lehman</u> (Main character, Lawyer, Quebec City)
- <u>Jean Leduc</u> (Lawyer, Quebec City)
- <u>Eric Marchand</u> (Lawyer, Quebec City)
- <u>Elizabeth Garner/Liz</u> (Main character, lawyer, Hobart)
- <u>Abraham Elliot Garner</u> (father of Elizabeth Garner, lawyer, Hobart)
- <u>Helen Garner</u>: (Wife of Abraham, mother of Elizabeth)
- <u>Jack Lewis</u> (Lawyer, Hobart)
- <u>James Lewis</u> (Jack's brother, Liz's ex-husband)
- <u>Harold Freeman</u> (Investigator, Hobart)
- <u>Yang Wu</u> (Engineer, Savage River mine)
- <u>Sackman, Bryan</u> (Lawyer, Quebec City)
- <u>Claire</u> (Henri Desgardes' first wife)
- <u>Uri Dudko</u> (Investigator under H. Freeman)
- <u>James King</u> (Suspect)
- <u>Irene</u> (Manager at Lips Waters Café)
- <u>Dominic Vaughn</u> (Also Yang Wu)
- <u>Ehuang Wu</u> (Yang Wu's wife)
- <u>Samuel O'Reilly</u> (Surgeon, North West Regional Hospital, Burney, suspect)
- <u>Upton Clay</u> (Investigator, Devonport)
- <u>Aleksei Yegorov</u> (Investigator under H. Freeman)

- <u>Gerald Harrison</u> (Also Alec Gilbert, environmental consultant at Savage river mine, suspect)
- <u>Alec Gilbert</u> (Medical student, Sydney)
- <u>Jeremiah Jones</u> (Shadow Man)
- <u>Shadow Man</u> (J.J.)
- <u>Xing Liu</u> (Mystery man, *Branched Resources* board of directors, suspect)
- <u>Xing Xu</u> (Xing Liu)
- <u>Henri Hartman</u> (Henri Desgardes)
- <u>Justin & Emma Swenson</u> (Lawyers for S. O'Reilly and G. Harrison, compromised)
- <u>Paul Desmond</u> (In-house doctor, Savage River mine, suspect)
- <u>William Dorset</u> (Engineer, Savage River mine, suspect)
- <u>Harriet Donovan</u> (Head of accounting, *Branched Resources*, suspect)
- <u>Jonathon Weisman</u> (Head engineer, Savage River mine, suspect)
- <u>Owen</u> (Liz's secretary)
- <u>Donald Weber</u> (Engineer, Savage River mine, suspect)
- <u>Thomas Landry</u> (Engineer, Savage River mine, suspect)
- <u>Mervin Saunders</u> (Engineer, Savage River mine, suspect)
- <u>Tony Sanchez</u> (Crewman, Savage River mine, suspect)
- <u>Gabriel Turner</u> (Crewman, Savage River mine, suspect)
- <u>Dimitri Osminin</u> (Security under H. Freeman)
- <u>Leopold 'Lelo' Eisenberg</u> (Defense attorney)

- <u>Bruce Martens</u> (AOW, suspect)
- <u>Kate Schmitt</u> (AOW, suspect)
- <u>Daniel (Danny) Woods</u> (AOW, suspect)
- <u>Derek Kline</u> (AOW, suspect)
- <u>Michael (Mickey) Stanley</u> (AOW, suspect)
- <u>Morris (Moe) Weiner</u> (AOW, suspect)
- <u>Stan Markalay</u> (AOW, arsonist)
- <u>Janice</u> (Caretaker for Abraham Garner's estate)
- <u>Jason Saëns</u> (Front Shield officer, Hobart)
- <u>George and Monique Swenson</u> (Attorneys from Adelaide, parents of Justin Swenson)
- <u>Karl Gilbert</u> (Surgeon from Sidney, father of Alec Gilbert aka Gerald Harrison, and Emma Swenson)
- <u>Alan Grieves</u> (Ground Sky Ground Ltd)
- <u>Raphael Montgomery</u> (Judge)
- <u>Alan Desmond</u> (Paul Desmond's father)
- <u>Robert Lewis</u> (Jack's father)
- <u>Edward Sexton</u> (Oxford University professor circa 1209)
- <u>August Alexander</u> (Law professor, London, circa 1899)
- <u>Jean-Pierre and Cecile Desgardes</u> (Henri's parents, lawyers)
- <u>Derek Gunn</u> (Deceased, homeless)
- <u>Tanya</u> (Xing Liu's niece, James King's girlfriend)
- <u>Pamela Liu</u> (Xing Liu's wife)
- <u>Oscea</u> (The Liu's keeper)

—— o ——

OTHER RELEASES
BY THE AUTHOR

— The Disappearance of Olaf Swyndle
(An Improbable Emergence Volume 1)
© 2016
— The Hektor Dilemma
(An Improbable Emergence Volume 2)
© 2016
— Ma-l's Grand Gathering
(An Improbable Emergence Volume 3)
© 2017
— Convergence of the Realms
(An Improbable Emergence Volume 4)
© 2017
— Escape from Inconsequence   © 2018
— Reyes & Leeds   © 2018
— Story of a Tale-Maker   © 2019
— Nine Amber Pieces   © 2019
— A Life Given, a Life Taken   © 2020
— Hello, my Name is Tunes!   © 2021

—— o ——